A
GRIM REAPER'S
GUIDE TO
CATCHING
A KILLER

– A –
GRIM REAPER'S GUIDE TO CATCHING A KILLER

Maxie Dara

BERKLEY
NEW YORK

BERKLEY
An imprint of Penguin Random House LLC
penguinrandomhouse.com

Copyright © 2024 by Maxie Dara Liberman
Penguin Random House supports copyright. Copyright fuels creativity,
encourages diverse voices, promotes free speech, and creates a vibrant culture.
Thank you for buying an authorized edition of this book and for complying
with copyright laws by not reproducing, scanning, or distributing any part of it
in any form without permission. You are supporting writers and allowing
Penguin Random House to continue to publish books for every reader.

BERKLEY and the BERKLEY & B colophon are registered
trademarks of Penguin Random House LLC.

Library of Congress Cataloging-in-Publication Data

Names: Dara, Maxie, author.
Title: A grim reaper's guide to catching a killer / Maxie Dara.
Description: First edition. | New York: Berkley, 2024. | Series: A
S.C.Y.T.H.E. mystery |
Identifiers: LCCN 2024011530 (print) | LCCN 2024011531 (ebook) |
ISBN 9780593815793 (trade paperback) | ISBN 9780593815809 (ebook)
Subjects: LCGFT: Cozy mysteries. | Paranormal fiction. | Novels.
Classification: LCC PR9199.4.D368 G75 2024 (print) | LCC PR9199.4.D368
(ebook) | DDC 813/.6—dc23/eng/20240325
LC record available at https://lccn.loc.gov/2024011530
LC ebook record available at https://lccn.loc.gov/2024011531

First Edition: October 2024

Printed in the United States of America
1st Printing

Book design by Jenni Surasky

For my mom: my greatest supporter, best friend,
and biggest Grim-spiration.
(And who I now need to apologize to for that pun.)

A
GRIM REAPER'S
GUIDE TO
CATCHING
A KILLER

1

438 Melrose Court

I tapped the address in my file with the lid of the pen I'd been chewing on. Beside the front door of the sandy beige new build, swirly metal numerals confirmed my location. Four three eight. Weird. Definitely the right number, but this was all wrong. I turned from the house and glanced down the manicured lawn to the street sign across the road. It promised in no uncertain terms that this was Melrose Court, just as it was supposed to be. I shut my file with a defeated sigh and went back in through the open door a second time.

"Hello?" I called yet again as I stomped through the kitchen. It was a kitchen that belonged on a show about kitchens more than in somebody's house: clean and white and open-concept, leading out into the high-ceilinged living room beyond. The "after" on a home renovation show. Not even a spoon in the sink or a crumb on the countertops. Which made the body sprawled across the tiled floor look even more out of place.

Now, slap a corpse on the floor of my dingy apartment

kitchen and you wouldn't bat an eye, at least in my line of work. But in a place like this, a dead body really spoils the ambience.

I rounded the island and reopened my file.

```
Case # 507032
Conner Mateo Ortiz
Age: 17
Cause of death: Seizure
Time to Collect: 4:30 p.m.
```

"Conner?" My voice ricocheted off the stainless steel and marble surrounding me. I crouched by the body and attempted to hover in a squat, but my left knee protested my weight with a defiant pop, and I wobbled forward. "Nope, nope, nope," I muttered to myself, "no falling on bodies today. Not after last time." I lowered myself to my steadily widening bum by 507032's head. His rich brown locks fell over one closed eye, a spattering of freckles on his nose. I sighed, one hand at my stomach. Poor kid. He looked younger than his age lying there, long lashes pressed above bronze cheeks still full with the last remnants of baby fat. I'd found his basement bedroom not ten minutes earlier; a gallery of posters and mess and potential. It always felt wrong when they were young. Like their bodies should still have some life left in them. But of course, they didn't. That's why I was there.

Still, he was going to make me late, and the last man to make me late was the very reason I needed to get back to the office and then on my way home on time.

"Conner?" I tried again. Nothing. The house shuddered at my voice and fell still.

My phone vibrated in my back trouser pocket and I nearly

puked, though I wasn't entirely sure the two were related. I scrambled for the phone and hauled myself to my feet.

Simon. He got the table for six thirty instead of seven. Of course he did. Shit. If we weren't already in the middle of a divorce, I'd consider filing over this.

This wasn't the way it normally worked—the way it always worked. Death, for all its unpredictability and unknowns, was remarkably routine on my end. It was one of the things I loved most about my job. Someone under my department's jurisdiction dies, I get the paperwork, carry out the collection, write up a report for Stu, and am on the couch watching *Family Feud* with a bowl of canned tomato soup by five thirty. That's how it was, how it always had been for the six years I'd been a Collections Agent with S.C.Y.T.H.E. But somehow today was different. Case 507032 was different.

I glanced back over the boy. My client files were always pared down to need-to-know information, and in my position, there isn't much I need to know. But it seemed clear enough from the body—long-limbed and dressed in faded jeans and a gray hoodie—that aside from his family's apparent wealth, 507032 was your average, unremarkable teenaged boy. So the question was, why wasn't he here?

I did a second tour through the house, Conner Ortiz's name bouncing back to me in my own voice from the high ceilings of every starkly furnished room. By the time I'd circled back into the kitchen, it was after five.

"Conner," I said into the definitively empty house, "I'm sorry."

I closed my file for the last time and left 438 Melrose Court.

2

Gemma Burke was still in her cubicle when I arrived at the office. She rolled her seat back and poked her head around our shared wall at the sound of my car keys hitting my desk. Her emergence was like a sunrise, the high dark blond ponytail and naturally veneer-white smile rising out of the mists of corporate gray. Gemma did Pilates and went to concerts and brought salads for lunch every day, which she genuinely seemed to enjoy eating. She had work friends she saw without the obligation of work. At a push, she might even consider me one of them, though I'd never braved one of her famous Friday bar nights. I had never been a Gemma Burke, but I was glad someone was.

"Hey, Kath!"

I placed file 507032 face down beside my computer and fell into my chair, a small bubble of anxiety rising in my stomach.

The anxiety bubble burst in a shaky, "Have you ever failed to collect?"

Gemma cocked her head at me, her brows creasing.

"I had a routine collection just now, and my client . . . wasn't there."

"Wasn't there?" Gemma repeated. "Oh no, Kath, that's not good. No, it's never happened to me. Ugh, I'm sorry, that's so stressful."

The look on her face, tight and pitying, confirmed my fears. I glanced down at my hands. They had a way of making a mess of things—I had a way of making a mess of things—and somehow I'd finally messed up the one aspect of my life I thought I'd had under control.

Gemma's voice snapped me out of my thought spiral. "Have you told Stu?"

"Not yet, I just got in."

"Oh, fair enough. Well, I mean, that's definitely not supposed to happen."

"No," I agreed, swallowing the lump in my throat. "It isn't." I took a breath and remembered the thing I should have said from the start. "How was the funeral?"

Gemma shrugged. "Like, typical funeral vibes."

I nodded uncomfortably. This was uncomfortable. Death was our job, and seeing it on a daily basis made us pretty blasé about the whole ordeal fairly quickly. But when death came to our own doorsteps, there was no telling how one of us would react, and I was not equipped with the skills necessary to handle big displays of emotion. I cast a cursory glance around me, noting the quickest exit in case of a tears-related emergency, and said, "That makes sense. For a funeral." I cleared my throat. "My aunt's somehow ended with a fire in the church cloakroom."

"Oh. Yikes."

"But your dad's was nice?"

"Nice enough, I guess," said Gemma. "I always find funerals kind of pointless. I mean, maybe it's because of the job, you know? Like, the whole idea of funerals is to say goodbye, but *we* know it isn't goodbye, that there's something else, even if we don't know exactly what."

I let out a small breath of relief as I realized there wouldn't be any shoulder crying, when the clock on the wall across from me caught my eye.

"Shit. I'm supposed to be having that dinner tonight," I said. "With Simon."

"Simon? Really?"

My shoulders sagged. "Yup." I slid the file back off the desk. The time had come. "Assuming Stu doesn't eat me alive first."

"He's really not that bad once you get past . . . you know . . ."

"His personality?"

Gemma gave a girlish giggle.

"Wish me luck."

"Good luck! See you tomorrow, Kath."

My knuckles rapped softly on one of the windows of Stu's office. Almost the whole thing was windows. He'd said when he installed them that he wanted us to feel he was more approachable, but those windows had shown him picking his teeth with empty file folders and blotting his armpits after lunchtime workouts enough times to make me avoid approaching him unless it was absolutely necessary. Well, a missing client seemed to fit that bill.

"Come in," Stu called from his desk on the other side of the glass.

I slid into the office.

"Kathy," Stu said by way of a greeting.

"Stu," I replied. "Mr. Calhoun," I corrected quickly, blinking hard in a futile attempt to Etch A Sketch away my slipup. Stu was only Stu when you weren't talking directly to Stu.

"What can I do you for?" Stu eyed me with his usual cool blue intensity, his over-attended muscles flexing impatiently beneath his pale button-up. I watched a bicep bounce, and for a moment I swore the sound of it rubbing against Stu's shirtsleeve was a sigh of disappointment.

"Well," I started, still eyeing that bicep in case it had anything else to add, "one of my scheduled collections today didn't go according to plan. This has never happened to me before, and it's been years since I was in training, so I need a bit of a refresher on protocol."

Stu pulled a stress ball from a drawer in his desk and squeezed, his massive hand enveloping the little ball until all that remained was a tight fist. "Didn't go according to plan *how*?"

"The client." I held up the file. "He wasn't there."

Stu's knuckles whitened. "Wasn't there?"

I shook my head.

"So you didn't collect the client."

"No," I said.

"I see." The bicep jumped again. I jumped slightly with it. Talking to Stu always put me on edge. He was disconcertingly good-looking in the sort of way that reminded me I was a pear-shaped forty-two-year-old near-divorcée, and yet he was perpetually disapproving in a way that made me feel like a first grader who'd just been caught eating crayons. It made for an awkward position to be in under the best of circumstances, and this was not the best of circumstances.

"I'm sorry," I whimpered at the bicep.

"This"—he tossed the stress ball into the other hand, which promptly ate it—"is unprecedented under my leadership. No client has gone uncollected for as long as I've been here."

"I looked everywhere for him—"

"This is bad, Valence."

I gulped at the sound of my surname. It sounded harsher, sharper than I was used to.

"Our company prides itself on having revolutionized the way these things are done. For almost two hundred years now, we've been the world's leading soul collection and transportation service, and do you know how? By making sure things like this don't happen."

"Right, yes, absolutely, of course. So what do I do?"

Stu sat frozen for a beat, the stress ball unsqueezed, the bicep unflexed. He repositioned himself in his leather-upholstered ergonomic chair, arms crossed over his desk. "I need time to run this upstairs. I hope you understand the severity of this situation, Valence. You know what happens when souls go uncollected."

I did know. It was one of the first things you learned in training; day one, hour one. Agents, whether day shift or night shift, collected their assigned souls and delivered them to a designated processing facility. If a soul wasn't collected and delivered within forty-five days of its body eviction, it would be relegated to stay on earth as a soul forever. In layman's terms, a ghost. There used to be a lot of these incidents, back when my field was more negligent and less knowledgeable than it is today. The last ghost created by S.C.Y.T.H.E. was due to a mishandled case in 1906. I didn't know exactly what had happened to that agent, and I wasn't keen to find out for myself.

I gulped in reply.

"Go home, Valence. Sort yourself out. I'll be in touch with instructions as soon as I've talked this over with my higher-ups."

I stood, the take-out lunch in my stomach rising with me.

"And, Valence?" Half a box of chicken fried rice marched up my throat. My hand was near the doorknob. So achingly close. I could feel the cold metal brushing my fingertips. I turned back to Stu. His bicep stared back at me. "I am not pleased."

I gave a somber nod of understanding and threw up in his garbage can.

3

Forty-Five Days to Ghost

The dim amber light of Papa Giuseppe's Pizzeria turned the pale blue and yellow flowers on my dress into splotches of discolored mud. I'd barely had enough time after work to run home for a shower, throw my poof of hair into a bun, and change into the only dress that still fit me. And now, in the lighting that had been romantic on my first date with Simon but currently felt like I was walking into an Italian-themed circle of hell, that dress looked like military camouflage. I ran my palm down the front, shoulders drooping, and hauled my way through the crowded restaurant to our usual table near the back.

Simon was already there, head buried behind a menu even though he never strayed from the chicken Parmesan. The menu dropped as I approached, and Simon clambered to his feet, one knee hitting the table as he tried to scooch around the patrons beside him without sweeping their spaghetti onto the floor with his butt.

"Kath." His arms were open to me before he'd finished

rounding the table. I let him envelop me in that tight, all-consuming strangle hug of his, wondering if he could feel anything different as he squeezed.

Simon pulled away, taking my hands in his and beaming up at me.

"Simon," I said back, breathing him in. He was a solid inch and a half shorter than me, several more rounder, with a hairline that had given up merely receding years ago and was now bent on a full, surrendered retreat. I peered around the glare in his glasses to the pale gray eyes underneath. My heart gave a reluctant flutter, and just like that I was back in the dairy aisle of the grocery store where we'd met; a pool of broken eggs forming a viscous puddle around my sensible loafers, at least one shell fragment inexplicably nestled in my hair, and a stocky stranger bent at my feet, ready to fearlessly tackle my mess before I even had time to right the now-empty carton clutched upside down in my hands. I was meant to be cooking for a date that night—a blind one, arranged by an old roommate, and one that I was having seventh thoughts about (second through sixth having taken place throughout work that day). Those thoughts had led me to distraction, which had led me to drop the eggs, and which in turn had led me to tears, which were flowing freely by that point.

The strange man pulled the eggshell from my hair, followed me home, and made a simple but delicious spaghetti dinner for me and my date while I scrubbed the yolk from my pantyhose. When I emerged from the bathroom, stuffed into my most presentable dress, sopping pantyhose hung over my arm like a pair of limp black snakes, he dropped the wooden spoon back into the pot he'd been stirring.

"You look exquisite," he'd said. Not that I believed him for a second. And then he left. And I had a perfectly average date with a bland law clerk who bred dachshunds. A week passed, then a second, without much thought given to the man with the eggs. Until I put on the black pantyhose for the first time since that night and remembered how it felt to have someone not only see the mess I made of life but be there to help clean it up. In many ways, he'd been right there cleaning up my messes ever since.

Simon looked at me now in a way that suggested if he had a spoon, he'd be dropping it.

"You look exquisite, Kath. You always do."

"Stop that," I said in reply, taking my seat. "Have you ordered?"

Simon rounded the table to his seat again, coming dangerously close to beheading a breadstick with his backside, and sat himself across from me.

"Chicken Parm for me, Alfredo for you. And I got a bottle of red for the table."

"Oh," I said.

"Oh? Bad oh? It was presumptuous, wasn't it? Red wine, especially after last time at my place . . . That wasn't very divorced of me."

"No, it's not that. I just . . . It's about why I wanted to see you tonight." My heart crashed against my rib cage as I began.

Simon reached out a hand and cupped it over mine. "Sweetie, you're shaking. What is it? What's wrong?"

I bolted up from my seat, pulse drumming in my ears. "Excuse me for a second." And with that I fled the table.

The ladies' room smelled like pine cleaner and stale air. I gulped it in until my wobbly legs re-solidified, bracing myself against the sink. The reflection in front of me was bleak. My soft brown eye shadow somehow enhanced my crow's-feet, my left bra strap was in no mood to be hidden away from the spotlight, and I'd very clearly forgotten to bleach my upper-lip hair.

"Okay," I said at the woman in the mirror. "You can do this. You have to do this. I'll get you gelato if you do this. Just go out there and get it over with. Rip off that bandage. You are a strong, independent woman. You can do this."

I dabbed some cold water on my neck and forced myself out into the dining room again. Simon tracked me with worried eyes as I walked back to the table.

"You okay, Kath?"

I sat down heavily.

"Yep," I said tightly. "Listen, Simon . . ." My phone pinged. "Sorry, sorry, this could be urgent." I slid the phone from my purse and laid it on the table in front of me. It was Stu. Shit.

"Kathy, please," said Simon.

"I know, I'm sorry," I said, my eyes scanning the text.

SPOKE TO HIGHER UPS. U NEED 2 GO BACK 2 CLIENT'S HOUSE ASAP. SEE IF U CAN FIND ANY CLUES RE: WHERE SOUL WOULD HAVE GONE WHEN ALIVE

"Kathy," Simon pleaded, the hurt in his voice as work once again consumed my focus reminding me that this divorce was necessary.

My phone pinged again.

CHECK PHONE COMPUTER SOCIAL MEDIA

"Kathy!"

"I'm pregnant."

Ping

FRIEND LIST PHONEBOOK ANY RELEVANT CONTACTS

"You're what?"

Ping

TRACK HIM DOWN THAT WAY

"Just over six months."

"Is it—"

Ping

I'VE BOUGHT YOU TIME. NOT MUCH

"It's yours."

"Are you—"

Ping

BOSSES NEED TO SEE UR DOING SOMETHING ABT THIS

"I'm sure. And I'm keeping it."

"Kathy, this is incredible! All this time we thought we couldn't, but we did. We did?"

Ping

GET OVER THERE TONIGHT. UR JOB DEPENDS ON IT

My eyes fluttered up from my phone screen. "I've got to go."

I pushed back my chair as a young man sauntered over with a tray of steaming food.

"All right, who's got the chicken Parm and who has the fettuccine Alfredo?"

"We're really pregnant?" Simon rose after me.

"Yes."

Simon took my hand. "Okay."

"Okay."

"Okay," said the server. "Alfredo?"

"I guess I'll take that as well," said Simon, his round face beaming. "I'm eating for two."

4

By the time I pulled up to the curb outside 438 Melrose Court, the sun had almost fully set. The driveway was empty, but I pulled my name badge from the glove compartment and pinned it to the collar of my dress just in case.

My job, especially since my promotion to Collections Agent, came with a number of perks: dental, a retirement plan, a gym membership I've New Year's resolutioned myself into using one and a half times, and my name badge. It was silver and shiny, with my name and position engraved just beside our company name and logo, and, most importantly, it enabled me to go wherever I needed to without being noticed. It didn't make me invisible, exactly, but when I put it on, I became part of the furniture, like a lamp or potted plant; there, but not worth paying attention to. It was like turning forty.

Name badge secure, I left my car and crept back into the Ortiz house, the door still open to me in the wake of the recently evicted soul. Easy Death Zone access was another perk of the job. The house looked almost like it had before; still and open and empty. But it was darker now, the kitchen so dim I had to feel my way around the island to the body. Or at least to where the body had been. Some funeral home had clearly come and taken care of that side of things, but the stillness of the air said they'd long since gone.

"Conner?" I tried again, expecting the same nothing I received. A lump had formed at the back of my throat. Not of vomit this time, which was a nice change of pace from Stu's office, but of worry. I couldn't lose this job. I loved this job. I *was* this job.

I'd found the client's bedroom during my last sweep of the house, tucked away in the well-furnished basement, behind a door leading off a room with a pool table and built-in bar. I retraced my steps down the stairs and through the door and felt the same disjointed jolt hit me again. This room was the only one like it in the house: red-painted walls where the rest were refined suburban beige, a gaming system crouched in one corner, a twin bed wrapped in navy blankets against the opposite wall, which was decorated by a hodgepodge of posters, magazine clippings, and printed photographs. An old lava lamp glowed orange from the bedside table and clothes drooped lazily over the chair by a wooden desk with a laptop on top. This room was messy and cluttered and alive. It didn't seem to belong to the house it lived in.

I dove for the jeans on the desk chair and felt the pockets for a phone but found nothing. Seating myself on top of the discarded clothes, I popped open the laptop. It opened directly to FriendChat without requesting a password. I clicked his profile and enlarged his photo. Conner Ortiz, standing at the peak of some hill, a tumble of brown and green below him, a pair of mirrored sunglasses tucked by the arm into the collar of his T-shirt.

It took me a moment to recognize him, even though he was the only person in the photo, arms spread, freckled cheeks lifted in a smile. That wasn't the boy I'd seen on the floor late this afternoon. He looked somehow both older and younger in the picture than he had in death, but what caught me most by surprise were his eyes: big and brown and so sparkling with life it seemed impossible that anything could dim them. The caption read: "Machu Picchu is lit af," with a date stamp of nearly two years ago.

My eyes prickled. I didn't usually have to get to know my clients like this. Alive.

I gave a sniff and sifted through the rest of the images on 507032's profile. A few pictures of him rolling his eyes at the camera during buttoned-down family functions, some shots from concerts, a few of Conner and some friends at a park, a few more of blurry house parties and red cups.

I shifted my focus to the messages that lined the bottom of the screen. A girl named Jessica wanted to know if he and Maddie S. were "a thing." Someone called Youssef just got a new car. But the majority of the messages came from an Ethan Orrick. I scrolled through the conversation until I was a month back in the archives and began to skim.

Ethan: **Priya told the other girls about that pic I sent her and now they all think I'm gross**
Conner: **Nice**
Ethan: **Be serious please Not trying to graduate a virgin here**
Conner: **Dude just lie and say someone else was using your phone and it was their junk**
Ethan: **You really think that would work?**

I skipped ahead.

Ethan: **We still good for Friday at Meadows?**
Conner: **Got nothing else to do**
Ethan: **Cool**

Two days later.

Conner: **Mom's pulling the same bullshit again I'm not going to waste four more years of my life sitting behind a school desk just so I can be like them**
Ethan: **Sucks bro**
Conner: **Not like they'd even notice either way**
Ethan: **Ha ya lol**

That evening.

Ethan: **Yo you good for Meadows? I really need it man**
Conner: **Ya mom and dad are out of town again anyways May as well**

Last night.

Conner: **Meadows?**
Ethan: **Can't man Mom's on me about my grades Gotta study**
Conner: **Pussy**
Ethan: **Yeah yeah**
Conner: **Fine I'll go solo**
Ethan: **You still got enough stuff?**
Conner: **Yeah like half a bag**
Ethan: **Niiice Blaze it for the both of us, brother**

As I read the messages, my mind was trying to translate Teenaged Boy into Middle-Aged English. Was "Meadows" some new slang I was too old to understand? Was it code for something? The name of a hangout, maybe? Did kids still call it hanging out anymore?

I exited the chat and scrolled through the rest of the profile. When I couldn't find anything of interest there, I clicked back through his pictures. Ethan was tagged in most of them. He was shorter than Conner, with the kind of moustache that looked like the facial hair equivalent of a training bra. Conner and Ethan with other friends at a pizza parlor, Conner and Ethan fishing at a lake, Conner and Ethan smoking at a park, Conner and Ethan toasting Gatorade bottles at a park, Conner, Ethan, and two girls illuminated by the camera's flash in the same park. I looked at the location tag. Blazing Meadows Park.

Blazing Meadows. I dug through my purse for my phone and opened up my GPS app. The park was only a ten-minute walk from 507032's house. I glanced back at the picture of Conner and his friends. That spark of life still leapt from the depths of his dark brown eyes. I shut the laptop and retraced my steps through the basement and up the stairs to the main floor, the silence of the empty house crowding around each footstep with a microphone in hand, amplifying every squeak of my shoes on the sterile marble. I'd walked through this silence countless times. Death, for all its wheezing, coughing, and final gasps, left a remarkable vacuum in its wake. And yet, there was something different in the silence that ricocheted off the walls of 438 Melrose Court that made me speed my squeaking steps.

It wasn't until I was nearly back at the front door that I was sure something was off. I couldn't pinpoint it at first. The stress of seeing Simon, maybe? Missing dinner? The tiny fetus rearranging my insides? But then I heard the crash. It came from the basement, from Conner's room. I heard footsteps tapping up the basement stairs, so I crept back through the kitchen and ducked behind the island just in time to catch the shadowy streak of someone dressed in black—and far too alive for my general comfort—dart across the living room to the back door. They gave one final glance behind them, as if searching for a secret only the house would know, emitted a guttural groan of frustration, and slipped through the door, their dark form quickly swallowed by the night.

I rose from my awkward crouch, heart thundering. I didn't know why I'd hid. My name badge meant I had no reason to hide. Yet something in my gut told me I'd done the right thing, for reasons I couldn't put a name to yet.

Just as my pulse returned to normal, my phone rang, shattering the stillness of the house. My prenatal Kegel training failed me.

"Hello?" I said into the phone, voice shaking.

"Did you tell him?"

"Tell who what?"

"Ah, so that's a no, I take it."

I sucked in a gulp of air as I registered the voice on the other end. Jo. She had been my mentor at S.C.Y.T.H.E. until she retired nearly four years ago and decided to fill her newfound free time mentoring me in every other area of life instead.

"Just a sec," I said. In that moment, creeping back through that oppressively silent house felt less daunting than facing the inevitable tuts of disapproval about to come down the phone line. I put Jo on hold and followed the same path down to 507032's basement bedroom, my focus shifting over my shoulder every few steps in case the someone in black reappeared.

This time, the teenaged mess of the bedroom was replaced by something more sinister. Every drawer lay open, their contents hanging out like taunting tongues. The computer screen stood awake, open to the same page I'd left it on, and the bedclothes were strewn in an even more haphazard way than they had been. My knees softened to jelly. Something was very wrong with case 507032.

"DODGING THE QUESTION, ARE WE?" I'D MADE IT TO MY CAR, TURNED it on, and sat there in the dark as Jo's husky, southern accent-tinged voice filled my ear with the comfort of a hot mug of cocoa on a stormy night.

"You mean Simon, about the baby?" I exhaled the words and let myself sink into the discomfort of this area of conversation for a moment while my brain raced to catch up with what I'd just seen.

Jo's tone was an eye roll. "No, the other life-changing errand you had today."

"I told him," I said.

"And?"

"And it went the way I thought it would. He was over the moon."

"I think you might be the first woman in history afraid to tell a man about a pregnancy because he'd be happy about it."

"Yeah, well, he was the one who always wanted babies." I flopped forward over the steering wheel. "I figured, after trying for so long, and then splitting up, it wasn't something I'd have to think about ever again. Especially at my age."

"You two never could keep it in your pants around each other. If you didn't get pregnant sooner or later, he would have. I did warn you about going over to 'talk' that night, didn't I?"

I petted my belly, which had been round long before that last hurrah with Simon. "What's done is done." The porch lights from the Ortiz house danced in my peripheral vision from across the street. "Hey, Jo, did you ever have a file sent to the wrong department back in your S.C.Y.T.H.E. days?"

"Is this some sort of metaphor?"

"No, no. Just . . . I have this case, it was sent to me at Natural Causes, but I feel like there's more to it. Something's off in a big way. The soul was missing, and someone was sneaking around his house just now. Maybe there's some . . . foul play involved?"

There was a pause at the other end of the line. "That can't be right. The higher-ups don't make mistakes like that."

I gulped. "I didn't think so."

"If you're worried there was a mix-up, tell Stu."

"I did—Stu's already on the verge of blending me up and adding me to his morning protein shake."

"That does sound like Stu. Still, you've had a lot on your plate with this baby situation. It'll ease your mind to hear directly from him that this is just like any old case. Talk to him again tomorrow morning."

"All right," I said. "I guess I'll do that."

"No guessing involved, sugar. Take my word for it, you'll feel better once you have your answers."

"I will. Thanks, Jo."

"Of course."

We hung up, and the sudden silence of my car sent my mind rushing back to that wrong silence of 507032's house. The overturned bedroom, which had obviously been searched. I had to find 507032, fast. But where would he go? Essences were creatures of habit. They could move about as they pleased, but preferred to stick by their body when they could because it was the home they knew best. I thought about the photos on the dead boy's computer. Maybe, for some, a stronger home came from the people they cared about. I set my GPS for Blazing Meadows Park.

THE PARK SAT ACROSS FROM A SMALL ROW OF COOKIE-CUTTER houses, the floodlights from a baseball diamond at the far end spilling just enough over the open field of the park itself to illuminate the tree line about fifteen yards away. The heat of the day was finally breaking, sending swirls of mist over the grass. I crunched across the pebbled square that made up the small parking lot and stopped a few feet from a line of cement parking blocks. 507032 glanced up at me from where he sat on one of the blocks, looking just as he had in the photos on his laptop but for a slight glow.

"Hello," I said.

Nothing.

I shifted my weight. Talking to youths had never been a skill of mine, even when I technically was one. I raised my voice an octave, adopting the tone I'd used when talking to my old cat. "I've been looking for you."

The boy's gaze slid from my face to my name badge, where it snagged.

"What the fuck do you want?"

"I . . ."

But before I had a chance to think of how to fill the rest of that sentence, 507032 interrupted with, "Fuck off."

"Hey now," was all I could think of in response.

He angled himself away from me.

"Conner," I tried again, "my name is Kathy Valence. I'm an agent with Secure Collection, Yielding, and Transportation of Human Essences. I'm here to help you."

"Help me?" the boy spat, whipping back around. "Fuck you."

I sucked in a deep breath. "Okay, I'm sensing some hostility here—"

"Ya think?" he said. "What do you fucking expect? What, you want a hug? Oh wait, can't give you one of those, I don't have a fucking body anymore."

"No," I agreed. "Look, it's natural for someone your age to feel anger at this time. You're upset about all the things you'll miss out on—"

"No," said 507032. "I'm upset because you killed me."

5

I stared blankly at the soul in front of me for a long moment. This wasn't the first belligerent client I'd ever encountered. If you have a job working with the public, you know it means dealing with all sorts—and being newly dead always seemed to bring out the worst in people. But being accused of killing someone was new.

"I *what*?" was the only thing I could muster.

The boy got to his feet, his freckled face bunched up into a scowl. "All I know is one second I'm alive, and then I see that thing"—he jabbed a finger at my badge—"and the next thing I know, I'm dead as fuck."

"Conner, I need you to calm down."

"And I need you to fuck off."

"What you're saying is impossible," I said, as much to myself as to him. "You shouldn't be able to see anyone wearing one of these badges pre-death."

"Yeah, well, no one was wearing it. It was in the grass over there." He angled his chin towards the tree line, but when I moved to investigate, he added, "It's gone now. But you would know that, wouldn't you?"

My skin prickled into goose bumps as the implications of what the boy was saying swirled in my mind. "Did you see a name?"

He shook his head. "Just that stupid symbol."

I ran a thumb over the engraving of the scythe and arrow on my badge. My mouth felt dry, as if someone had come in and vacuumed up all of the saliva.

"You must be mistaken. I have you down as death by seizure. I can show you the file if you'd like—"

"Save it. I don't want any of your bullshit. I just want you to leave me the fuck alone."

"Conner, I need you to come with me. There are consequences to not following procedure. You'll end up trapped here."

"Fine by me." He shoved his hands back into the pockets of his hoodie. "I was actually happy here. And then you sick fucks took it all away."

Before I could reply, his back was towards me as his soul faded into the bruised-indigo summer night.

I DIDN'T SLEEP THAT NIGHT. FOR ONCE MY UPSTAIRS NEIGHBORS' late-night escapades (having sex? Moving furniture? Performing intricately choreographed modern dance numbers? I still hadn't figured out which) were a welcome distraction from my thoughts. If what 507032 said was true, then someone from my company, someone I knew and trusted, had murdered a teenaged boy. But why? And how? I'd seen the body. There was no sign of violence or injury, so he *must* have died of a seizure like his file said. And if he hadn't, our system would have picked it up and logged his death accordingly.

I turned onto my side and tapped my phone, letting its light pick out the details of my room: the bookcase by the window, the dress slacks and dark purple blouse I'd hung over my closet door for work tomorrow, the antique mirror and dense oak vanity inherited from my grandmother. It was a tight squeeze; most of my furniture came from the town house I'd shared with Simon, and it barely fit into my dingy divorcée apartment. In some ways, I barely fit too.

This wasn't how I'd pictured my forties, but I told myself the divorced life was for the best. Or at the very least, it was inevitable. When I was growing up, my dad always said I had the "Sadim touch." It took me until my senior year of high school to realize that was "Midas" spelled backwards. The opposite of a golden touch. Everything I turned my hand to, I ruined. From messing up lines in a school play to failing out of college twice before graduating, I could never seem to get anything right. For most of my life I couldn't keep friends for more than a year, jobs more than six months, and I considered past relationships a success if they made it beyond the second date. Even my own family seemed to disappear once I moved away; Mom's calls lessening every year, Dad only emailing on my birthday, their focus ever more concentrated on a brother and sister who never put a foot wrong, the memory of my parents' disapproving looks in response to each of my failures my main connection to my roots.

Then S.C.Y.T.H.E. came along, and they wanted me. *I* was exactly what they were looking for. *Me*. My unremarkable, downright mediocre life meant I could blend into the scenery; could handle the extraordinary because I lacked any of my own. For once, I wasn't bad at something; wasn't even just okay. I was good. I got my souls where they needed to be, my reports on Stu's desk by end of day, and suddenly I knew my place in life. But it was a place no one outside S.C.Y.T.H.E. was allowed to know about. Not even Simon.

And at first that suited me fine. I only ever knew how to keep him at arm's length so my Sadim touch couldn't ruin things, and this job gave me permission to keep him there. But over the years, this secret became so big and took up so much room in my relationship with Simon that I knew I'd eventually ruin us anyway. Every day I'd come home to questions I couldn't answer, pleas to open up, and sad gray eyes filled with hope and love for someone I could never be. Which meant I had to choose. Love, which I sucked at, or a job I could actually do. Between secrets and the oak vanity, there was room for only one in my cluttered life, and I knew which one Simon deserved. Where a baby fit into the mix, I had no idea. When I was honest with myself, I didn't think it fit much at all.

I sighed and flopped onto my back. Tomorrow I would talk to Stu, just like Jo told me to, and he'd all-caps SORT THIS OUT, just like he always did. Whatever the real story was, he'd get to the bottom of it, and I'd write up the report. I just needed to get through one more morning of judgmental biceps and pleading for my job and then everything would be back to normal. With me *and* my job.

On that thought, I fell asleep.

WHEN I GOT TO WORK IN THE MORNING, GEMMA WAS PERCHED ON the edge of my desk, scrolling through her phone with one hand and nibbling a manicured pinky nail with the other. For a moment I wondered if I'd walked into the wrong cubicle, but there was no mocking yoga mat rolled in the corner, no gallon jug of water on the desk, no kitten calendar thumbtacked behind the computer. Just the desk waiting for my laptop, the chair waiting for my butt, and Gemma Burke.

"Good morning," I said.

Gemma leapt from the desk, her hands falling to her sides. "Stu's on the warpath," she warned.

"Shit."

"Yeah. Everything all right after that weird collection thing yesterday?"

I could feel my cheeks warming as her eyes searched me. I wondered what was behind her gaze. Judgment? Pity? Could she see me reaching out towards case 507032 with my Sadim touch, about to ruin something else?

"Oh, nothing to worry about," I lied. "You know Stu."

Gemma gave a light laugh. "Yeah. You know, I hear he keeps a stack of spare shirts under his desk for when he gets so pissed he Hulks out of the one he's wearing."

I pictured those angry biceps tearing free of their light cotton prison, bulging veins pulsing curses at me in Morse code.

"Anyway," Gemma continued to my blank face, "just thought I should give you the heads-up, what with the sitch last night and all."

"Thanks," was the best I could muster.

Just then, Stu's hulking voice boomed. "Valence!"

I bolted up and padded cautiously down the hall towards his glass sanctum. Through one of the windows I caught a glimpse of his morning smoothie. Greens-forward, with something mealy floating through it. Shit. I'd angered him into a cleanse.

"Sit," Stu said as soon as I was through the door.

I sat.

"Well?"

I took a big inhale. I'd practiced this speech my whole drive in to work. "I found the missing essence, but he claims he was killed by someone from S.C.Y.T.H.E. As absurd as that sounds, is there any possibility of truth to it?" was what I had planned to say. Perhaps what I should have said. But I didn't. Instead I shrugged.

"No luck," I mumbled, though I didn't know why. I was shooting myself in the foot, but for some reason I just couldn't bring myself to say my speech. The words just wouldn't come.

Stu wheeled himself closer to his desk, propped his elbows on the surface, his face in his hands, and rubbed his temple. "Kathy," he said, "I gave you a chance with this—"

"You did," I jumped in. "And I went back to the address; I followed your directions to a T. I just . . . I think I just need more time."

"And I need to know you have this under control. This is serious. This is important. I need to know it's being handled as quickly and effectively as if I were handling it myself."

"It will be," I promised.

"All right," Stu said through an exhale, taking me by surprise. "You have a good track record. This situation is an anomaly, I can appreciate that. It will be taken care of promptly or there will be consequences, but you will be the one taking care of it. For now. Am I understood?"

My eyes flitted from Stu's angular face to his left bicep, which regarded me with a patient stillness through his light pink button-down.

"Really?" I blurted in spite of myself. I'd braced for a verbal smackdown. I'd braced for Gemma's promise of a Hulkian explosion. I'd braced so hard I didn't know what to do with all this energy I'd been bracing with. My knee bounced. I should tell him. I should tell him about finding the boy and what he'd said. But still I didn't.

"Be quick about it, Valence. The higher-ups are not happy. Mess this up and I'll have to decide whether or not you still have a place at this company."

"Okay," I said, wondering if someone had laced his smoothie with sedatives. "Thank you."

"Don't thank me yet," said Stu.

"Right. No. I won't. I mean, I did, but it was more of a placeholder thank-you. I just—" I scrambled to my feet. "I thought you'd be mad."

"I'm furious," said Stu.

"Oh."

"But I need to conserve calories for my new fitness program later. I'm not wasting them yelling at you."

"Oh," I said again.

"Now get out of my sight and get to work."

IT HAD BEEN A FAIRLY EASY DAY: TWO HEART ATTACKS AND AN eighty-four-year-old cancer patient who kept up a running commentary on what he would say when he saw his wife again. It sounded sweet at first, because I was half tuned out, my mind on the 507032 problem. When I actually started listening, it quickly became apparent that he wasn't planning their romantic reunion but was rehearsing how to tell her he'd been sleeping with her sister for the past forty years. I dropped him at the warehouse with one of the processors on duty and a tight "good luck."

It was just after five when my car crunched over the unpaved parking lot of Blazing Meadows Park. The boy wasn't on the parking block this time. In fact, he wasn't anywhere, as far as I could tell. I trudged across the open field, the smell of recently mown grass on the breeze, but only a man playing Frisbee with his dog was there to greet me. I swallowed a sudden lump of desperation. Where was he? If he wasn't here, I had no idea how to find him. What was I going to tell Stu? "I lost an entire soul. Again." My job was hanging on by a thread already, and 507032's disappearance was a ball of knives hurtling towards it. At the tree line, I pushed into the densely woven woods without searching for a path to follow. My feet kicked up dry leaves as I marched deeper into the forest, calling the boy's name. I was so distracted by my mission to find him, I nearly missed the cliffside I was barreling towards. I froze at the edge of a steep twenty-foot drop-off, the hillside covered in lush trees and tangled roots. I backtracked a few steps and noticed a bench beside me, looking out over the tree-filled dip. A half-full Ziploc baggie of what appeared to be weed sat on the far end of the bench. I wondered briefly if it had belonged to Conner or one of his friends. This had been their spot, after all.

When I emerged from the woods, the man and dog were gone. Someone nearby was barbecuing, the humid air ripe with smoke. My stomach gurgled. I hadn't eaten since breakfast, and neither my belly nor its current resident was happy with that choice. I scanned the park one last time before slinking, defeated, back to my car. The boy had already been so distrustful last night that even had he been here I was sure I would have had a tough time. Now, with him missing again, I was right back where I'd started on Melrose Court.

6

sailed out of the suburban maze of lifeless, cookie-cutter houses and headed towards home.

When I opened the door, Jo was sitting at my kitchen table wrapped in a floral housedress, her yellow Lab Seeing Eye dog, Chap, at her feet. The overhead light turned her short, cottony, snow-white curls into a halo. A half-eaten plate of my leftover fettuccine lay in front of her.

"You're late," she said, frowning.

I threw my purse onto the free edge of my file-cabinet-turned-kitchen-counter. "I wasn't expecting you."

"You should always expect me."

She was right about that. A few months back I'd given Jo a spare key so she could water my plants while I was away for a weekend conference, and I had been coming home to surprise visits ever since. Each time it happened I told myself I'd sit her down and tell her to stop, but I never did. In truth, it was nice having someone to come home to every now and again since my separation from Simon, even if she did eat more of my food, borrow more of my toiletries, and complain more about my attempts at cooking than he ever did.

"So?"

I slid into the chair across from her. "So?"

"So how'd it go with Stu, you silly thing?"

Ah. I should have known it was gossip she'd come for.

"Did he sort it out for you, then? He didn't bite your head off too badly, I hope."

I took her weathered hand and placed it on top of the shapeless frizz sprouting from my head down to just below my shoulders. "It's still there," I said lightly. I wasn't ready to tell her I'd chickened out of telling Stu the truth, or for the lecture that was sure to follow. And I certainly wasn't ready to tell her I'd lost the boy again.

Jo pulled her hand away, exasperated already. "Well, that's something."

"He's letting me handle it," I said.

"Remarkably levelheaded for Stu."

"I thought so, yes."

"And?"

"And?" I repeated blankly.

"And what is it you aren't telling me?"

I grimaced. Jo didn't have to be able to see the expression on my face to know there was more to the story. She'd known me for too long. She knew me too well. She knew too much in general. All she needed was the slight crack in my voice before she pounced.

"I lost him."

"You what?"

"The essence. I found him, and then I lost him, and I don't know where else to look." The words poured out of me like tomato soup from a can, rushed and sloppy and splattering. "He said things. When I found him. Impossible things. He said he was murdered—"

"Bullshit! The company just doesn't mix up Murder with Natural Causes!"

"I know, but there's more. He insists that someone at S.C.Y.T.H.E. killed him. That right before he died, he saw our logo. He was so sure. And it made me . . . less sure. About everything. And now I don't know what to do. About anything. I could lose my job over this, Jo. And then what? I'm back to being hollow except for this exhausting, hungry thing growing inside me, and I can't let that happen. I can't have *nothing* again."

My lips wobbled closed and we sat for a long moment in the echo of my rant. Finally, Jo cleared her throat.

"Well, that is a mighty pickle you're in."

I rubbed my freshly throbbing temples.

"Souls are funny things," Jo continued. "They're raw, vulnerable, naked without their bodies to wear. From what I know of them, they don't stray far from where they feel safe. Wherever you found your boy once, you'll find him again. Just give it time. He sounds scared."

"But what does he have left to be afraid of? He's dead."

"True. But he's young, isn't he? Could be that. Could be he hasn't fully come to terms with being dead yet. But . . ."

"But?"

"But none of that explains how he'd have seen a S.C.Y.T.H.E. logo when he was alive. Now that, my girl, is strange indeed."

7

Forty-Three Days to Ghost

Work felt different the next morning; like I was inside a fishbowl and all my colleagues were watching me, distorted and unfamiliar, from the outside. I could feel the comfort and sanctuary of this place I thought I knew slipping away. Which was absurd. I'd known this place and the people in it for the better part of a decade. Sure, I didn't spend time with them outside of these four walls. And okay, I couldn't remember most of their partners' names under threat of death. And admittedly, I may have lied about the demise of an uncle I didn't have in order to get out of the annual interdepartmental softball tournament. Twice. But I knew my colleagues, and the notion that any of them could go against policy, much less the law, and actually kill a client was bonkers. And yet, no matter how many times I told myself as much, I couldn't shake my uneasiness.

By one thirty I had barely mustered more than the occasional, wary "working hard or hardly working" to any of my colleagues, which suited my newfound discomfort just fine.

Fortunately, Gemma was too busy to chat, her focus on her phone, tapping away in a flurry of manicured thumbs and intensity, girlish smiles occasionally fluttering across her face. She was back on the dating apps again, I guessed—a place someone like Gemma would undoubtedly thrive. I was always so grateful Simon had come along before I'd had to venture into that world, because I was certainly no Gemma. Yet still, somehow, he'd chosen me.

I kept eyeing Stu through his office windows but couldn't bring myself to tell him my concern that one of his employees could be involved with 507032's death. What would I say? "Hey, any chance the system we've relied on for centuries could be faulty and someone here could be a murderer?" He'd already downed three troughs of water in place of food. Low-blood-sugar Stu was my least favorite Stu even on a normal day. I decided to wait.

The lunchroom was empty when I got there. I popped my pasta into the microwave and sat down at one of the peeling square tables with my phone. Three texts from Simon. The first was a picture of a stack of parenting books, the second was an emoji with a smile taking up half its yellow face, and the third simply said "BABY!!!!!!!"

I sent a thumbs-up emoji back, fighting off a grin of my own. That was Simon in a text: boundless care, an all-encompassing smile, and seven exclamation points' worth of enthusiasm all bundled into a compact, slightly clammy man. I sighed, turned my phone off, and pulled my lunch from the beeping microwave.

A moment later Caroline and Abdul from Accidental Deaths strolled in with Jesse Hare from Murder. The AD twosome were chirping pleasantly about some new show they'd started streaming last night. Caroline gave me a wave without stopping her chatter as she joined me at the table. Her short, dirty-blond curls and electric-blue glasses offset her vest of the day: a twine-brown crocheted number hanging open over a T-shirt rather bravely displaying unicorns in outer space. Jesse popped a frozen meal into the microwave and sat down a few feet away as Abdul made a beeline for the fridge. Jesse seemed to have checked out of the conversation that was still ping-ponging between the others, his arms crossed over his broad chest. I didn't talk to Murder much, but today I had a reason. Today I needed answers. I slid my chair towards him.

"Hey, Jesse," I greeted, as naturally as I could. "How's it going over in Murder?"

"Oh, same old grind," he responded, sliding a wooden toothpick from one side of his mouth to the other. He had recently been promoted to manager of the department, which coincided with a decision to quit smoking, and the stress of both meant a toothpick had become a staple of Jesse's otherwise nondescript face. He wasn't a particularly tall man, but between an inexplicable year-round tan, thick dark hair, and a wardrobe of polo shirts that smelled like lemon-scented laundry detergent, there was something on the cusp of attractive about him. Today's citrusy shirt was a rich blue that matched his eyes. "How's Natch Cause?"

"Yeah, yeah, same there too." I scooched closer. "You're still getting all your cases okay? Paperwork-wise? No filing mix-ups or anything?"

Jesse cocked a brow at me. "Of course not. That doesn't happen here."

"No, you're right," I said quickly. "Just . . . I was watching this report on the news last night about how frequently corporations mix up files and send things to the wrong department and all that, and I just thought . . ." *I just thought I might have gotten a case meant for one of your people instead*, was what I wanted to say, but instead what I said was, "I guess it got into my head."

Jesse nodded. "Good thing we work where we do."

"I agree," I said through a forced smile. When I shifted back to my original spot, I realized the other conversation had stopped. Abdul was up at the counter, stirring something and seemingly oblivious, but Caroline was sitting with her sandwich still in its wrapper in front of her, staring at me with wide eyes.

I DIDN'T KNOCK ON STU'S DOOR UNTIL FIVE MINUTES AFTER THE workday was done. He beckoned me in with a "come" and was typing something on his laptop when I opened the door.

"Progress?" he asked, his eyes leaving his computer screen just long enough to register that it was me in his office.

"Getting there," I lied. "I have a question for you. I know our death system is foolproof by all accounts. But, hypothetically, in a crazy, backwards world where that wasn't the case, what would happen if, say, someone from Natural Causes was assigned a case from Murder or vice versa?"

Stu narrowed his eyes at me. "This is all hypothetical?"

"Entirely. It's just something I've often wondered about. You know me, Curious Kathy."

Stu blinked at me for a beat and then nodded. "Hmm. Hypothetically, that soul would be prevented from crossing over because they couldn't be processed correctly. A Collections Agent would need to determine the actual cause of death and the case would proceed from there accordingly. Were that process to fail, the essence would be bound to earth just like any other uncollected soul. Which is why S.C.Y.T.H.E. has invested so much time and money into creating the system it has. We can't afford to risk the scenario you've just described."

"And in that scenario," I said, "a Collections Agent should do whatever it takes to learn what happened to the essence?"

"Absolutely that should be the priority, yes," said Stu. "But enough hypotheticals. How's your actual case coming along?"

I hid a gulp under what was meant to be a casual chuckle but emerged instead as the deranged croak of a frog on the first day of mating season. My actual case was growing more complicated by the moment, and if I let the increasingly strained smile slip from my face, I might show as much. But I couldn't do that. Not with my job on the line.

I croaked again. "Everything's going exactly according to plan." And in truth, it was. It just wasn't my plan. Instead it was the plan of a messed-up teenaged boy. Or maybe, if I was really unlucky, the plan of a murderer.

8

It was just after one a.m. when I parked my car. For a minute I stared out into the thick, humid darkness, slippered foot still on the brake. When I emerged, I inadvertently slammed the car door shut, the sound ripping through the air like a gunshot. I grimaced, nearly biting the inside of my cheek. I was in my plaid pajama pants, my dense, frizzy hair springing sideways in defiance of gravity.

After more than two hours of tossing and turning and trying and failing to sleep, I'd given up altogether. And now I was here. I lowered myself to the cement parking block I'd found 507032 sitting on two nights ago and hugged my knees, my back to the field and the forest beyond. The moon was high overhead, its pale glow dimmed by the nearby floodlights. A light breeze brushed my cheeks, its touch wet and warm. My pulse was a jackhammer in my ears. I was a woman alone in an empty park in the middle of the night. Each of those factors individually was enough to set off alarm bells, and mixing them together seemed like a recipe for the kind of cocktail that left you hating yourself come morning. But this was where 507032 felt safe, so I breathed in and tried to feel whatever he had felt here.

I sat with my eyes closed for ten, maybe fifteen minutes, a cricket loudly requesting a one-night stand from the nearby grass. My pulse had steadied by the time I opened my eyes again, but this time I wasn't alone.

"Fucking things don't shut up." The boy tipped his head in the direction of the cricket.

"Hello, Conner," I said, forcing a calm smile over my relief and eagerness.

"Yeah. So, what do you want from me?"

"I want to help you." I rose to my feet, and he still towered above me. I wondered, not for the first time, what sort of elephant hormones kids these days seemed to be born with. My hand drifted to my stomach and I willed this baby to be whatever size was easiest to squeeze out.

"That's rich," the boy spat.

"Because you think someone at my company killed you," I said before he could. "I don't know whether or not that's the case, Conner, but I do know that I had nothing to do with whatever happened to you. And I promise that I'm going to find out exactly what did."

"Yeah, right, and how do you plan to do that?"

"I have no idea," I said. "But I'd have a much easier time of it with your help."

"You want me to help you, like, solve my murder?"

"Yes."

"Like the Miss Marple bullshit my nanny used to watch?"

"Exactly." I shrugged. "What do you think? Help me figure out what happened to you?"

He looked through me as though I was the one without a body, half his face alive with moonlight, that incomprehensible sparkle still lighting his eyes. Finally, his focus returned to me.

"Fuck," he said. "Fine."

"SO WHAT ARE YOU, LIKE, SOME KIND OF GRIM REAPER?"

We'd fallen into step in the open field, the boy's hands in his pockets, his hood up, eyes on the dew-soaked grass. I'd just finished the usual spiel I used with my clients when I came to collect them, more out of habit than anything, though nothing about this case was usual.

I grimaced. "Essentially. We underwent some reorganization around the turn of the last century. The field was still working out some kinks and we dropped the ball more than we should have during the 1800s. All those ghosts stuck on the earthly plane meant new souls had become reluctant to work with us, so we dropped the cloaks, went corporate, and brought on some of the best minds in science, technology, and image consulting to help turn things around. We prefer to be called Collections Agents these days. 'Grim Reaper' has negative connotations."

"So you *are* a grim reaper."

I exhaled sharply through my nose. "Can you run me through what happened on the day you died? Anything out of the ordinary?"

The boy shook his head. "Nah, Grim. Typical day. I woke up around one, played some video games for a bit, got stoned, went into the kitchen to make a grilled cheese, and before I'd made it to the fridge, boom, dead."

"Just like that?"

"Yeah. I mean, I had a seizure first, I guess. I got real dizzy and blacked out, like I used to when I had them as a kid, but this time I didn't wake up again."

"So you've had seizures before?" My pace slowed, my mind picking up speed.

"Sure. Used to get them all the time as a kid. Full-on epilepsy according to my doctor. Then a few years back they just kinda stopped."

"Just like that?" I asked again.

"I guess. Like, I think I kind of made them stop."

I cocked my head at him, and the boy took a deep, airless breath.

"Like, they're scary, right? Like fuck, I always thought I was gonna die when I had one. Which, irony, I know. But as long as my nanny was around, I knew someone would at least be there to call 911 or whatever if I needed it, right? But then I got too old for a nanny and I wasn't about to have a seizure on my own, so like, they just kinda stopped after that."

At this point I'd stopped walking altogether.

"What?" the boy asked from a few paces ahead, turning once he realized I was no longer beside him.

"Conner," I said, trying to keep my voice steady, "is it not possible that your epilepsy didn't just go away? That maybe it was dormant for a while and came back with a grand mal seizure strong enough to kill you?"

"No," he said, his hands out of his pockets and waving animatedly in front of him. "Absolutely not. I told you, I got rid of them."

I closed my eyes for an extended blink and tried to think calming thoughts. "Right, but you also said that someone at

S.C.Y.T.H.E. killed you. How is that possible when you died from a seizure?"

"I don't know," said the boy. "But it happened. I swear to you. I'm not making this shit up. I don't remember how it happened. It's like there's this blank spot in my brain from the night I saw that logo, but somebody killed me. I know they did."

"Conner," I tried again, "the way you died is nothing to be ashamed of—"

"I'm not ashamed!"

"Let me take you to processing. You can move on; we can all move on."

"No! Fuck you. I was murdered and you don't even care. Nobody ever fucking cares."

"Conner—"

"No! God. What is it with you people? What, you hit thirty and suddenly nothing said by a teenager means anything? I'm telling you what I know. I don't know how I know it, but I do. If you won't believe me, then fine, fuck off forever. I'm better off out here alone."

"You don't understand how this system works," I said through clenched teeth. "You have a very limited time to be processed and moved on or else you end up trapped here permanently."

"Good," said Conner. "I hope I do get trapped here. At least I was happy here. And you know what? I hope you get fucking fired for like, negligence or whatever."

I chewed the inside of my cheek to keep from yelling. "I don't think you're thinking this through."

"Yeah? Well, I'm seventeen. I shouldn't have to think this through. I should be, I don't know, at a party or, like, planning my future or some shit. But I'm not. Because I'm dead. Because one of your guys fucking killed me and not some stupid, pointless seizure, and you won't do anything about it, so we're done here."

Before I could even think up a reply, the boy had returned his hands to his pockets and was making a beeline for the dark web of trees beside us. As much as I needed him processed, and as sure as I now was that this was a straightforward case after all, I couldn't bring myself to follow him, unarmed and pajama-clad, into the woods. Instead I swallowed a lump of frustrated tears and walked alone through the park to my car as my one hope of keeping my job disappeared into the forest.

Forty-Two Days to Ghost

Things looked different in the daylight, by which I mean they looked the same as they had before 507032 and his stoned, teenaged paranoia had gotten into my head. The S.C.Y.T.H.E. offices hummed with the familiar, fluorescent buzz of the migraine-inducing lights above. The halls smelled faintly of cleaning supplies and yesterday's lunch. Gemma flitted past with a dainty wave and a rolled yoga mat under her arm. Everything was normal. Everything was right. I bypassed my desk and went straight into Stu's office without knocking. He was hunched over the remnants of some sort of egg white and spinach concoction that smelled like a wet dog rubbed in feet and which he was now picking from his teeth with an open safety pin.

I cleared my throat and Stu put the pin back in his drawer and nodded for me to sit down.

"I've located the essence," I said as my butt hit the seat across from his desk.

Stu's eyebrows bounced with surprise. "And?"

"And as of this time he remains where I found him, so we know where he is. I've also confirmed his cause of death, which is as his file stated."

"Of course it is," Stu said with a note of annoyance. "That was never in question."

I breezed past that with an enthusiastic clap of my hands against my lap. "It's exciting, isn't it? The case is nearly closed. All that worry for nothing."

"I don't see anything exciting about you doing your job correctly, but I am relieved to hear we can put this episode behind us. Get the essence to processing and I'll inform my superiors that no internal investigation will be necessary."

"Internal—?"

"In fact, why isn't he already in processing, Valence?"

"He will be," I promised. "Soon."

"Hmm," was Stu's reply.

Gemma and Caroline were chatting in the hallway as I passed through to get to my desk. It was something I'd always envied Gemma for—her ease in befriending colleagues, even from other departments, like Caroline, whose current vest glimmered with enough sequins to costume half a decent drag show. Though, frankly, this was one conversation I didn't much regret missing out on.

"I guess I just figured losing a parent would be easier considering my line of work, you know?" Gemma was saying. "Mortality just feels so . . . It all feels so different when it's someone you care about, I guess. So confusing."

"It's something you get past once you've been in the game as long as I have," Caroline replied as I snuck by. "No more worrying about what happens next and all that. No room for squeamishness when you've dealt with hundreds of souls or stood over hundreds of bodies. No, when it comes to death and all that surrounds it, I no longer have any squeamishness at all. In fact, between you and me, I—"

Gemma broke from the conversation and rushed over to me as I passed. "Kath! A bunch of us are going out after work tonight. A new club just opened downtown and I'm totally dying to check it out. Come with?"

This was the third time in as many weeks that Gemma had tried to get me to socialize. It was a nice thought, but I was always so tired these days, and I couldn't drink due to the baby situation, which meant I'd be stuck sober at a table watching drunk colleagues half my age gyrate at one another. The thought made my bile rise, though that didn't take much lately. Besides, I had never been much for social gatherings even when I didn't have a fetus rearranging my organs.

"Thanks," I said. "But I think I'm going to make it an early night."

"Aw, if you're sure."

"Maybe next time," I said.

"I hope so, but I totally get it. My mom can't stand staying up later than ten p.m. anymore. I'm super not looking forward to that."

I smiled politely in reply, wondering what she'd have thought of me in my early twenties: home by nine every night so I could catch the second airing of that day's *Jeopardy!*, then a chapter from whichever Brontë book I was rereading before sliding into bed at eleven.

Gemma was the kind of girl I'd always thought I should be but could never quite figure out how. At twenty-five I bought myself a pair of skintight jeans as a middle finger to my pear shape, dyed my hair platinum blond, and went on a weeklong trip to France with a couple of girls I knew from work. I hated every minute of it: the blisters I got from my fashionable shoes, the constant hangovers from barhopping every night, the sound of one girl or the other getting laid across the hostel room. I even tried having a one-night stand myself, with a German tourist we met while at a little café, but I'd gotten bored halfway through and we ended up playing cards instead.

The moment we got home, I dyed my hair back to its usual strawberry blond, traded the jeans for slacks, and have stayed the same Kathy ever since. Sometimes I regretted it, but I'd accepted some time ago that I'd passed the expiration date for wild adventures, and with this baby on the way, I couldn't ask for much as far as new experiences went unless they revolved around motherhood, something I was in no way suited for or particularly looking forward to.

SIMON WAS OUTSIDE MY APARTMENT UNIT WHEN I GOT HOME, AND he wasn't alone. Beside him stood a stack of packages cloaked in silver and yellow wrapping paper, his hallmark over-taped edges glistening in the fluorescent hall lights along with his ever-lengthening forehead, which, as always, begged for a kiss. It had been our ritual every day before we each left for our respective jobs; a kiss on my cheek, a kiss on his forehead, and one on the lips that almost always held the promise of something more waiting at the end of a long workday. I pulled my gaze away and closed the space between us.

"I know I shouldn't have come without calling first," he said before I'd reached him, hands out in front of him as if he was expecting a swift knee to the ballsack responsible for my current condition. "But I was in the area and couldn't resist."

"Resist what?" I said as I wrestled my keys from my purse. "Turning my hallway into Santa's workshop?"

"You're glowing," Simon said.

"It's sweat," I assured him. "Did you want to come in?" I regretted the words as soon as they were out of my mouth. I was playing with fire now. Every moment we spent together weakened my resolve and made me question my decision to leave him, no matter how much I knew it was for the best.

Before I could say anything more, Simon nodded and scooped at the parcels until his arms were crowded with them. I reluctantly opened the door and he waddled in behind me.

"What is all this?" I asked as he placed the packages on my kitchen table.

"Nothing to get too excited about, just some things for the baby. There's diapers in there, and that one"—Simon tapped one of the bigger packages—"is a Diaper Genie. One of these has bottles, and there's a bulk tub of coconut oil in case you decide to breastfeed and your nipples get sore."

"Let's not talk about my nipples," I said.

"Right, right." He held a hand up to the swell of my stomach but thought better of it before letting it land. "Do you have a birth plan worked out? Midwife or doula? I think both have pros and cons, but a lot depends on what kind of birth you're having. And I've learned some relaxing breathing techniques. I've tried them out and they definitely help relieve trapped gas, so that's a promising sign—"

"Simon," I said before he could continue.

"Too much?"

"Too much."

"Right," he said. "I should go. I'm sure you had a long day . . ." His tone shifted, weighted with years of emotion, as he added, "At work."

I shot him a look that was meant as a plea to drop the subject that ended our marriage but might have come across more as mild constipation. And there it was; the reminder I needed that we couldn't be together. My line of work required secrets to keep my job, my Sadim touch required secrets to keep Simon from seeing just how much of a mess I truly was, and my secrets hurt him. And I couldn't be the one to hurt Simon. His hands were raised defensively again. "I mean it, I'm not trying to start anything, I'm sure you're tired is all."

"Thank you for the baby things," I said, trying to match his earnest tone.

He gave a modest shrug. "I was just in the area."

"You're going to be a good dad, Simon," I said. I wasn't sure I'd managed to keep all the sadness from my voice, but he didn't seem to notice. Instead, his face lit up in the sort of all-encompassing smile that had made me fall in love with him in the first place.

"You mean that? Oh, Kath, I really hope I will be. And you? You're going to be an amazing mom. The best there is."

Those words made my stomach turn, and I ushered him out in just enough time to make it to the bathroom before retching up my lunch.

10

That night I was a different person than I had been the night before. No pajama pants and slippers, no wild-eyed insomnia, no inky midnight keeping me on guard. I pulled into the gravel parking lot of Blazing Meadows a good half hour before sunset, in my work outfit of black bootcut slacks and an eggplant blouse. I was a professional. I was here to do my job. I straightened my name badge as I exited my car, debating where to start the hunt for my reluctant client. This wouldn't be easy, I knew that much, but if nothing else it might give me a chance to prove that I deserved to keep my job. That my Sadim touch didn't extend to my work. That I could do something right.

"Conner?" I called into the ether. "I know I'm probably the last person you want to see, but if we could just talk for a minute, I—"

"Will you shut up, you crazy bitch?" came a hiss from behind me. I whipped around to find Conner there in the dying sunlight, sparkling eyes darting around like two dark flies buzzing on his face. I swallowed back my distaste for his greeting.

"Conner. Now, I know we didn't get off on the best foot—"

Without letting me finish my rehearsed speech, 507032 attempted to grab me by the forearm, growled when his hand went through me, and instead tipped his head for me to follow him.

"I know we didn't get off on the—" I tried again, faster this time, but the boy tipped his head again and had already begun storming away a few words into my sentence. I grumbled to myself but followed him, his pace picking up until we were both tucked behind the fat trunk of an oak tree.

"I know we didn't—"

"They came back," 507032 interrupted, his voice an urgent whisper.

I sighed, knowing where this was headed but unable to help myself all the same. "What are you talking about?"

"Your . . . your grim reaper pals. The ones who killed me. They came back."

I took advantage of a long blink to steady my breath, calm my voice, remind myself that this was an essence with no body left to throttle. He would be out of my hair soon. Tonight. I'd be making sure of that. Just talk the stoner kid down from his paranoia and dump him at processing and then sleep. Sweet, beautiful sleep. Eight whole hours of it.

"No, they didn't, Conner. That's in your head. I know you're scared. I know 'death by seizure' isn't what you want all your little friends to read in your obituary because it isn't 'cool' like murder is, but I assure you that's what happened. Now, if you'll just come with me, I'll take you to a better place."

It was a bit of a lie. Processing was an industrial warehouse that didn't have much in the way of ambience, but it was the next step on every soul's journey. I started walking back to my car, hoping Conner would follow like a trained puppy. I had said my piece. The car ride was what naturally followed.

"But I saw the van."

"I don't know what you think you saw, but . . ." I stopped walking and turned back to the soul by the tree. "What van?"

"I don't know, a van," said the boy. "I didn't . . . I couldn't remember it until I saw it again, but it was here the night before I died, and it was here again today. Right there by the curb. One of those big white perv vans old guys with moustaches drive so they can lure kids into the back with candy. But it had the same logo on it I saw on that badge in the grass. The same one over your right tit."

I cupped my name badge and part of my right tit.

What he was saying didn't make sense. Our vans were only deployed for large-scale collections: hurricanes, tsunamis, the occasional cult suicide. Mass deaths. There was no reason for one to be anywhere near a quiet park in the middle of the suburbs, and if there was, I would have heard about it.

"Did you see anyone?" I asked.

"Nah." 507032 kicked the tree with a sneakered foot, making no impact. "I saw the van and took off running when I heard them call my name."

My stomach sank to my knees, sending my fetus on an elevator ride. "Conner, I need you to be honest with me now. This is crucial. You heard someone call your name?"

"Jesus Christ, Grim, yes, okay? Why doesn't anybody listen to me? It's not like I want this to be happening."

"Okay," I said. "I'm listening. Can you tell me what happened? All of it, don't leave anything out."

"Fine, whatever." Conner lowered his hood. "So I'd been

walking near the trees and heard something big pull up. I looked back and saw the van, so I hid behind one of the trees, because that was *the* van, you know? Like, I know what I saw, and I'm not some pussy and I know I'm dead and whatever, but I figured if whoever it was wanted to kill me, who knows what else they'd do, right? So anyway, I'm behind a tree and then I hear my name. And I knew it wasn't you, I've heard enough out of you to know your voice, so I bolted. Tried going home but figured the killer would look for me there and besides, I didn't need to see my parents celebrating finally being rid of me, so I booked it to my buddy Ethan's and just chilled in his backyard until I figured they'd be gone."

I leaned myself against the tree as the boy's words sunk in. No one else from S.C.Y.T.H.E. should know his name. Even Stu would be more likely to have looked up his case number than his name, and besides, this was my case. I was in charge of collecting this essence. There was no reason for anyone else from my company to know who Conner was, much less where. But I had told Stu this morning that I'd found him. Anyone from the office could have heard that if they'd walked by at the right time. Or Stu himself could have . . . I pushed the thought aside. It couldn't be Stu. I wouldn't let it be Stu. Even if he *was* the only person I knew at S.C.Y.T.H.E. with the proper authority to sign out a van. But if someone *had* killed Conner, someone who'd met him here, then they would have a good idea where to find him again.

"You good?" 507032's voice floated up from beside me. I opened my eyes. I hadn't even realized I'd closed them.

"Shit," I said in spite of myself. "Conner, come with me."

"What the fuck?" he yelled. "You said you'd listen. I told you, I'm not gonna have anything to do with your sketchy-ass job, Grim, just le—"

"I'm not taking you to processing," I said. "I'm getting you away from here. It's not safe."

"Wait, so you believe me?"

I swallowed. "Yes."

"Fucking finally. Now what?"

"I don't know," I said. "But we need to get you somewhere secure. Somewhere no one will find you. And then we need to figure out what the hell is going on. Good?"

"Good."

My armpits were sweating. I hated everything about this. I wanted Conner Ortiz and his angst out of my life. I wanted sleep. I wanted to go back to the way things had been a few short days ago when none of my colleagues were potential murderers. I did not want to have to play detective with a teenager. I wanted my life back.

11

What is this place? Some kind of safe house?"

The essence trudged through my apartment, scrutinizing the dirty dishes piled on the counters of my tiny kitchen, the small, round dining table stacked with paperwork, the boxes by the door filled with knickknacks and a blender that I kept neglecting to unpack.

"This is my apartment," I said, tossing my purse to the floor.

"What, like, you live here?" 507032 looked viscerally disturbed. "Like, all the time?"

"Yes."

"But you're . . ."

"I'm what?"

"I dunno, you look like you should have a house or some shit. This looks like my cousin Marco's apartment, but he's in college. And you're ol— I mean, you're definitely not."

"No," I agreed through gritted teeth. "I'm definitely not."

"Huh. So what do you do around here for fun?"

"We aren't here to have fun, Conner, we're here to keep you safe. If the wrong people get their hands on your soul, they could see to it that you never move on, or worse. They could destroy your essence altogether."

"Right, right." Conner's fleshless face paled. "So it's just you alone here, then?"

"Yes," I said. "It's just me alone."

"And your work buddies, they don't know where you live?"

I shook my head.

"I guess it'll have to do."

"Sorry it isn't up to your usual standards," I grumbled, slumping into one of my dining chairs. "Now, we need to talk about why on earth anyone from S.C.Y.T.H.E. would want you dead."

The essence slid into the chair across the table from me. "I told you, I don't know. I can't remember. It's like the night before I died just kinda . . . like, didn't happen. Or got erased or some shit. Like I got roofied. All I know is that was the night I saw the van, and the next day I died."

I closed my eyes and conjured up an image of Stu in my mind. Beefy, dress shirt–clad, macro-counting Stu. He knew about Conner, but why would he want to do him harm? And even if he did, surely he would have just needed to wrap a meaty fist around the boy's scrawny neck and be done with it. I'd seen the body. There were no visible injuries. It just didn't make sense; none of this did.

My phone rang and my eyes flew open, heart thudding in my ears. I scrambled to my feet and ran to my purse, dug through the carnage inside, and pulled my phone free.

SIMON MOBILE, said my caller ID.

Shit.

"You gonna get that?" asked 507032.

"No."

"Okay."

I gave a hard exhale. "Yes." I answered the phone. "Not a good time, Simon."

"No, sorry, right, I was just in the area and thought—"

"Really not a good time, Simon."

"Sure, all right. Anything I can help with?"

I looked at the dead boy in my kitchen.

"Not this time," I said.

"But sometime, maybe, huh, Kath? You know I'm always happy to. If you want me to. If I can. Help, I mean."

"You really can't," I said.

"Right. Well. Maybe next time, then?"

"Sure, yeah, maybe next time." I hung up the phone to find Conner staring at me like a snake at a mouse.

"Who was that?"

I wobbled to my feet. "What? That? That was no one."

"Didn't sound like no one."

"That was my soon-to-be ex-husband, though it really isn't your business. I'm your Collections Agent, you are my client. I understand these are unusual circumstances, and you're in my home, but that doesn't change the nature of our relationship."

"Why is he your soon-to-be ex?"

"Conner." I sat back down at the table and glared at the soul across from me.

"What? I'm just making conversation."

"And I'm just trying to figure out how you died so we can get you moved on."

"Yeah, well, I've already told you everything I know. Besides, it . . . it sucks to think about. Like, I'm dead and I'm still in danger? That's . . . It just sucks."

"Is there anyone else who might know more?"

"Whoever killed me."

"Aside from them."

The boy shrugged. "My buddy Ethan, maybe. He was the last person I spoke to the night before."

"Great." I eyed the wooden clock on my wall: 9:09 p.m. "I'll look into him tomorrow and see if he has any pertinent information for us."

"Sweet," said 507032. "So, why's your husband a soon-to-be ex?"

I sighed, exasperated.

"I could really use the distraction, Grim."

I closed my eyes and Simon's face swam up through the blackness, his eyes begging me to let him into my world in ways I couldn't. Wouldn't. Not if it meant him seeing what everyone in my life before him had seen in me. He'd loved me in ways I never thought possible, that no one ever had, and I knew as surely as I knew my own name that if I let my guard down and my mess out, that love would be ripped away from me. At least this way I could imagine it would always be there. And he'd have the chance to be happy without my Sadim touch inevitably ruining everything. I opened my eyes again. "Because he deserves better."

507032 said nothing.

"Satisfied?"

The essence looked away and shrugged.

"Right, well, make yourself at home. I'm going to bed."

This snapped the soul's attention back. "What? Bed? It's barely nighttime. What the fuck am I supposed to do?"

I ran my hand over my face. "I'll leave the TV on for you. See you in the morning, Conner."

"Do you at least have Netflix? Hulu? Kathy? Hey, come on, throw a dead guy a bone here."

I LAY IN BED WITH MY BLANKETS PULLED UP TO MY CHIN, THE TV humming outside my closed door and Jo's raspy voice in my ear.

"You brought him *home*?" I pulled the phone away as she erupted. "Oh sugar, if this gets found out, are you ever in hot water!"

"I know," I whispered. "But what other choice did I have, Jo? There's no reason for a mass transport truck to have been in the suburbs, and even less reason for anyone from work to go looking for Conner. There's clearly more going on here, and I can't get him to processing until I know what. Besides, his soul could be in real danger."

"You're really sticking your neck out for the boy. I hope he appreciates it."

"He's a rich seventeen-year-old brat, Jo, of course he doesn't. But that doesn't matter. I just need to keep an eye on him and figure out what caused his death so we can both move on. At this point it's as much a risk to my job if I don't do this as it is if I do."

"What are you gonna tell Stu when he starts asking about the boy's case?"

I rolled onto my side and stared at the door of my room. Beyond its peeling white paint sat the boy in question, currently parked in front of what sounded like an infomercial for a temperature-adjusting toilet seat on whatever channel I'd left on for him. "I hadn't thought that far ahead."

"Well, you'd better start thinking. You and I both know Stu

is not a patient man. He's going to start asking questions sooner rather than later."

"I know," I said, choking down Stu's potential involvement in Conner's death like a dry cracker. "Any ideas?"

"Sorry, sugar. I think you've stumbled onto a nut even I can't crack."

And there it was. Even Jo couldn't untangle this. Jo, who had been through it all twice and wouldn't hesitate to tell you if it was worth a third time. "Thanks anyway," I said.

"Good night, kiddo."

"Good night, Jo."

I hung up my phone and stared at the shadows on my stucco ceiling. What the hell had I gotten myself into?

12

That morning I awoke to the sound of . . . nothing. No alarm screaming at me from the cell phone on my bedside table, no early-morning birdsong from just outside my window, no honking horns as the first round of road ragers shuffled off to work. Just the hum of the TV in my living room. Where 507032 was.

I rolled over and grabbed my phone. It was 8:23 a.m. And it was Saturday. Somehow, in the chaos of the past few days, I'd lost track. Saturday meant a reprieve from the office. From Stu and all the question marks surrounding him. But not from work. I wouldn't be getting a break from that so long as a potentially murdered client was in my home.

I tossed off the covers, shoved my perpetually icy feet into their awaiting slippers, and shuffled out into the living room.

"Morning, sunshine," the essence greeted lazily from where he lay flung over my couch like an unfolded blanket.

I gave him a sleepy nod and continued to my kitchen to put on a pot of coffee, which I intended to down in its entirety.

507032 wafted in after me, leaned his lack-of-weight against my fridge, and watched me wordlessly.

"Yes?" I asked as I crossed him to retrieve the milk.

"We're talking to Ethan today, aren't we?"

"I'm talking to Ethan today," I corrected. "Yes."

"Well," said Conner impatiently, "go talk to him, then."

"Conner, it's Saturday. Not a workday. And even if it were, I wouldn't be on the clock for another half an hour. I'm going to sit down to a nice breakfast of coffee and Cheerios, take a shower, change into something more socially acceptable, and then I will proceed with your case."

"And what the fuck am I supposed to do, just stand here and watch?"

"If you like," I said, then quickly added, "I'll be showering and changing on my own, thank you."

"No arguments here," said the boy. "But you're wasting time. Like, you get that, right? Ethan could know something about what the fuck happened to me, but instead of finding out you're just sitting around eating cereal. It's not like I can do this without you, okay? I don't like it any more than you do, but I fucking need you on this, Grim. Whoever did this to me is still after me."

I stared down into my bowl of beige hoops, the bottom layer already soggy with milk. I watched them shift and bob and ultimately plummet down the drain alongside the remaining half of my first cup of coffee before heading back to my room to change.

"YOU'RE SURE THIS IS IT?"

"Yes. Dude, I spent more time here than I ever did at home. This is it."

"All right." I stared through the driver's-side window at the house tucked behind a short, well-kept yard. Inoffensively beige, with a tasteful salmon-pink door and a bright array of carnations lining the stone walk from the driveway, it wasn't the suburban castle 507032 had lived in, but it was certainly nothing to sneeze at either. I readied myself, knees weak as I tried to imagine what I could possibly say to this strange teenager to make him talk to me about a dead friend without giving anything away. "You wait here," I said to the boy in the passenger seat. "I'll be as fast as I can."

"Fuck that," he said. "I'm coming with you."

"Conner," I began, but relented. It wasn't like anyone else could see him anyway. "Fine. But behave yourself, all right?"

He shrugged.

I squeezed my jaw and got out of the car.

The doorbell echoed through the house twice before the door opened and a thin, stern-looking blond woman in her late fifties appeared in its wake.

"That's Marta, the housekeeper," the boy said from beside me on the front stoop.

I smiled at the woman. "Good morning. Is Ethan around? I know it's a little early, but I . . . uh . . . he goes to school with my . . . daughter and I need to . . . talk to him . . . about that."

"Nice," said the essence.

"No," said Marta.

"No?"

"Ethan isn't here."

"Oh," I said. "Do you know where I could find him?"

"He's with his family at a funeral."

507032 and I exchanged a glance. "Conner Ortiz's funeral?"

"Yes, I think so," said Marta.

"Holy fuck," said Conner.

"Well, thank you for your time. I'll try again later," I said quickly, and began to turn around, but Conner didn't budge.

"I want to go."

I looked back at him.

"To the funeral. To *my* funeral. I want to go."

I wanted to argue with him that this could be a bad idea, but I couldn't work out the logistics of arguing with an incorporeal essence in front of a living human without drawing suspicion, so instead I said, just before the door closed, "Do you happen to know where the funeral is being held?"

Marta's head reappeared from behind the door.

"My . . . uh . . . daughter knew him too. Conner, I mean. She misplaced the information about the funeral. You know how kids are. But we'd like to make an appearance. For Conner's sake."

Marta gave me a hard stare for the length of two full breaths but said at last, "One moment."

She disappeared into the house and returned a few seconds later holding the obituary section of a newspaper. Halfway down the first column was Conner's obituary.

"Holy fuck," 507032 said again, more breathily this time.

I found the name and address for the church where the funeral was being held, made a mental note, and handed the paper back to Marta.

"Thank you," I said.

Marta gave a nod and closed the door.

"The funeral only started fifteen minutes ago," said Conner. "It isn't far. That's my parents' church. It's like five minutes from here."

"Conner, this is a bad idea."

"My mom says I'm full of them."

I could feel a knot forming deep in my stomach. Taking a client to their own funeral would be another unprecedented event in a week chock-full of them. It wasn't that I hadn't been asked before. In fact, funeral visits were right up there with last messages to loved ones as far as client requests went. But one of the core tenets of my job was to keep things professional and keep things moving. Start seeing a client as more than a package to be delivered and you could end up getting attached. It was always best to get an essence moved on as quickly as possible and save the sentiment for the living. Besides, I wasn't playing postmortem tour guide here.

"Look," I said carefully, "I understand the temptation to see your loved ones one last time, but I promise it's for the best if we just stay focused on the task at hand."

"Ethan'll be there," said Conner. "Talking to him is the task at hand, right?"

"We won't be able to talk to him until the service is over anyway."

"And we won't know when it's over unless we're there."

"Conner," I said sharply. That knot in my stomach tightened as I imagined the boy's best friend sitting in the church, saying goodbye to someone who'd barely been on this earth long enough to say hello. "We can't."

"Suit yourself," said Conner, turning his back on me and trotting down the sidewalk.

I swallowed a shout and waddled after him. "What the hell are you doing?"

"Going to my funeral." Conner picked up his pace.

"But I just said—"

"Heard you loud and clear, Grim. You said 'we can't.' Not that I can't."

"Conner, it's dangerous for you out here alone. We still don't know who's after you, or why."

"Yeah, well, some things are more important than your immortal soul."

"What?" My raised voice bounced off the neatly trimmed lawns of the quiet street we were practically sprinting down. "What could possibly be more important?"

"That obituary lied."

I said nothing and braced for another rant about Conner's misidentified cause of death.

"It said 'beloved son.'"

THE CHURCH WAS AS FULL AS YOU'D EXPECT FOR SOMEONE WHO'D died so young. I chased Conner through the front doors and into an empty pew at the back as a projected slideshow skittered across the front wall to an instrumental rendition of "Over the Rainbow." Photos of Conner, his sparkling eyes leaping off the makeshift screen, at each stage of his short life. I averted my eyes.

"This is pure cringe," said the essence from beside me, a picture of him in the bathtub as a toddler filling the wall in my periphery. I had hoped this would be enough to get him away from the building, but his focus had already been pulled to the crowd, his dark eyes dancing over the rows of people sitting rigidly on the wooden pews. My pulse hadn't slowed since we'd left Ethan's house. There were too many dangerous variables here. I just wanted to speak to Ethan and get back home.

"Not a bad turnout," said 507032. "That's Hailee Glass over there. We hooked up a couple times. I think she's actually crying. Nice."

I clenched my jaw but kept my eyes trained on my lap.

"Whoa, that's totally Rileigh Hanson two rows up. Man, she's so fucking hot. I can't believe she's here. I figured she didn't even know I existed. Fuck, I miss having a body."

This time I shot him a quick warning glance.

"Right, sorry, sorry." He kicked back in the pew and propped his feet up on the back of the seat in front of us. I closed my eyes and mentally begged the fetus growing in me to be a girl.

The slideshow ended and the music stopped, the sounds of shuffling bodies and clearing throats filling the void. A gray-templed man in a well-tailored suit stepped to the microphone, calling my attention towards the front of the room in spite of myself.

"That's Uncle Sidney," said Conner. "He lives in New York City doing some kind of real estate thing. I guess he flew over for this. Probably on his own jet."

We needed to be gone. I wanted to be gone.

"Wasn't that beautiful?" said Uncle Sidney. "A few of Conner's cousins put that slideshow together. You know, it was a privilege for all of us to watch him grow up into the wonderful young man he was. He's the baby of the family, and as you saw from some of those pictures, my girls definitely took advantage of having their own living baby doll around to dress up and play house with." A soft rumble of laughter from the crowd. "Unfortunately, we moved away a good few years ago now, and I didn't get a chance to know Conner as well as many of you, but seeing so many people here today tells me he was just as special as I always knew he would be."

"He's always been real good at this shit," 507032 said. "Like, saying the right thing. I guess that's why he's so rich."

"Now," continued Uncle Sidney, "I'm sure you can all appreciate what a painful time this is for his parents, but they'd like to say a few words in memory of their son. Sergio? Tabitha, honey?"

Uncle Sidney walked back to his seat with the poise of an Academy Award winner as a tall man with bronze skin and thick black hair ushered an elegant blonde in a silver-gray skirt suit up to the microphone.

"Fuck," 507032 barely whispered.

His parents were young, attractive, and remarkably composed. Sergio spoke first, a concise vignette of stories from Conner's early life: his first year playing peewee soccer, ski trips with family friends, eating ice cream dinners they swore to never tell Tabitha about.

I was ready to bolt. This was too much. 507032 fidgeted beside me but otherwise seemed rooted to his seat.

Then it was his mother's turn to speak.

"What can a mother say about her son?" Tabitha began. "Every mother thinks her own child is the best, doesn't she? Well, mine truly was. He was smart and kind and handsome. We, Sergio and I, knew he had great things in store for him. So much potential. He was only one short year away from college. He surely would have gone to one of the best schools in the country, gone on to do great things. It's always hard to see someone so young robbed of those chances. Conner, you were the apple of my eye, and you will be so missed."

I couldn't breathe. This was why it was against company policy to get too close to your clients. The life presented in front of me, and the reminder of its absence beside me, felt oppressive.

Suddenly 507032 was more than a case file or a package to be delivered. He was a child. I let my hand flutter over my belly. A child who had everything, and yet still ended up a guest at his own funeral. If having such perfectly put-together parents wasn't enough, then what chance did *my* baby stand?

I glanced towards Conner, but he was no longer at my side. Before his mother had finished speaking, 507032 was up and storming to the door. When his hand slipped through the door handle, he gave a low growl and walked right through the door and outside the church. I scrambled to my feet and raced after him as quietly as I could, but when I got outside, Conner was nowhere to be seen.

13

Shit. I'd somehow managed to misplace the same soul three times now. And this time I couldn't exactly start calling for him without raising alarm. The knot in my stomach had contorted into a noose; one that wrapped tightly around my career.

I choked back the emotions the funeral service had forced into my throat and scanned the parking lot in front of me. No Conner. I rounded the side of the church, where a neat lawn bent into a hill and gave way to a soccer field rimmed by a row of identical houses. Still no Conner. My pulse quickened, the fetus in my gut now accompanied by a thousand razor-winged butterflies.

I knew this had been a bad idea. Who the hell lets someone go to their own funeral? S.C.Y.T.H.E. had rules, and it had rules for a reason. Maybe I wasn't as good at this job as I liked to believe. The thought was like a punch to my stomach, sending the butterflies up into the back of my throat to mingle with the tears that already resided there. I had always kept a professional distance with my clients before. Always. Don't get involved. Just get them from point A to point B. But I wasn't distant now. Now I was mad. I was enraged. I was traipsing through a churchyard on a Saturday morning on an empty stomach, a shitty night's sleep, and emotions I wasn't supposed to feel, searching for a dead boy who had been nothing but trouble. I'd had enough.

When I finally found 507032, he was slumped on a bench in the graveyard across the street. A weeping willow bowed over him, a sea of jagged tombstones in various states of upkeep sprawling around the bench towards the horizon. I stomped over, hands on hips, lecture locked and loaded on my tongue, but as I neared him, I realized his head was buried in his hands. His back was heaving.

He was crying.

I readjusted the set of my jaw and reassessed my approach. This didn't change anything. I was still pissed. But it was jarring to see all that teenaged bravado gone, a vulnerable child left in its wake. Shit. I hated vulnerability.

I sank down beside him, my gaze focused on the nearest grave. Thomas Winslow, 1946–2011. I wondered briefly if he could have been one of Jo's pickups back in the day.

"You can't run off like that, Conner," I tried.

"Fuck off," came the weepy reply.

"I mean it. We already know you're in danger from someone at S.C.Y.T.H.E. and I can't keep you safe if I don't know where you are. Besides, you dragged me here to get answers from your friend, remember? I can't talk to him if I'm out here running around after you."

"Fine, whatever." 507032 scrubbed at his face with the sleeve of his hoodie.

"Good," I said, though that wasn't exactly the answer I'd

been hoping for. Still, from what I knew of Conner, it seemed to be the best I could expect.

He leaned back on the bench and stared out across the graves, our uneasy silence interrupted only by an occasional sniffle and the rustle of a squirrel in the willow tree behind us. I drummed my fingers on my thighs, impatient to talk to Ethan and unsure of what to say to Conner. Crying children frightened me as it was, but a crying teenager was utterly terrifying.

"Conner—" I started.

"She didn't even cry."

I turned towards him, brows furrowed.

"I mean, neither of them did, but fuck. You expect at least your mom to cry at your funeral, don't you?"

"Oh," I said.

"It's stupid. I'm an idiot. I've always known she didn't care about me. But like, she didn't even *know* me. Fuck. Never mind."

I just looked at him, blinking. No words would come. Even the lecture I'd prepared had long ago melted on my tongue. The only thing I could think to do was listen and hope that was enough. I was not prepared for this. Not by work, not by life. This was new, and awful, and I wanted to run but I couldn't, so I just listened.

"It's just . . ." Conner continued, as if prompted. "They wanted me to go to college. They wanted me to be like them. But they knew—she knew—that I didn't want any of that. And yet her last words, her last fucking words about me were about what *she* wanted me to be instead of who I actually am."

I tried to swallow, but my mouth was too dry. All I could muster was a weak, "So who are you?"

"I don't even know, man. I thought I had time to figure it out, you know? I was gonna take a year off, maybe travel. Do that stupid thing rich kids do where they, like, backpack through Europe and stay at hostels even though they can afford resorts or some shit. I thought I might try something in the trades. You can make bank in some of them and you don't have to feel like an idiot trying to write stupid essays. Or DJ. Like, I know that's something only douchebags do, but I just really like music. I don't know, it's like it's this whole other language that I've just always known how to speak. What I didn't want is to be some stuck-up lawyer or something. That's bullshit. But that's all they had me for. To be a mini-them. Some people just shouldn't fucking have kids."

My heart jerked, my hand instinctively coming to rest on my protruding stomach. "I—I like music," I blurted.

"Yeah?" said the boy, brightening a little. "What do you listen to?"

"I like a lot of Bryan Adams's greatest hits."

He gave a choked laugh. "Jesus."

"What?"

"Nothing. Just, when you said you like music, I thought you meant good music."

I couldn't bring myself to be offended; I was too relieved the crying was over. "All right, fine, what constitutes good music to an expert like you, then?"

"There's this sick underground band called Dead Sparrow that fuses rap with orchestral music. Sometimes even opera. No one's heard of them in the mainstream yet, but they're gonna be huge one of these days." He shifted on the bench, stuffed his hands in his sweatshirt pockets. "I can play them for you sometime. I don't know if they'd be your speed. I mean, they're no Bryan Adams, but they're pretty cool."

"Okay," I said.

"Cool."

The door of the church across the street opened and an ocean of black clothing began flooding out. I jumped to my feet. "Shit."

Conner followed my line of sight and sat upright. "Shit," he echoed.

"You didn't hear me say 'shit,'" I said quickly, trying to regain my professional composure. "Come on, we've got to hurry if we want to catch your friend."

I scanned the parking lot, one hand over my eyes to shield them from the midmorning sun. "Do you see him?" Bodies eddied around the horde of cars, some stopping to chat with their fellow mourners, most opening doors and starting engines.

"Over there!" The boy pointed across the lot. I spotted the underdeveloped moustache right away. Ethan was with who I assumed to be his parents: a bald man with dark brown skin and broad shoulders, and a woman near my age in a tasteful black lace dress. I nodded and marched towards them as they reached a silver SUV.

"Ethan," I called, waving an arm as I approached.

"Yeah?" said Ethan. His parents joined him in turning my way, all three sets of eyes looking me over expectantly.

I froze. I couldn't tell them why I was there, but I didn't know what else to say to compel Ethan to talk to me. So instead I said nothing for longer than was appropriate, and gaped like a water-starved trout as Ethan and his parents watched me with growing confusion.

"Tell them you're my tutor."

I peeled my eyes away from the family I was frightening and looked at Conner, my own expression confused.

"Yeah. My parents hired a tutor for me last year. I only actually went to her twice, but my mom would have definitely told Ethan's mom about it. She was so convinced a tutor could cure me of dyslexia and get my grades up, I swear she bragged to all the moms who'd listen. Tell them you're my tutor."

I swallowed and looked back at Ethan's family. "I'm sorry to bother you. I was Conner's tutor."

"Oh yes." Ethan's mother reached out a hand. "Tabitha mentioned you. Nancy, isn't it? I'm Alison. This is my husband, Charlie, and you know Ethan?"

"Yes. No. Not personally, but Conner mentioned him a few times."

"They were very close," said Alison. "The boys grew up together; they were like brothers."

I looked over at Conner, who was still lurking a few paces to my left.

"Look at that stupid suit they made him wear," he said, jutting his chin at Ethan. "What a jackass."

"I was wondering if I could have a quick word with Ethan?" I addressed this question to Alison, but it was Ethan who replied.

"We can talk."

His parents gave a nod and we walked back towards the church, stopping in front of an arched stained glass window.

"You're not Con's tutor," Ethan said before I could open my mouth.

"What?"

"Don't bullshit me, he went to that lady like once before bouncing. No way someone would show up at a funeral for somebody they barely knew and start sniffing around his friends. So who are you really?"

Conner let out a chuckle.

"You a detective?"

The question caught me almost as off guard as Ethan's own detection skills.

"What?" I asked blankly.

"A detective. There's more to the story, right? No way Con just up and died like that."

Once again, I snuck a look at Conner, though this time it wasn't a warning, it was a question. Namely: What the hell was going on? But Conner just shrugged.

"What makes you think so?" I asked, trying to keep my voice steady.

"You a detective?" Ethan asked again.

"I am investigating Conner's death," I said. It wasn't a lie. "But this isn't public knowledge, all right? Just between us. Not even your parents can know."

"Fuckin' dope," said Ethan, eliciting another laugh from Conner.

"What makes you suspicious about Conner's death?"

Ethan scratched his chin thoughtfully. "We were gonna meet up the night before he died, but I had to bail."

"At Blazing Meadows, right? To smoke marijuana?"

Ethan's eyes widened. "Hey, look, I'm not out here trying to get arrested, all right?"

"And I'm not out here to arrest anyone. I just need to know what happened that night."

"Ah shit," said Ethan. "Yeah, all right. I owe it to Conman. Better to get in the shit than end up dead, I guess. He didn't deserve that, you know?"

"Goddamn right," said Conner, but there was a sadness in

both boys' voices that stabbed at my heart in a way I wasn't expecting.

"I know," I said.

"'Kay, so I finished my studying early," Ethan said. "I texted Con I was on my way. He said 'good, 'cause there's some weird shit going on,' but when I got there, he was gone. And he'd left his bag of pot behind on our bench. It was good stuff, too. Expensive. No way Conner would've just left it there. I mean shit, if I wasn't so freaked, I'd have grabbed it for myself. Fuck, okay, you didn't hear that from me, all right?"

I gave a nod.

"Anyway, I was in the woods by that bench where we like to . . . you know . . . smoke . . . and there were all these lights down the hill. And like, there is a road down there, but it's never used, and it was already after midnight, so I don't know what the fuck was going on. I heard voices, too, and car doors slamming. It freaked the shit out of me, honestly. I figured Conner got spooked too and went home and just forgot to text, but then the next day he was dead."

"Do you remember anything else? Did you hear what the voices were saying, maybe? Or see anyone's face?"

"Nah." Ethan shook his head. "But like ten minutes before I got to Meadows, Con texted me this."

Ethan plucked a cell phone from his jacket pocket and opened it to a photograph. The picture was dark and grainy and hard to make heads or tails of at first, but as I held it closer, the splotchy images began to make sense.

And in doing so, suddenly nothing made sense.

The pixels on Ethan's phone merged together into the unexplainable image of at least a dozen essences among the trees, walking towards a light on the road.

14

My apartment door was unlocked when I got home. I motioned to Conner to stay behind me and held my breath as I pushed the door open, unsure of exactly what I expected to find, but fairly confident it would fall into the category of "bad" after the morning I'd had. When I stepped inside, a wave of relief washed over me. I threw my purse to the floor and exhaled.

"What the hell're you doing out and about before noon on a Saturday?"

Jo was at my kitchen table, her voluminous figure filling one of my flimsy fold-out dining chairs. She was wearing another housedress, this one robin's-egg blue and speckled with happy daisies. At her feet sat Chap, her Seeing Eye dog, and on the table in front of her was three-quarters of a microwaveable chicken potpie from my freezer. I grabbed a fork, slammed the cutlery drawer closed with my hip, and dug in.

"Thank god you're here," I said through a mouthful. I was so hungry I barely noticed the freezer burn. 507032 stood by my fridge, blandly examining the novelty magnets and looking between me and Jo with the expression of a bored kid whose mom had just run into a friend at the grocery store. I caught myself before I could blurt out what I really wanted to say: that everything was a mess and I was in over my head and about to ruin things again. He was still my client, after all, and I had to maintain some professionalism here. Besides, I didn't want to panic him. I could panic enough for both of us.

"I've encountered some . . . unexpected difficulties in that case I was telling you about," I said finally.

"That who's hovering behind me?" Jo asked, pulling my attention from the pie and Conner's from a sleeping kitten magnet. "The boy feels like a whole stew of angst and sadness and loneliness and fear. That is him, isn't it?"

"Wait." 507032 rounded the table, his voice bouncing eagerly. "She can see me too?"

"He wants to know if you can see him, Jo."

Jo smiled. "Ah, not quite, puddin'. I can't see anyone. But I can feel just as well as anyone can see."

That's why S.C.Y.T.H.E. had recruited Jo to begin with. Most of us in collections had to be given special clearance to be able to see souls for transport. When our time with the company ended, so did our clearance. But Jo had always been able to sense an essence by what they were feeling. When she retired, S.C.Y.T.H.E. tried to revoke whatever it was that made her more sensitive to the dead, but they never could figure out how.

"So just what exactly is going on here, sugar?" Jo asked. "You do have a habit of bringing work home, but this is really something else."

I explained, as calmly as I could, what we'd learned from Ethan that morning. When I described the picture on Ethan's phone, a thought occurred to me. I turned over my shoulder to Conner, who had drifted closer as I spoke.

"What did you see in that picture that made you send it to your friend in the first place?" It hadn't struck me as odd at the time, not compared to the far odder occurrence of a roaming herd of souls, but now it was yet another question to add to my ever-growing collection. Very few people outside of my line of work could see the dead unless they'd officially transitioned into ghosts, but the essences in the picture were fresh, not ghosts. They were too crisp, lacking in the trademark white, misty auras and hollow, translucent quality of trapped souls.

"I don't know," Conner said. "I didn't even remember taking that picture until I saw it."

"What did you see in the picture when Ethan showed it to us, then?"

"Nothing, really. It was all grainy and dark. But hazy, I guess. Like some sort of misty, horror movie shit; you know, fog machines and stuff. And then that light."

"What's he sayin'?" Jo asked.

"That it looked like mist."

"Get enough souls together like that and I guess even regular folk are gonna see something's up."

"So the question," I said, "is what were they all doing there, unrecorded by S.C.Y.T.H.E.?"

"Whatever it was," Jo said, "seems like it was enough to kill our young man here for stumbling into it. You need to find out what happened in that forest, sugar. And you know as well as I do that an essence can't kill anybody, so you'd better find out what living person was out there too."

The chicken potpie churned in my stomach. Ten steps to the

toilet, I reminded myself. I'd counted more than enough times by now. The warm light from the overhead lamp above the table seemed aggressively bright all of a sudden.

"And when I do find out who they are?" I asked.

Jo put a weathered hand over mine. "Make sure they don't find out who *you* are."

Forty Days to Ghost

Sunday morning emerged slowly through the thick haze of night. I'd dozed on and off to the sounds of the TV outside my bedroom door, but barely managed more than half an hour of sleep at a time. When dawn finally pierced the dark, I was out of bed and making a mess of my kitchen.

507032 strolled in from the living room as I sat down to my scrambled eggs and toast. I wouldn't be caught on an empty stomach again today if I could help it.

"You need better channels," the essence said, taking the seat across from me.

"Good morning to you too," I said through a mouthful of egg. In fairness to him, I had left the Shopping Network on overnight, which probably wasn't his entertainment of choice. Hell, it wasn't my entertainment of choice either, but it was that or reruns of a sermon, so I opted for $39.99 handbags and called it a night.

It was just after seven thirty by the time I'd shoved my dishes in the sink. I still had two hours before I was picking Jo up from down the street; plenty of time for a long, Conner-free shower and a leisurely getting-ready routine. I turned the channel to the local news and escaped to the bathroom.

We pulled up to Jo's house ten minutes early. A pale yellow clapboard bungalow with an overflowing English garden that spilled onto the sidewalk in sunny daffodils and pansies, it had been purchased by Jo's fourth husband and left to her when he died twelve years ago. She was on the porch in her rocking chair when we arrived, listening to the finches and robins playing in her birdbath, Chap dozing peacefully at her feet.

"Early as always," she called down from her perch. "The boy with you?"

I glanced at Conner in my rearview mirror; I'd relegated him to the back seat. He was staring out his window at the kids playing in a driveway a few doors down.

"He's in the back," I replied through my open window. "You all set?"

"I've got nothing better to do," she said, and rose from her chair.

BLAZING MEADOWS LOOKED DIFFERENT EVERY TIME I SAW IT. I parked in the same place in the gravel lot I always did and helped Jo out of the car. 507032 reluctantly abandoned the back seat, where he'd been trying to coo over Chap as subtly as possible, and landed beside me at the edge of the park. The morning sun was still thin, but the air was already heavy with the heat of the coming day. In the wary light, and in the wake of the photograph on Ethan's phone, everything looked a little surreal. The trees looked denser, the field more exposed.

This was not a safe place. Not for any of us, but especially not for Conner. I'd tried to convince him to stay home, but he refused, insisting he'd die of boredom if he weren't dead already. It seemed like a flimsy excuse. In truth, I think he wanted to be here for something more. Company, maybe. Jo's if not mine. Or a growing desperation for answers. Then again, he was a teenager, so boredom wasn't an impossible reason.

This had been Jo's idea, as most things that went well in my life were. She thought that by returning to the park, and especially to where that picture had been taken, we might get a better sense of what the hell was going on. As we trudged across the field, I wasn't so sure, but I was too relieved to have someone else making the decisions, to have someone else in this with me, to care.

Conner guided us through the woods to the bench where he and Ethan used to meet.

"This is where the boy used to come smoke up?" Jo asked, running a hand along the back of the bench. "Smart kid, always going to the same place. It's helpful to know your surroundings. One time I dropped acid at a music festival in Vegas and spent three hours lost in the desert, chasing a talking badger with an Australian accent who I was pretty damn sure had taken my bra."

The boy's face lit up. "Wait, what?"

I sighed. "You got his attention with that one, Jo."

"Because I lost my bra? Honey, my bosom is lower than my center of gravity these days."

Conner grimaced. "What? No, that's not . . . What was the festival?"

"He wants to know about the festival," I said absently, bending down to look under the bench for anything relevant.

"Ah. I was following the Grateful Dead with my third husband, Phil. It was the late eighties. It seemed like a good way to pass the time."

"Guys," I interrupted, dusting my pants off. "Can we focus?"

The baggie of pot was gone from the bench, but there could have been any number of explanations for that. There were too many leaves on the ground to see footprints, and even if there hadn't been, I didn't exactly have the resources to do anything with them. Still, Conner had seen a S.C.Y.T.H.E. name badge out here, so I had hope that something else might have been left behind.

We walked through the trees, scanning for anything out of the ordinary, until we rounded another nondescript portion of the trail and Conner froze.

"Here," he said, his face somehow paling despite a lack of blood flow.

"Here what?" I asked, stopping a few paces behind him, Jo and Chap at my heels.

"This is where I saw it. Whatever *it* was. That light, that . . . thing."

"Conner said this is where he took the picture," I said to Jo.

"You sure, puddin' pie?" Jo asked.

Conner nodded.

"Are you really sure?" I pressed. "I thought you said you couldn't remember anything from that night."

"I couldn't. I can't. But . . . it was here."

"Okay," I said warily. "Well, what's around here?"

"I dunno, trees."

I closed my eyes on a sharp inhale.

"What makes this spot different from every other spot in the forest, Conner? Why would a group of essences be visible from this exact spot?"

The boy blinked at me for a second, then glanced around us, dark eyes glittering in the dim forest light.

"There's a path," he said finally. "It links up from some trail down that way and goes straight down to the road. It's a bit over-grown now, but like, it's the only way to get down the hill without going through a fuck-ton of trees. There." He pointed at a fat shrub lazily leaning its branches towards the ground.

"Conner says there's a path," I told Jo. I pulled the branches back, and a narrow dirt path appeared where the leaves had been resting.

A tiny bolt of anxiety ran through me. Somehow, the exis-tence of that little path made this all feel real in a way I didn't want. I was built for a safe, boring life of routine and solitude, not the mystery and danger that Conner's presence had thrust upon me. That path was a metaphor for everything I'd been dealing with. If I followed it into the unknown, there was truly no turn-ing back. This was not a decision to make lightly. I had to weigh my options, assess the risk—

"Off we go," said Jo, interrupting my thoughts as she trudged ahead with Chap in front of her and Conner behind. Shit. And just like that, I was walking the path I'd always resisted.

15

The road at the base of the hill was a single lane of crumbling neglect. On the side opposite the hill, an overgrown field grew up around a sign for a coming subdivision, weeds tangling around the sign's posts. It was eerily silent here. Even the nearby birds seemed to sing a little more quietly.

"Where are we?" I asked.

"No idea," said Conner. "I never really bothered coming down here. It was all farms and shit until a few years ago when the land got bought up for new houses."

"Someone want to fill me in?" Jo said.

"It's an abandoned road, Jo. And some land up for development."

"Empty road and empty land," Jo said thoughtfully. "Sounds like a perfect place for some nefarious goings-on."

"Right, but what? What would someone at S.C.Y.T.H.E. be doing at a place like this? Some sort of land development scheme? With a bunch of souls, for some reason? And why would they be after a child from the suburbs?"

"I'm seventeen," Conner scoffed.

"The boy's a teenager," Jo said at the same time.

"Right, fine, but that still doesn't answer my question."

"How much do you know about souls?"

"About as much as any agent," I said.

"Maybe that's the problem, sugar. There's clearly an agent who knows more, and you won't be getting your answers until you know whatever they do."

I took a picture of the road and the surrounding fields on my phone and then, with nothing more to do, I climbed back up the hill to my car with Jo, her guide dog, and my stowaway soul.

"I have a thought," I said as we pulled up to the curb outside Jo's house. I couldn't look at her in the passenger seat beside me as I finally let the idea that had been forming in my head over the past few days solidify into words. "A thought I hate. About Stu. It was just after I told him about finding Conner that the S.C.Y.T.H.E. van showed up at Blazing Meadows. He has access to those vans. He has access to my case numbers. He's the only one I told about finding Conner. If he was the one who . . ."—I instinctively lowered my voice—"*did this*, he knows about the park. I don't know what he'd want with Conner's soul, but I can't write all that off as a coincidence, can I?"

"Hmm," said Jo. "Stu was always something of an odd one when I was there. Never knew much about him beyond what he left on show. Trust your gut. See what you can dig up. And sugar, be safe."

"Safe is all I know how to be."

BY THE TIME I'D PARKED IN MY APARTMENT LOT, I WAS READY FOR lunch, a nap, and all the alcohol I couldn't drink. Conner followed me off the elevator, as quiet and contemplative as he had been since we'd left the park, but as we turned the corner to my apartment, we found the door blocked by the short, round silhouette of my ex-husband.

"Simon?"

The ex in question turned around, his face breaking into a smile as he caught sight of me. He held up two take-out bags from the Chinese restaurant down the block.

"Hey, hi, Kath. Hey. I was in the area. Don't know what your cravings are, but I know Kung Pao chicken is always a favorite. Have you eaten?" My face fell and Simon somehow started talking even faster. "Oh god, does chicken make you sick now? I've read about that happening. Is this a bad time? You're busy. I can just . . ." He put the bags down on my doorstep. "It'll be like I was never here."

I sighed, but couldn't suppress the smile pulling at my lips despite my best efforts. It was like we'd never left the grocery store where we'd met; he was still cleaning egg yolk from my feet. "It's fine, Simon. Come in. And thanks for the food."

"Who's this guy?" Conner asked as I unlocked the door and ushered Simon in. I indicated my ring finger and mouthed "ex."

"You sure about that?" Conner laughed. "I've never brought surprise Kung Pao chicken to girls I've actually been with."

I rolled my eyes, threw my purse on the floor, and went off in search of dishes. Conner was circling Simon by the kitchen table when I came over with plates and the only place mat that was clean. It was like watching a fox stalk a rabbit. I tried to give him a warning look, but he wasn't paying attention.

"Does he always wear his pants this high?" Conner asked.

"Yes," I said without thinking.

"Yes what?" Simon cocked his perfect balding head at me.

"Uh . . . yes, Chinese food. Yes! Very exciting." I sat down quickly and started dishing food onto the plates.

"Like old times, huh?" Simon said, then quickly corrected, "Sorry, no, I didn't mean . . . We just used to eat a lot of Chinese food, is all. Remember that first place on Cherry Street? That little studio apartment without a working stove? I think they knew us by name at every take-out place in the neighborhood." He laughed to himself.

"Fuck, this is awkward," said Conner from the corner of the room.

I chanced a look at Simon over a forkful of fried rice. His cheeks were rosy and full, his eyes soft and intent on holding mine for as long as possible. I ached for him in ways I wanted to yell at myself about. We were getting divorced for a reason. He had wasted enough of his life cleaning up my messes and waiting for me to let him in. Last time I let my guard down, I ended up pregnant. I wasn't prepared for the consequences if I succumbed to his bumbling, damp-palmed charm again.

"I was wondering," said Simon, "if you've had an ultrasound yet? According to my reading, they recommend one around five months for anyone over thirty-five; since you're well past both of those . . . Oh! No! Sorry, not well past. Just the right amount past. I just meant . . . if you haven't had one yet, I'd like to be there, maybe? If I could? See our little one with you?"

"Simon—"

"Holy shit, wait, you're pregnant?" Conner waltzed over to the table. "You're gonna be a mom?"

My fork dropped from my hand, rice confetti decorating my half of the place mat. "Bathroom emergency," I said to Simon, holding my stomach bump as an excuse. I indicated for Conner to follow me with a tip of my head from just behind Simon's seat.

Conner furrowed his brows obtusely. I cleared my throat and bobbed my head more forcefully.

"Gross, no," Conner said.

I exhaled sharply and gave him the sternest look I could muster. Conner still seemed reluctant, but he followed me into the bathroom all the same. I closed the door.

"Okay," I whispered, "yes, I'm pregnant. Yes, it is my ex's baby. This is not something we will be discussing beyond this point, understood? It's unprofessional and, frankly, none of your business. So get it all out of your system now, because the second we leave this bathroom, the subject matter is off-limits."

"Wait, so did you get knocked up before or after dumping Mr. High Pants?"

"Neither," I said. "I didn't dump Simon. We had an amicable breakup due to incompatibility."

"Fine, sure, but were you already split up?"

I clenched my teeth. "Yes."

"Ho-ho-holy shit, you hooked up with that guy after you broke up?"

"Yes."

"Kath-ay! You fucking wild thing."

"Stop that." I hated teenagers. "We are consenting adults and—" I caught myself. "I told you, this is unprofessional and none of your business."

"So, you gonna keep it?"

"Conner!"

"What? You just don't seem super pumped about the whole thing."

"Yes, well, not everyone has to be excited about their pregnancy."

Conner's shit-eating smile faded. "No," he said. "They don't." He stuffed his hands into his hoodie pockets. "We done here? Feels kinda weird being stuck in a bathroom with a middle-aged pregnant lady. No offense."

"Yeah," I said. "We're done here."

"Cool." Conner turned away and walked through the closed door, leaving me alone in the bathroom with my thoughts and my baby.

Conner was wallowing in angst on my living room sofa when I rejoined Simon.

"Everything okay?" Simon asked, a grain of rice stuck to his chin. I reached over and absently wiped it away.

"Fine. Fine. Just . . . baby stuff," I said.

Simon gave a sympathetic smile and raised a hand to pat my stomach, but quickly thought better of it.

"You know," he said instead, "if I can do anything to help make this time easier, bring you whatever you're craving, or drive you to appointments, or—"

"I'm okay," I said, poking at a piece of chicken with my fork. "Really. I've been getting by just fine for this long."

"Of course," said Simon, his words slipping into an uncomfortable, lingering silence as we both stared at our plates. And suddenly we were back in the home we'd shared, stewing in the silence that always followed his attempts to bring more of me out of me: the feelings I wasn't brave enough to share, the job I couldn't talk about, the failures of my past or the ones I worried would be in my future that I kept tucked away so he wouldn't think less of me the way so many others had before him. His voice echoed with the same hurt it used to. Even split up, I was still hurting him. I wanted to run into my bedroom, shove my face into a pillow, and scream until my lungs hurt.

Instead, I blurted, "How's your mom?"

"How's work?" Simon said at the same time. We both gave a small chuckle. This was starting to feel like a first date, only I was already pregnant and in love with the man across the table.

"How's work?" Simon tried again.

I felt my jaw tense at the word that had caused so much turmoil. "Fine," I said.

"Just 'fine'?"

"Yes. Just 'fine.'"

"You can vent about it, if you want to. No job is perfect. Or sing its praises! Maybe it's the best job in the world and you want to brag about it a little. You can do that with me, Kath. You can tell me anything."

My whole body had stiffened. "How's your mom?" I said tightly, building my wall back up with sturdier bricks. This sent Simon to his feet, pacing the kitchen.

"You don't have to do this, you know. Shut me out. I feel like I've only read one chapter of your story, Kathy. And it was a great chapter, really riveting, but I want the rest. I want the oversharing narrator and the clumsy metaphors and the plot twists you don't know what to do with. I want it all. I want you."

"Simon, we've been over this a million times." I rose, and so did my voice. "You can't accept that there are things I can't talk about. My life will always be complicated, and messy, and that made things too hard. That made *us* too hard. That's why I'm living in this dingy little apartment and you're across town. That doesn't change just because I'm pregnant, because *I* haven't changed just because I'm pregnant. We're both still who we were before. The only difference is I'm nauseous more often now. That's it."

"Okay." Simon stopped pacing, his chest deflating, any hope or confidence he had in that moment leaving his body on an exhale. "Okay. You're right. I wasn't trying to . . . Well, maybe I was, but you're right. We're divorcing for a reason. It's just that . . . I love you, Kathy."

I love you too, I thought, but what I said was, "I know."

"You'll call me if you need anything? Or want anything? From a friend, nothing more."

"I will," I said.

"Okay."

"Okay." Simon gave me a nod and a sad smile and left me to a tableful of half-eaten Chinese food. I slumped back down in my chair, a sob escaping my throat. This was enough to summon every tear I'd been choking back for months, and before I knew it my cheeks and upper lip were drenched, my chest heaving as I wailed.

"Shit."

I turned around and saw Conner through the wall of tears.

"Shit," he said again. "That was fucking intense. You good?"

I gave him a look that I hoped read "Are you fucking kidding me? Of course I'm not good," but that was hard to convey through all the snot. To my utter dismay, Conner sidled up to Simon's abandoned seat and slid in across from me. I just wanted to be alone. I wanted him to go away; not just now but forever. But before I could protest, he reached across the table and placed a hand over my forearm. It felt like nothing more than a slight shift in the air, but as I stared at his hand, my sobbing eased.

"Hey," he said. "Your life is total shit right now, huh?"

I couldn't help it; I laughed. Of all the things to say, that was what he chose. Of course it was. But he wasn't wrong.

I bobbed my head in a clumsy nod.

"It really sucks, man. Sorry."

"Thank you," I said weakly. Somehow that helped to hear. Not that he was sorry for me, but that he saw how hard this situation was. That it wasn't just in my head.

"Sure," he said. His face was tight, his lively eyes dodging mine. He was clearly uncomfortable. A crying woman often had that effect. But he stayed with me, in an unexpectedly easy silence, until my tears stopped and I could muster up the strength to stand up and go pee for the fourth time that hour.

16

Thirty-Nine Days to Ghost

I held my laptop case tight to my chest like some sort of shield as I walked through the office the next morning. Every colleague I passed in the halls could be Conner's killer. Every colleague, but especially Stu. I needed to learn more about him, something he'd made difficult at the best of times. It had occurred to me on my drive in that, from what I'd seen, Stu's life was almost as focused on work as mine was. His only distraction seemed to be the gym, for reasons I could never understand.

What if his dogged focus meant he'd do anything for this job, and what if that "anything" included transporting souls in bulk to make the process more efficient, even if it went against policy and ethics? What I needed, I'd decided, was some time alone in his office. With any luck, there'd be some answers there. With extra luck, there'd be something to disprove his involvement entirely. The thought of working so closely with a murderer made my skin crawl. And that crawling only grew itchier at the prospect of someone I'd worked with for so long—and considered such a muscly constant in my life—being the culprit. But getting into his office was easier said than done. Despite all the inviting windows and Stu's official open-door policy, no one ever went in there unless invited.

My belly ached as I reached my desk, sending a flame of heartburn into my chest. The combination of pregnancy stomach and anxious jitters was enough to compel me to keep my garbage can nearby. Flouting authority did not come naturally to me, especially when that authority could cost me my job. Or, if the worst was true, my life.

I sat down and ran an eye over today's files. Cancer. Peanut allergy. Cancer. Aneurysm. Cancer. A standard workday. I tried to focus on the information in front of me, but my mind kept flicking back to Stu, currently sitting in his office with a kale smoothie moustache. If I could just figure out how to get him out of there . . . but it wouldn't be that easy. Stu's office was his sanctuary. He ate all his meals in there when it wasn't a fasting day, so it wasn't like I could just sneak in during lunch, and he always locked his door at the end of the day. I tapped my bottom lip with a pen.

"Morning, Kath," Gemma chirped as she walked past. I checked my watch. She was ten minutes late, something I could never dream of being, though I could never dream of being a lot of things Gemma was. When I turned around to reply, the reason for her tardiness quickly became clear. Her eyes were cloudy and bloodshot, lids heavy. She had very clearly been up all night, no matter what her sunny floral blouse or bright pink lipstick had to say about it.

"Morning," I said back. "Nice weekend?"

Gemma leaned on my desk conspiratorially. "It was nuts! A

few of my besties and I got a little wild after brunch on Saturday and ended up partying all weekend. Just between you and me, I'm, like, barely here right now."

"Glad you had fun," I said, for lack of anything else to say. Then a thought occurred to me. "How's your annual report coming along? You struggled with your first one, didn't you?"

"Oh *god*." Gemma rolled her eyes. "I can't think about that today."

"I understand," I said. "It's just, the deadline's getting close. It's already almost the end of August. I struggled with them too my first few years, but Stu was able to help me out a lot."

Gemma gave me an incredulous look. "Really?"

"Yes," I lied. "He doesn't look busy right now. I'm sure he'd be happy to look over what you have so far."

At this, Gemma glanced between me and Stu in his office. "I guess. I just don't know if I have it in me today. Maybe tomorrow. Thanks, Kath." She rose to leave, but in a sudden desperate panic to get answers, I grabbed her arm before she had the chance.

"I just want to make sure you have enough time to make any necessary changes," I said, and forced a smile.

"Well . . ." Gemma gave a little sigh and smiled sweetly back at me. "I appreciate you looking out for me. Let me just down some coffee and I'll see if he'll help. You're a good friend, Kath."

My heart sank at that. "Happy to help."

Ten minutes later, Gemma left her cubicle and knocked on Stu's office door. I stood and faked a stretch, watching her ponytail dance as she spoke, her gestures graceful and animated. Stu, by contrast, seemed carved out of stone, his features unmoving, but his head nodded and a moment later they were walking past me. I gave a polite smile to them both, waited a moment for them to settle at Gemma's laptop, and quickly abandoned my cubicle.

Stu's office felt wrong without his hulking torso looming over the stark, utilitarian metal desk. I tossed a look back over my shoulder and closed the door, heart racing.

Despite the late-summer heat, a charcoal-gray windbreaker hung on the coatrack by the door. Stu always wore it around his waist on his daily jog to work, and it always served to remind me never to jog anywhere. I dove for the windbreaker pockets, trying my best to avoid the office windows, which was no easy feat with size 14 hips and a growing baby bump. Still, my colleagues outside Stu's lair seemed oblivious; everyone glued to the laptops at their desks or out doing collections. I had just shy of ten minutes until my first client of the day was ready for pickup, and little confidence that Gemma's report would hold Stu's attention for long. I had to be quick.

The left windbreaker pocket was empty, the right holding only a nickel, a bent paper clip, and a receipt from a health food store for three containers of unflavored protein powder. Nothing suspicious, other than the lingering mystery of why anyone would buy their protein powder unflavored. I returned the items and slunk over to the desk, my pulse thundering in my ears. Somehow this—not entering Stu's office uninvited or rummaging through his pockets, but this—felt like a breach of trust and professionalism. A desk was a sacred space.

I braced myself, squeezing my increasingly sweaty hands into fists at my sides. This could play out one of two ways: either there was some sordid piece of evidence in one of those desk drawers and my boss was a murderer, or there was nothing more than a forgotten half of a stale protein bar and he was back to being reliable, terrifying Stu again. I needed to find out which it was, not only for Conner's sake but, in truth, for my own. I needed to know that this job was what I thought it was. What I needed it to be. That it was some low-level asshole who'd hurt Conner and not the man I'd been answering to for the better part of a decade.

With that, I took the plunge. I plucked open the first drawer, and a herd of stress balls jittered nervously at me in an endless variety of colors and states of wear. I recognized a few and wondered how many I'd inadvertently contributed to destroying. The next drawer down was harder to open; as soon as I'd managed it, I realized why. Three sets of dumbbells were wedged inside, a medicine ball and two resistance bands piled on top. The drawer down from that spilled open with a whoosh of air, ruffling files of neatly aligned printer paper. I thumbed through the first few files but found nothing more than reports on collection data and a one-page handout entitled "LeaderSHIP: How to Steer Your Crew to Sunny Shores." I closed the drawer.

There was only one drawer left, on the other side of the desk, but when I pulled at the handle, it wouldn't budge. I braced my foot against the desk and pulled again, but when it still wouldn't open, I realized it wasn't jammed, it was locked. It was then I noticed a blue Post-it note lying crumpled beneath the drawer, along with a toothpick and a protein bar wrapper. I squatted awkwardly and reached out for the paper. Scribbled across the Post-it in Stu's hand was the address for Blazing Meadows. I clutched the note, my eyes unblinking. There was no reason for Stu to know about the park, much less have its name and street address etched in ink at his desk. And yet, there it was, proof he knew where to find Conner in life and in death. I wobbled back to my feet, but as I stood, I realized I wasn't the only one in Stu's office anymore.

Caroline was in the doorway, eyes as wide as mine as they flicked between me and the paper in my hand.

"What are you doing?" Her voice was tight. She wore a vest embroidered with cats, her brown skirt skimming the floor. Her short blond hair was neat as always, but her pale eyes, usually ready for laughter, were on me with an intensity I'd never seen in her before.

"I . . . uh . . ." I was unsure whether the next thing to come out of my mouth would be words or vomit. Shit, shit, shit. What was she doing here? This wasn't even her department. "I . . . uh . . ." I said again, fiddling with the Post-it note. "Uh, this." I waved the paper triumphantly. "I dropped it when I was meeting with Stu before, so I just came back to grab it."

Caroline hmm-ed at me, her eyes still sharp. A lump grew in my throat.

"What, um, what brings you over to Natural Causes?"

"I had something important I needed to discuss," said Caroline. "With Stuart." She glanced again at the note in my grasp, eyes wilder than I'd ever seen them. "What is that?"

"Anything I can help you with?" I deflected.

"No, only Stuart." Caroline crossed her arms over her chest, decapitating a white kitten playing with a ball of yarn. This was all very odd. Unless . . . Ethan had said he heard voices in the woods that night. Not a voice; voices. There had been someone else. Someone who might be looking to clean up loose ends.

What if there was something important in that locked drawer in Stu's desk? The same important thing Caroline had come to talk to Stu about? Come to think of it, Caroline had been over here last week chatting with Gemma, despite Accidental Deaths being on the other side of the building and two floors up. She had been standing just outside his office door when I told Stu I'd found Conner. And that day in the lunchroom when I'd asked Jesse about any possible mix-ups in Murder, she'd seemed shocked at the suggestion. That such a thing could happen, or that I knew it had?

I peeled my lips into as convincing a smile as I could muster. "Well, I'll let him know you're looking for him," I said, sliding past her through the door.

"See that you do," Caroline called after me. "And Kathy? Stuart doesn't like people in his office when he's not here. Remember that. His things are not to be rifled through. Snooping around where you don't belong can come with very nasty consequences."

I threw a thumbs-up over my shoulder and walked back to my desk as fast as my perpetually full pregnancy bladder would allow, Caroline's sharp stare hot on my back.

17

Thirty-Five Days to Ghost

I ripped off a hunk of pizza crust and mopped it through the puddle of ranch dressing on my plate. It was a rainy early evening and I had just finished recounting my Caroline run-in to Jo and Conner around my dining table. I'd successfully avoided Caroline after the incident in Stu's office for the remainder of the week. Her uncharacteristic intensity that day unsettled me almost as much as Stu's Post-it note and locked drawer, though he'd been more difficult to avoid. I'd made a second home of the ladies' room and used Gemma as a human shield three times. Time may not have been on my side, but I wasn't willing to make any more moves alone. Conner and I spent the next few evenings online, looking into Caroline and Stu for anything of use, but despite our best efforts, our search turned up nothing relevant. What I needed was to talk to Jo. And I couldn't do that until she was back in town from an impromptu camping trip with her aerobics instructor, who she'd recently started seeing. He was Italian and kept bees.

"I think he's the one," she'd told me over the phone before she left on her trip.

"Really?"

"Well, the one for now." I had half expected her to come back with news of an elopement, but instead she'd brought a pizza and a declaration that "for now" had passed.

I grabbed another slice and fought the urge to add peanut butter to the toppings as Jo contemplated my experiences.

"I wouldn't have thought Caroline capable of something as bold as murder," Jo mused. "Though if I'm honest, honey, I wouldn't normally think of Caroline much at all. She always seemed fine when we were colleagues. Not good, not bad, just fine. Like oatmeal."

"Well, that could be good, right?" said Conner. "Like with spies. You never get the guy who looks like a spy. He's gotta blend."

"Conner thinks she could be using her oatmealness to her advantage," I relayed to Jo.

"Smart kid," said Jo. "Could be. I can't think what her motive would be, but the best way to know would be to learn more about her. See if she knows about our boy, find out what she's involved in."

"Right," I said. "How do I do that?"

"Well now." Jo lowered a piece of pizza crust under the table for Chap. "When I was in my early thirties, I was working at a pub after I followed a temperamental mime to the festival in Edinburgh, and there was this lovely fella there who was a regular. But for the life of me I couldn't get a word about him out of any of my coworkers. They were worse than the mime. At least until the day I caught the boss watering down the beer supply.

Suddenly he was only too keen to tell me the man's marital status, along with some other information that made me reconsider my pursuits. Which was just as well, since my mime and I made up for a while. He was always very good with his hands."

"Great," I said. "So I just need to catch Caroline watering down some souls and I'm all set."

"You could get her drunk," Conner suggested.

I shot him a glare. At this rate I'd have better luck finding a mime to run off with.

"What?" Conner said defensively. "People are idiots when they're drunk. That's why I stopped drinking after I turned sixteen. Like, fuck, do you know how many dumbasses end up, like, crying in the bathroom at a house party or some shit? Nah, I'll take weed over that mess any day."

"Conner, I am not going to . . ." I stopped, an image playing in my mind's eye of Caroline talking to Gemma about grabbing drinks with some people from the office, right before I turned down the invitation to go myself. It was the kind of thing Gemma organized regularly. She liked spending off-hours with coworkers for some reason. And from the looks of things, Caroline liked to join in. "Shit," I said.

"What?" asked Jo.

"I'm going to get Caroline drunk."

Thirty-Two Days to Ghost

That morning had a dreamy quality to it—a subtle, Vaseline-on-the-camera-lens haze that made me wonder if I'd actually woken up. The golden sunlight beaming through my windshield seemed to be filtered through frosted glass as I pulled into the office parking lot and stepped out into the already blazing heat of the day. Within seconds I had sweat patches growing in the armpits of my lime-green blouse and the whispered threat of a matching line under my boobs, which were no longer a B cup for the first time in my life and seemed eager to share the news no matter what blouse I put on.

I found Gemma at her desk, head bent over her cell phone, thumbs flying furiously.

"Morning, Gemma," I greeted. She dropped the phone to her desk with a bashful expression and gave me a wide smile.

"Hey, Kath! Cute blouse. Love the stripes!"

I looked down. The line of boob sweat had somehow been joined by a line of stomach-roll sweat even though I'd been in air-conditioning for a good five minutes now.

"Thanks," I said. "Say, you're not planning on organizing drinks for this weekend by any chance, are you?"

"Oh god, after last weekend?" Gemma gave a demure laugh. "No way. Besides, Stu said some parts of my report need reformatting, so I really should buckle down and get that done."

"Of course," I said. "Maybe next weekend?"

"I'm away next weekend," Gemma said.

"Oh. Right. Well." I needed to find out what Caroline's role in all this was, and I needed to find out fast. If I was on the wrong track, I was wasting valuable time, and if my gut was right, well . . . if it was right, that meant I would have a whole new set of questions to find answers to.

Gemma flashed another smile, swiveled her chair back towards her desk, and was just reaching for her phone when I blurted, "Only, I really need this."

This got Gemma's attention, for a moment anyway. With half her focus still on her phone, now resting in her lap, she said, "Wait, you *want* to go for drinks?"

"Yes," I said. "I need . . . um . . . I need to unwind. Which is something people do at bars."

"You okay?" Gemma's eyes were full of concern. "You always struck me as more of a homebody."

"I am," I said. "Usually. But things have been difficult lately and I could really use something different."

"Aw, Kath. That sucks. But I really should—"

"I'm pregnant," I said, louder than I'd planned to. The sound of it stung my ears.

"What?"

I hadn't planned on telling anyone at the office until it became unavoidably obvious, which my already curvy shape and loose blouses helped prolong, and Gemma's face was exactly why. Her expression kept oscillating between horror and unabashed joy, clearly unsure which she should be feeling. Both annoyed me equally.

"It wasn't planned," I continued.

"Is it . . ." She lowered her voice. "Simon's?"

I nodded.

"Holy shit."

I nodded again.

"Are you guys still going through with the divorce?"

"We are."

"Oh, Kathy." Gemma was on her feet, throwing her perfectly toned arms around my neck. "Men are such scum. Use 'em and lose 'em is what I say." She pulled away, still holding me by my upper arms. "You poor thing. But you can't drink if you're pregnant, right?"

"No," I said, swallowing a rising tidal wave of bile. I couldn't tell if it was Gemma's sickly-sweet perfume or her sickly-sweet tone, but either way I knew we had to wrap this up quick before I added my own pattern to her polka-dot blouse. "But I thought being out with people might help me get my mind off of things."

"Of course," said Gemma. "Of course it would. God, what a total nightmare. I'll throw something together for Friday, all right? I may have to bail early, but at least you'll be with friends. We're gonna get you through this."

"Thank you," I said, and I did mean it. As much as I hated pity, Gemma truly wanted to be there for me, even if it inconvenienced her own life, and I appreciated it.

"Anytime, girl." Gemma slid back into her chair.

"Oh, Gemma," I said as I turned to head back to my own desk, "can you make sure to invite Caroline? I'd like to get to know her better."

"Oh, totally," said Gemma. "She loves this kind of thing. And she's divorced too, so you'll have loads to talk about."

18

Thirty Days to Ghost

We'd already lost two weeks of Conner's grace period and I still had yet to confirm Caroline's involvement in the case. Try as I might, I couldn't find anything helpful about her despite quizzing coworkers, and my nights of online research had amounted to little more than the discovery of her blogger alter ego, "Caro-Wine." Time was marching away from me like ants at a picnic, slipping off with crumbs of precious hours I didn't have to spare. Friday somehow felt farther away as each hour passed, and suddenly those thieving ants were up my pant leg, tickling me into restlessness.

It was a quarter past five and most of the cubicles around me sat empty, the late-afternoon sun beckoning my day shift colleagues from their desks to do whatever it was people did outside on bright summer afternoons. Picnics? Hikes? Something involving helmets and boards on wheels? The outside world was decidedly lacking in couches and played too fast and loose with bees, so we saw very little of each other. Regardless, the night shift had yet to file in, dour and sleep-deprived, which left the office in tranquil silence. I dropped my laptop into its case and let the quiet nestle against me, the half walls of my cubicle surrounding me in a familiar embrace. I sat unmoving at my desk for a moment, attempting to feel as soothed as usual by the comforts of this little gray world I knew.

My leg bounced, unbidden. The ants again, crawling past with their stolen morsels of time. I slid my rolling desk chair back and took in the emptiness around me. A department all to myself. A building all to myself. I jumped up, knocking my rolling chair onto its side. Its wheels spun impotently in the air like the legs of an upended turtle.

"A building all to myself," I said slowly to the no one that surrounded me. The chair wheels stopped spinning in response.

That meant, if I was very lucky, that Caroline had gone home for the night. That her cubicle sat empty. That anything connecting her to Conner was there, unguarded and easily accessed.

I crossed the hall and slammed a fist against the button for the elevator. A ding and the doors parted. I shuffled in and pressed the third floor button. I'd only been to the third floor—which was shared by the Murder and Accidental Deaths departments—a handful of times. Around here there were very few occasions that made venturing outside of your department necessary, except for socializing, which I did my best to avoid, and accessing the lunchroom, which was on my floor anyway.

The doors opened and I stood just outside them for a moment, taking in the slightly larger cubicles in a slightly darker gray. There were fewer agents up here, leaving enough room for a battered brown leather couch against a far wall. Posters of encouraging kittens and upbeat slogans hung thumbtacked to the walls in a way that said, "Stu doesn't have any authority here."

I ventured into the belly of the office. Each of the cubicles sat identical in their crisp gray rows like well-ordered tombstones, and it occurred to me I had no idea which belonged to Caroline. I crept into the first I came to and quickly retreated at the sight of David from Murder in a Speedo, surrounded by other Speedo-wearers smiling up from a frame on the desk. This was definitely not Caroline's cubicle. More desks with more family photos sent me away from the center of the office to the left-hand side, where the closed offices of the department managers and team leaders sat. I dove into another cubicle and then a second, but came away empty. The third was where things changed. Three notebooks sat on the desk beside a photograph of a pair of ferrets. The top notebook was embossed "Caroline Daughtry." A small thrill ran through me. I flipped the cover open. The first page was scribbled with work notes and shopping lists. Whole milk was circled twice, though it was hard to tell which list it was connected to.

The pages that followed were equally cluttered with information of all sorts. I skimmed a few until something caught my eye and made my heart leap. Stu's full name. His home number, which I didn't even have despite working in his department. Beside this, barely comprehensible scribbles and corresponding dates. Including the day of Conner's death. I pulled out my phone to take a picture when a voice boomed behind me.

"Kathy?"

I swung around to find Jesse Hare, manager of Murder, in front of his office door, arms crossed over his chest, brow cocked.

"What the hell are you doing?"

I quickly slammed the notebook shut and shuffled out of the cubicle.

"Jesse. Hi. Hey. Hey there. You're . . . working late, huh?" My voice was tight, and at least an octave higher than usual.

"It's five thirty."

"Huh."

"What are you doing up here? What were you doing in there?"

I could feel the cogs in my brain rusting over as I tried to think of something, anything, that could possibly make for a believable excuse.

"In there?" I repeated dumbly. "I . . . uh . . . looking for you!"

"For me?"

"Yes."

"In Caroline's cubicle?"

"Um, yes. Well, no. What I mean is, I didn't know whose workspace was whose. It's all so confusing up here. With all the, uh, kitten posters and everything."

Jesse's expression was unreadable.

"Why were you looking for me?"

"To ask you . . . to be sure . . . to be sure to ask that you were coming out with us on Friday. For the office drinks, I mean. I'm just . . . going around . . . trying to get a sense of numbers."

"Oh," said Jesse blankly. "Yeah, I'll be there." As he spoke, his eyes shifted behind me; a patter of soft footsteps first grew louder, then immediately retreated, leaving a waft of some perfume I vaguely recognized. I whipped around, expecting to find Caroline staring in all her intensity again, but whoever had been there was gone.

* * *

POSSESSION ISN'T REAL. WE LEARNED AS MUCH AT S.C.Y.T.H.E. ORI-entation. It's very much a one-body-per-essence deal, and when that body is used up, an agent swoops in and shepherds the essence onwards. That's just how it works. And yet, even with that highly classified information etched on my brain, I was half convinced the soul of someone far bolder than I was had been wearing me all afternoon like one of those inflatable dinosaur costumes. Because it almost definitely wasn't me. I wasn't the action type. I was the thinking type, immediately followed by the overthinking type, which inevitably turned into the well-now-I'm-definitely-not-doing-that type. And yet I'd done it. I'd barged onto the third floor and into Caroline's cubicle without thinking. Without planning. Without Jo's insistence. With only my own uncharacteristic spontaneity to blame.

My hand shook as I slammed my key into the lock of my apartment door. I trudged in on air-filled knees to find Jo at my kitchen table and Conner lounging on a chair beside her, his attention rapt on whatever bawdy tale she'd been spinning. She paused at the sound of my footsteps.

"Christ, honey," Jo said to me. "I haven't heard someone drag their feet like that since I busted Enrique out of the drunk tank after Carnivale in '96. We still somehow managed to outrun three cops and one very boisterous German shepherd, but something tells me there was less rum and illegality involved in whatever's weighing you down."

"You're half right," I said weakly, slumping into an empty kitchen chair. "Conner, feet off the table."

The essence in question gave an eye roll but did as requested.

"I don't know what's wrong with me, Jo," I continued. "I think Caroline might've spotted me."

"Spotted you where, exactly?"

"In her cubicle."

"You were in her cubicle?"

"Yes."

Jo blinked at me. "Well, that's quite the development. I thought you had a plan for Friday night."

"I did," I moaned. "I did, I always do, and I always stick to the plan so I can't ruin anything. And yet somehow I was upstairs, digging through Caroline's things. And Jesse caught me. And I heard someone behind me, and . . . and I don't know what's come over me, I really don't. What the hell was I doing?"

"You were *doing*," Jo said after a beat.

"But why?" I was certifiably whining now. "Every time I *do*, I mess things up."

Jo gave a slow nod. "Sure, sugar, so you say. So you were taught. But some things are worth the risk of making a mess. I reckon the best things usually are." I thought I caught her gaze shifting slightly in the general direction of Conner. "Hell, a life without risks is like . . ."

"Being a ghost," Conner finished.

My breath caught. I ran my eye over the calendar held to my fridge by a banana magnet. For Conner, not taking a risk right now was the biggest risk of all. But that didn't make me feel any better about what I'd done. I'd been reckless. I could have compromised this whole amateur investigation. I said as much to Jo, but she wasn't having it.

"Plenty of time for thinking yourself into a tizzy when you're dead," she said. She turned to Conner. "No offense, kiddo."

Conner shrugged as Jo continued. "Life is for making messes, my girl. That's living. That's a privilege we only get for maybe eighty years at a go. We're given this wonderful, beautiful sandbox to play in, and what a waste it is to never try and build something from it, even if the rain sweeps it away in the end."

I shook my head. This was all fine and good for Jo to say. Despite her age, she'd never left the playground. She lived for sand under her nails, for castles made of earth and imagination. I didn't have that luxury. Not with my Sadim touch.

"It's not that easy, Jo."

Jo said nothing. Instead she took my hand and gave it a squeeze as the last bit of adrenaline left my body and a rush of hollow sadness filled the space left behind.

19

Twenty-Eight Days to Ghost

B y the time Friday night rolled around, I had worked myself up into such a state I could barely stomach anything but crackers and jam for dinner. It wasn't just that time was slipping away from us, or even the thought of spending an evening with a possible murderer that made my palms sweaty. As much as I hated to admit it, there was something far less ominous twisting my stomach into knots. It had been more than a decade since I'd been "out" in the way people under thirty say they're going out, and every ounce of "out" etiquette was suddenly eluding me. I couldn't begin to imagine what to wear, I had no clue what kinds of small talk to lean on, I barely knew most of the colleagues Gemma had invited along, and if by some miracle I could even get Caroline's guard down enough for her to talk, I didn't know where to begin with an interrogation.

My mind was spinning so dizzyingly when I got home from work that I barely even noticed something amiss. The local news was blaring from my living room as I sat down to my crackers, forcing each one down my throat with a grimace as a swell of butterflies rushed up to meet them. It was only as I was shoving my plate into the sink and dusting the crumbs from my trousers that it hit me.

Where was Conner?

He'd usually be by the door complaining about the change-over from sitcom reruns to the news by now. But he wasn't. He hadn't come out of the living room at all since I'd come home forty minutes ago, and something told me it wasn't the spinach recall the TV was droning on about that had him rapt.

I practically leapt the few steps from the sink to the living room, jaw clenched with preemptive rage, and sure enough, as I stepped through the doorway, my hunch was proven right. Conner was gone.

Shit. This was a nightmare. I was supposed to be at a bar across town in an hour, I still needed time to shed my work clothes and find something socially appropriate to wear, and now I had to find Conner. Again. If my apartment walls weren't so thin, I would have screamed, but instead of risking my neighbors calling for a welfare check, I dialed Jo's number as I raced into the hall.

"Evening, sugar," Jo answered, as carefree as a cat on a sunny porch. I nearly hung up.

"He's gone."

"Oh dear," Jo said. "You really need to microchip that boy."

I hit the elevator button. "Not funny, Jo. Tonight's bar night. I don't have time for this."

"That's tonight? Goodness, you must be going out of your mind."

The elevator was still three floors above me, with no indication it would be moving anytime soon. I growled and raced for the stairwell across the hall, threw the door open, and started down the steps.

"Jo, focus," I said, already winded. "I need to find Conner. He could be in danger. I can't think. I need help. Where the hell could he be?"

"Well now, let's see," said Jo. "What've you got nearby? A pizza place—"

"He's too dead for pizza."

"There's that elementary school down the block."

"Jo, he's a teenager. He's not going to go to any school by choice."

"That school has a park, though, I believe."

I reached the main floor just as the structural integrity of my legs gave out.

"Shit. Jo, you're brilliant."

"I know, pumpkin."

We said our goodbyes and I ran down the block to the school as the sky erupted in a pastel blaze. It was even later than I'd thought. Shit, shit!

Behind the empty school lay a mini-basketball court and a crumbling asphalt play area painted with hopscotch squares. Beyond the asphalt was a small patch of grass littered with potato chip bags and several deflated old basketballs. In the middle of the grass stood a rickety metal playground structure composed of a small slide, a dome-shaped climber, and a swing set. On one of the swings I spied the back of a familiar gray sweatshirt.

My relief lasted the length of my inhale. As soon as I breathed out again it was gone, replaced by the same anger that had taken hold of me when I was in my apartment.

"Conner," I hollered, marching across the grass.

Conner peeked over his shoulder. "Shit," he muttered.

"This is unacceptable." I was still marching, my momentum barely allowing me to stop as I rounded the swing set and came to face him. "What the hell do you think you're doing? Is this some kind of game to you?"

Conner's eyes landed everywhere but on me.

"No, you look at me, Conner Mateo Ortiz," I continued. "And you listen to me. I'm doing this for you, do you understand? Everything . . . all of this . . ." I waved my arms. "I'm doing it for—"

"For me?" Conner shot back. "Bullshit. You're doing it for your dumb job and you know it. You have to find out what happened to me so you can get rid of me and make your boss happy. Admit it. You couldn't give two shits about me, so stop pretending anything you're doing is for anything other than your fucking job, Grim."

I stood there for a moment, sensible work shoes slowly sinking into the candy-infested sand around the swings, heart thumping hard against my rib cage.

"Is that so?" My voice shook. "That's what you think? Conner, my boss could be the one who did this to you. Or could at least be involved somehow. Do you get that? Do you get that I'm not only risking my job but my *life* to get answers here? Do you get that I'm going to a *bar* tonight? A bar, Conner. Me. With people I barely know. And I'm going to have to pretend to care about CrossFit and potty training and mortgages, and watch while everyone around me gets drunk because I can't, and wear a bra that barely fits while the underwire pokes my ribs all night and I sit in a loud room and confront a possible murderer, and I have to be there soon and I don't even know what to wear or how to act . . . and . . . and . . ." But by this point any "and" left was thoroughly muffled by a heavy blubbering that I didn't immediately realize was coming from me. "And I hate all of that, Conner. All of it." I sank down onto the swing next to his, exhausted. "But I'm still doing it. I'm doing it because of my dumb job, yes, but for you, too."

Conner kicked his feet in the sand, slowly twisting his swing from one side to the other with whatever residual energy from our plane his soul still harbored. I turned away from him and mopped my cheeks with the sleeve of my blouse. I really needed to stop crying in front of this kid. Between my pregnancy hormones and the stress of this whole situation, I was basically a ticking time bomb of tears, but it was unprofessional, and worse yet, it was embarrassing. More for him than for me though, I guessed.

"Sorry," Conner said quietly.

I turned back to look at him and noticed his eyes were rimmed red. He wasn't high. That wasn't a possible postmortem activity. And then it hit me. He'd been crying too.

"Conner," I said, my voice still unsteady. "Are you okay?"

Conner shrugged.

"What are you doing out here?"

Another shrug.

"You must have left the apartment for a reason."

By way of reply, Conner drew back in his swing and released his feet, sending him up into the air.

"Conner," I called, mentally adding *passersby catching sight of a haunted playground* to my growing worry list. But he was away, pumping his legs, gaining more height each time he passed me, his lanky form silhouetted against the cotton candy sky. A smile tickled my lips in spite of myself, and without thinking, I pulled my own swing back and joined him in the ether. I hadn't been on a swing in years; decades. I'd forgotten what it was like to shrug off gravity as the ground rose and fell away beneath me and a hit of wind brushed my cheeks. It was an unfamiliar sensation: easy and careless and free. As I watched Conner's profile ebb and flow from the corner of my eye, I realized that this was him. This feeling. Whatever else he felt, all the angst and fear Jo had sensed from him, this was what made Conner's eyes light with so much life despite his death. This was who Conner was at his core. His true essence. A boy soaring through the twilight sky on an easy summer night.

Conner's legs stopped pumping. He slowly returned to earth.

"You really don't know what to wear to a bar?"

I slowed beside him and shook my head, still somewhat dazed.

"Show me what you've got," Conner said. "Let's get you ready for the ball, Cinderella."

20

Conner made a beeline for my closet when we got back, while I detoured to the living room to turn off the TV. I had just dug the remote control out from between the overstuffed cushions of my thrift store couch when something on the news caught my eye. The anchor was recapping the day's stories on one side of the screen, with relevant footage rolling on the other. Amid a cacophony of news camera flashes and just behind the shoulder of a local councilman embroiled in some scandal or other was a pretty woman in a silver-gray skirt suit. The same skirt suit she'd worn to her son's funeral. Her expression as she herded her client into a waiting SUV was as poised and composed as it had been the first time I saw her.

"Jesus, do you have anything in your closet from the last decade?"

I turned from the TV to find Conner behind the couch. His face fell as soon as he looked at the screen.

"This is why you ran away," I said quietly, "right?"

"I didn't run away. I was just down the street. I'm not a child, I can go down the street."

"Conner."

Conner looked away with a shrug.

"She's already back at work," I said, nearly as shocked as he must have been the first time that footage rolled. "Less than two weeks after burying you."

"Fuck, Grim, you don't have to fucking say it."

"I'm sorry, Conner." I rounded the couch and landed directly in front of him, but he kept his focus on his feet.

"You people and your fucking jobs."

My hand fluttered reflexively to the swell of my stomach.

"I know," I said.

"Do we even matter at all? Or are we just accessories until we're too old to be cute? Just something you have to check off your 'Successful Boss Babe' to-do list? Like, had a kid: check. Moving on."

Something deep within me lurched, twisted, stabbed at every part it could reach. My heart, the backs of my eyes, my gut, all stinging with the impact of his words.

"You matter," I tried weakly.

Conner angled his face away and ran his sleeve across it. "My parents clearly didn't get that memo."

"Maybe they were scared," I said, looking down at the swell of my belly.

"Scared of what?"

"Nothing. Never mind. You know what? Fuck your parents."

Conner's head whipped back to face me. "Whoa, what?"

"You heard me. You're a good kid, Conner. If they can't see that, that's their loss." It was what my guidance counselor had told me when I was being bullied in school, but somehow it seemed to apply here.

"You . . . think I'm a good kid?"

"I do," I said. "I could do with a little less cussing, and I don't approve of drugs. But yes, Conner. I think you're a good kid."

Conner scrubbed his face with his sleeve again. "God, we're both such pussies. First you blubbering and then me."

"Language, please," I said.

"Sorry, we're both vaginas, then."

"Conner."

"Come on, Grim. This is stupid. I'm done talking about it. Besides, we've got a bar to get to and you only have granny clothes to pick from. We'd better get a move on."

"*I* have a bar to get to," I corrected.

"Not a chance," said Conner, already halfway to my bedroom. "I know how to navigate a bunch of drunk idiots better than anyone. You're screwed without me there and you know it."

"But if Caroline or one of the other agents sees you—"

"No one's gonna see me," said Conner. "You said you're meeting at Brewster's on Sycamore Street, right? My buddy's cousin manages the place. He snuck us in more times than I can count. There's a stall in the men's room that's always out of order. I'll just stay in there and you poke your head in when you need me, cool?"

"Not cool," I said. "Not cool at all. What if—"

"Grim. You know your job, I know partying. We work this thing together, all right? Nothing's gonna happen. Now, do you have any clothing from after I was born? Because I'm not letting you go for drinks in shoulder pads."

EVERYONE WAS ALREADY AT THE BAR BY THE TIME I SHOWED UP IN a drapey T-shirt with floral appliqués and my most casual pair of black slacks. Conner had slipped in through the back while Gemma ambushed me with a hug and a kiss on each cheek.

"You look great," she yelled into my ear over the blaring rock music and the thrum of patron chatter, her hand patting my belly. "Come sit down. What can I grab you? Virgin cocktail? Nachos? I was just headed up to the bar."

Gemma guided me to a crowded table in the corner, beneath a wall of exposed brick covered in classic rock posters and a neon sign glowing yellow with the word "bar" helpfully reminding me of my current location. The table was already littered with drinks and baskets of gingham paper half-full of fried foods. The room was dim and red-tinted, a garish chandelier above me with crimson bulbs spitting out just enough light for me to make out the faces of my colleagues: half of my department and a good portion of Accidental Deaths, Jesse from Murder, another man I recognized but couldn't put a name to, and Caroline. She was in a brown suede vest with fringe down the shoulders, a cream turtleneck poking out from underneath despite the season, looking perfectly at home laughing with the group. I, on the other hand, could not have felt more out of place if I were naked at the grocery store.

Everything about this place—the loud music, the loud voices, the darkness, the expectation of some wild outcome to talk about at work—made me long for my pajamas and a cup of tea.

"How about a round of shots for the table?" I said to Gemma. "On me."

Gemma beamed and wiggled off in her skintight cobalt-blue dress. If I had to get Caroline drunk, I was going to be quick about it. If I played my cards right, I could be home for the *Star Trek: Voyager* rerun at eleven.

I squeezed myself in between Caroline and Jesse and tried to think of something clever or interesting to say.

"It's hot in here," was the best I could come up with.

"Scorching," Jesse agreed, pulling the collar of his navy polo away from his neck.

Neither comment seemed enough to steal Caroline's attention away from whatever the rest of the table was talking about.

"How's the family?" I asked Jesse. He had two kids, I thought, maybe three, and a wife somewhere in there too.

"Ah, fine," said Jesse, popping one of his trademark wooden toothpicks into his mouth. "Melissa's been home with the girls for a few months now. I think they're all enjoying it."

"How nice," I said, and turned to Caroline. "How about you?"

Caroline pulled away from the group conversation and looked me square in the eyes.

"What?"

"How's your . . . uh . . . family?" I wasn't even sure she had one, but the turtleneck told me it was worth a shot.

"Gary's fine," she said.

"Good, good," I said. I had no idea if Gary was her husband or her son, or possibly her cat, but Caroline didn't seem keen to elaborate. She had already turned back to face the other end of the table when Gemma came back with a round of bright pink shots laced between her fingers.

"The bartender's specialty," she said as she placed a shot in front of Jesse. He quickly rose and wrapped a broad hand over hers.

"What, his specialty doesn't come with a tray? Let me help you with those."

"I'm fine," Gemma shot back. Her face quickly softened into

a smile as she pulled away. "You keep my girl Kathy company, I've got this."

Jesse sat back down beside me. "One of those 'strong, independent women,'" he said, rolling his eyes. "Hey, she didn't give you one." Jesse waved his shot at me.

"Yeah, no, I'm . . ." My hand slunk to my belly despite myself. "Mormon."

Jesse raised a brow.

"Half Mormon. On my dad's side. You go ahead though."

I wanted to keep sinking lower in my chair until I had melted to the floor and could crawl away from the table and out of the bar. Jesse downed his shot with a "cheers" from around the table and I eyed the exit sign glowing orange above the door. It was all feeling a bit pointless. Caroline was still glued to a conversation about— from what I'd managed to gather through eavesdropping—some new video game called *Legacy 5*. Whenever I tried to steal her attention, the best I could pull out of her was a one-word answer and a pinched look before she joined back into the video game talk.

The smell of bacon from the loaded potato skins a server had just dropped in front of Jesse made my stomach turn. This evening was a nightmare. I excused myself and nearly made a clean escape, but as my hand grazed the bar door, I remembered I had a soul stowed away in the men's room who would need retrieving before I could go anywhere. I forced myself from the door and pushed through the crowded tables to the narrow hallway at the back of the bar. The men's and women's bathrooms sat beside each other at the end of the hallway, with an employees-only door off to the side. I gave a quick look around the space to make sure I was alone and quickly slipped in through the door with the little stick figure not wearing a dress.

"Conner?" I hissed into the bathroom. There were three stalls, I noted as I slid inside, with an out-of-order sign tacked to the stall on the far end. Graffiti littered the black-painted walls; some intentional, some clearly patron additions. It smelled like weed and soap tinged with cheap cologne. I gave one more glance over my shoulder and marched to the last stall, punctuating my arrival with a knock.

"Conner?" I whispered again.

"Yo," came the reply.

I pried the door open and closed it behind me in case anyone came in. Conner sat perched on the toilet tank, his feet propped on the closed toilet lid, face long with boredom.

"We're leaving," I said.

His face brightened. "You got what you needed?"

"No," I said. "But there's no use. I must have been out of my mind to think this would work."

Conner dismounted the toilet tank. "You choked?"

"I did not choke," I said. "I'm just . . . not in my element. Besides, Caroline is too wrapped up talking about some video game to even—"

"What game?" Conner's bright eyes were dancing.

I ran a hand over my face, already sick of this conversation. "Something called *Legacy 5*." I shrugged.

"Shit, she's got good taste for a murderer," said Conner.

"You know it?"

"Well, I don't live under a rock, so yeah."

I gave him a sharp look.

"*L5* is the latest release from the Legacy series," Conner explained, arms waving animatedly. "It just came out like a month ago. Hell, it was the last game I played before I kicked it. One of my biggest regrets is that I'll never get to finish that game. If this chick really did kill me and she gets to play it through, I'm gonna be pissed."

"Right, well." I did not want to go back out there. I really did not want to go back out there. "I guess now that I know what it is, I can try talking to Caroline about it."

"Whoa, whoa," Conner said. "Knowing what it is and talking about it are two very different things, Grim. This game is complex."

"Fine, so break it down for me."

"You got a pen?"

"A pen? Why?"

"You're gonna wanna take notes."

I sighed but dug through my purse all the same. Sure enough, among the mints and loose change at the bottom, I had a pen.

"I have nothing to write on," I said as I fished the pen out.

"What are you talking about?" said Conner. "You have a perfectly good left hand."

"Conner, this is not a ninth-grade biology exam. I'm trying to gain the trust of a potential killer here."

"Hey, if it works, it works."

I sighed. "And does it work?"

"Put it this way: if I wasn't dead, I'd be graduating high school next year, and that sure as hell isn't because I was a good student."

"Fine," I said, the pen poised over my left palm. "Tell me about the game."

"All right, class, listen up."

CAROLINE WAS TALKING TO GEMMA WHEN I GOT BACK TO THE TA-ble. I squeezed into my seat, ink-covered hand in my trouser pocket, and started to wonder if all my scribbled notes were for nothing as I listened to the chatter. They were reminiscing about some club they'd been to a few weeks ago; something about a light-up dance floor. If I thought I was a fish out of water during the video game conversation, I was a carp catapulted into space now. My focus bounced between Gemma and Caroline as they chatted easily, completely unencumbered by any sort of agenda, while I stewed in the juices of my rapidly failing mission. Caroline was throwing back a cocktail, so that was promising at least, but this was not the conversation I'd prepared for.

Finally, both women stopped talking long enough to burst into laughter and I jumped.

"*Legacy 5*," I blurted. My cheeks immediately ran hot as half the table turned to look at me. I cleared my throat and addressed Caroline. "Uh. I overheard you talking about the new Legacy game?"

"Yes," said Caroline, with a "what of it?" wedged between each letter.

"I love it," I said. "Can't stop playing it."

"I didn't know you were a gamer," Gemma said.

"I am," I said. "I love them. Games."

"You're an *L5* fan?" Caroline's icy blue eyes narrowed under her pale lashes.

"Uh-huh."

"Cool," said Gemma. "Well, I'll leave you guys to it and mingle a bit. Gaming isn't really my thing, but Kathy, you dark horse, I never would have guessed."

I gave a polite laugh as Gemma found an empty seat at the other end of the table and seamlessly knitted herself into the existing conversation.

"Well, that's something, I guess. I've already played through it twice," Caroline said, her cool tone warming by nearly a degree. "First time as Owen, obviously, but I just finished a playthrough from Stella's POV, and in the last few chapters it was like playing a different game."

I slid my hand from my pocket and glanced at my palm from the corner of my eye.

"I, um, I couldn't believe what happened in chapter eleven, with the prison guard."

"Oh, I know." Caroline was more animated now, her features softening slightly, but she was still too sober for my liking. "No one saw it coming. It was the only thing the forums talked about for weeks."

"Yeah, uh-huh. Hey, let me get you another of whatever you're drinking before we carry on."

Caroline downed the last drops of her existing cocktail. "Don't mind if I do."

Three more drinks and two shots later, and the alcohol finally seemed to be doing its job. Half the table had emptied. Jesse sat picking at the remains of an order of fried pickles, Gemma was saying goodbye to one of the remaining stragglers, and Caroline was slumped sideways on her chair, one arm slung across the back, her words fusing together in a mild slur.

"No, no, you don' understand." She waved her empty glass at me to punctuate her point. "The purpose of Owen's journey izzin love, iss about proving to . . . to . . . to the world you're more'n, you know, what they think. That's why it ends that way."

"Uh-huh." I nodded as though I understood a word of her speech, but I was just waiting for the perfect opportunity to shift the topic to something more productive. Conner never made it to the end of the game, so neither did my notes, which were steadily blurring with the sweat of my palms as I tried to steady my nerves. I smiled and hoped that that would be enough for Caroline.

It wasn't.

"Well . . . well now, what do you think?"

"Me?"

"About the way it ended. Everyone's so divided on it."

"Right," I said, my pulse quickening. "Very controversial. It . . . um . . . I liked it."

"No, no," Caroline wailed. "What do you *think*?"

In panic, I glanced back down at my notes. The few words still legible were of no help. My heart thudded in my ears. I had finally gained Caroline's trust; I had her where I needed her, I couldn't afford to blow this now. This whole night could be for nothing, and I'd be no closer to finding Conner's killer.

"The . . . the prison guard," I said, feeling my way along this narrow conversational ledge like a linguistic Indiana Jones. "That was really shocking. And then at the end, when Owen and Stella . . ." I racked my brain for everything I knew about this game. "When they kiss . . ."

This sobered Caroline up enough for her drowsy eyes to narrow at me.

"They don't kiss," she said.

"No," I said quickly. "What I meant was, I wanted them to kiss."

"But they're brother and sister."

Shit. I vaguely remembered that from my notes.

"Kiss and make up," I tried desperately.

"Make up about what?" Caroline said slowly. "Did you . . . did you even play the game? What is this?"

I swallowed hard.

"Oh hey, Mr. Calhoun!" Gemma called from across the table, waving in the direction of the front door.

I turned around and sure enough, Stu was walking towards us, the slight metallic sheen on his cream shirt catching the dim bar light. Caroline's head whipped around at the sound of his name and, despite her drunken state, she was on her feet in a flash, straightening the hem of her turtleneck and giving him a somber nod. I stood too, looking between Caroline and Stu. Why would she be so flustered by a superior from a department other than her own? It didn't make sense. Unless he was her boss too, but on a very different sort of job.

Caroline kept switching between giving me a suspicious side-eye and watching Stu approach until Gemma came up behind us both and said, "He never comes out to these kinds of things. You must be special, Kath." She elbowed me playfully in the ribs and walked over to greet Stu. When I turned back to Caroline, she was gone.

I did a slow-motion turn in place, wobbling to my toes to peer across the crowded bar, but Caroline was nowhere to be seen. Shit. How did I keep losing people?

I grabbed Gemma's arm. "Did you see which way Caroline went?"

"Bathroom, I think," Gemma said as Stu landed in front of us and opened his mouth in what would likely have been a greeting. I was off and into the crowd before I had the chance to be sure. Shuffling between drunken bodies crowding the web of table-made pathways, I pushed through and into the emptiness of the back hall, making a beeline for the ladies' room.

Caroline was still wasted, but she must have had something

to hide, or else why would she flee? This was it. I needed to confront her now, while I had her cornered, and hope the drinks she'd downed would make her careless enough to admit something useful to me.

I could've vomited. This night had become an all-you-can-eat buffet of everything I hated most; it seemed only fitting that a direct confrontation with a coworker would be the dessert I'd have to choke down at the end.

I pushed the bathroom door open. Sure enough, there was Caroline, leaning weakly against a wall by the stalls, arms folded. She scowled at me as I entered.

"You bitch," she spat. "All those lies back there. To . . . to distract me."

My heart clenched. I was right. Was I right? What was happening?

"Caroline, enough. Just tell me your involvement in this," I tried.

"My involvement? That's rich. You know full well all about my *involvement*."

"I think I do." My mouth was dry. Was this real? Was I actually on the verge of hearing a killer's confession? They did not cover this in Collections Agent training. I could feel my hands begin to tremble. "But I need to hear what you did, Caroline."

Caroline gazed at me through bleary eyes, her look unreadable. And then she burst into tears.

"Oh," I said. "Uh." I crossed the bathroom to where she stood and tentatively patted her shuddering shoulder. "Hey now. That's, um . . ." I really wished people would stop doing this.

Before I could think of anything more productive to say,

Caroline had folded into me, the neck of my shirt dampening with her tears.

"I just . . . I want . . . and I tried . . ." she wailed.

"Caroline, you're not making any sense. Tell me what you've done. Tell me what Stu did."

Caroline peeled away from me. "I love him."

I took a step back, jarred. "You . . . ?"

"Stuart," Caroline said through a sob. "He . . . he took me out for lunch . . . after Larry, one of my beloved ferrets, died last month, and . . . and that's when I knew. I love him. And you . . . you . . . he loves *you*!" She pushed me away from her and tried to stand at her full height but quickly slumped back against the wall, narrowly missing a dried wad of gum.

"What the hell makes you say that?"

"First you leave your number in Stuart's office. His own private office that *no* one can enter without his permission—no one but *you*. And don't tell me that's not what you were doing with that Post-it note. You were too cagey for it to be anything else." Caroline gave a big, snot-rattling sniff. "And when I went by his office the other day, I heard him on the phone talking to someone about you. About how he had done something bad, something that could cost him his job or worse, and I very clearly heard your name. And then he shows up here, something he never does, when it just so happens to be your first time coming out for drinks with us. As if that's a coincidence. Well, dating a subordinate is against company policy."

"Caroline," I said, still struggling to find my words after this revelation, "Stu's gay."

Caroline dabbed her turtleneck sleeve across her wet upper lip. ". . . What?"

"Yeah. He's with Ivan from Processing. You don't remember them dancing together at the office Christmas party last year?"

"I . . . I thought they were brothers. Affectionate brothers."

I shifted my weight.

"You're really not having an affair with Stuart?" Caroline asked pathetically.

"Really not," I said. "Is that why you've been spending so much time in our department? Because you wanted to see Stu?"

Caroline nodded, her tears easing slightly. "I know I'm a little old for him, but I . . . I thought . . . if he saw me around enough . . . Oh, you don't know what it's like to love a man you shouldn't love."

My jaw tightened. "You'd be surprised," I said. "But sometimes it just can't work out. Sometimes you know you'd only mess things up for him in the end."

Caroline blinked at me.

"And sometimes he's gay," I added quickly. "But that doesn't mean we can't still love them in our way, it just means we can't do anything about it."

"Love is a dangerous thing," Caroline said somberly. "Like ferrets."

I nodded and mentally crossed Caroline off my suspect list. But even if Stu didn't have a rodent-loving accomplice, that didn't put him in the clear. He still had that Post-it note with Conner's file number in his office, not to mention the locked desk drawer. And now he'd been overheard saying he'd done something bad, and that I was involved. He could have killed Conner and swiped the file from Murder to give to me, a quiet, reliable worker who wouldn't ask too many questions. Until I did. He had the access.

He had the resources. Was that why he'd come tonight? Was he keeping an eye on me? He certainly wasn't here for the fried food.

I left Caroline to clean herself up and crept back into the men's room. Conner nearly accosted me as I entered the out-of-order stall.

"Final-fucking-ly," he said. "If I wasn't dead already, I'd have died of boredom in here. What the hell took you so long?"

"It's a long story," I said on an exasperated sigh. "There were dead ferrets involved."

"Huh," said Conner. "So did she do it?"

I shook my head.

"Seriously? So all that waiting around in a nasty-ass bathroom all night was for nothing? What I—"

I held my hand up to shush him as the men's room door creaked open.

"Nobody can hear me, dumbass," whispered Conner.

Shoes squelched on the sticky floor. I peered under the stall and found a pair of burgundy, top-of-the-line Hoka sneakers staring back at me.

My eyes widened. "Stu," I mouthed. I could have wrung Conner's neck. Anyone from S.C.Y.T.H.E. could see and hear Conner as clearly as I could; that was what made his insistence on coming tonight so dangerous. And yet I'd let him talk me into this.

Stu's footsteps inched closer to our stall door.

"What do we do?" Conner whispered back.

I squeezed my eyes hard. This was not a good night for my work reputation.

"Stay here," I mouthed, and held a finger to my lips. "Do not make a sound."

I sucked in a deep breath and pushed the door open just enough to squeeze through.

"Kathy?"

"Mr. Calhoun," I greeted, my voice chipper. "Hi. Great bar, isn't it?"

Stu squinted at me, more unsure of what to make of me than usual. He glanced over his shoulder to the wall of urinals and then back to me, head cocked.

"This is the men's room."

"Yes," I agreed.

"I shouldn't make assumptions," said Stu.

"The, uh, the ladies' room was full," I said.

"You were in an out-of-order stall," Stu said slowly.

"I was," I said. "Because . . . I just had gas. Didn't want to hog a working stall over that, you know?" I tried to give a casual chuckle, but it came out as more of a whimper. I would have to transfer to a new department after this. The thought of facing Stu again at work started to give more credence to the gas story than I'd like.

A snort of laughter came from the stall behind me.

"Is there someone . . ." Stu tried to navigate around me to the stall door, but I blocked him as nonchalantly as possible.

"Oh shoot, I must have left my phone in there," I said. The back of my neck was sweating. Stu's attention didn't shift from the door.

"So, what brings you here?" I tried.

This brought Stu's eyes to me.

"Were you looking for a specific number, Valence?"

My cheeks warmed. "Oh, oh god. Oh no. No, no. Not the

bathroom. I mean, what brings you to Brewster's? It doesn't seem like your kind of place."

"No," said Stu. "It isn't. But Gemma informed me that you'd be here . . . that you've been having a difficult time of late." He cleared his throat. "And I thought it would be beneficial to make an appearance. Show some support as department leader."

"You're here for me?" I wondered how much of that idea came from one of those leadership guidebooks Stu had in his office, if there was any truth to it at all.

"If I'm honest, Kathy, I was hoping we might have a word. I hadn't planned for it to happen in a men's bathroom, but you've been avoiding me at work. Kathy, where is the boy?"

I swallowed. "The boy?"

"507032, I believe."

"Oh," I said, my voice too high-pitched, "that boy."

"This is a dangerous case, Kathy. If you can't close it, I will."

"What's so dangerous about this case?"

Stu's face hardened, his eyes icing. "That is not your concern. And if you value your job, and your general well-being, you won't ask it—or anything else about this case—again."

"Sir?"

"I won't say it again, Valence. Bring me the boy, and quickly, or else you may find yourself in a similar predicament to his. Is that clear?"

Without waiting for a reply, Stu swept out of the bathroom as I stood alone in the echo of his words and the steady dripping of a leaky faucet.

21

My hands were still shaking as I wrapped them around my steering wheel five minutes later.

"Did Stu's voice sound familiar?" I asked Conner as I started the car.

"I don't remember." Conner was in the passenger seat, his gaze on his lap. "Sorry, Grim."

"That's okay," I said. He was shaken too. It was written across his face. He'd barely said a word since we'd left the bar. In Stu's dark warning that night, things had become a little too real. A little too much. Playing drunken cat and mouse with Caroline was one thing, but Stu's words had an edge of very real danger, and that edge cut right through any of the fantasies I had left that this was some harmless Sherlock Holmes role-playing game. No; there was a very real killer out there—my own boss a prime suspect—and that meant my life was on the line, along with Conner's soul.

"Radio?"

Conner nodded but still didn't look at me. I turned on the

radio and pulled out of Brewster's parking lot. Finally, my soft rock station did its job and Conner's head snapped up.

"Barry Manilow? Dude, seriously?"

"What's wrong with Barry Manilow?"

Conner just stared at me, brows raised.

I suppressed a smile. "All right, fine. I'll flick through, you tell me when to stop. But you'd better make it a good one. Impress me, DJ."

I skipped past some smooth jazz, a handful of country songs, and "Total Eclipse of the Heart" before Conner held up a hand.

"Holy shit."

"What?"

"Holy shit, holy shit."

"What? What?"

Conner's eyes were electric, beaming with excitement. "This is Dead Sparrow. Oh my god, what station is this? Fuck, turn this shit up."

I turned up the volume, my small car filling with the boom of lyrical rap set against a single, somber violin. Conner bounced his head to the rhythm, impossibly filled with life. My smile grew as the beat washed over me. I would never seek out this music in a million years, but there was something magical about the seamless blend of genres, and about Conner's unabashed enthusiasm for the band, and for music, and for the naive but endearing dream of being a world-renowned DJ—a dream he could no longer chase. My grin grew broader and I found myself bopping along in spite of myself.

"Aha!" Conner waved an accusatory finger at me. "You like this."

"I don't *dis*like this," I said.

"It's good shit, right?"

"It's good shit," I agreed.

Conner flashed a smug smile. "There may be hope for you yet, Grim."

I smiled back. "So I'm not a lost cause?"

"Nah," said Conner. "You aight. I think I can train you up. Get you ready to raise that baby of yours on some decent music."

My jaw clenched. "Conner, no baby talk."

"Right, sorry. But like . . . why?"

I sighed, biting back the swell of tears. But before I could reply, a pair of headlights in my rearview mirror caught my attention.

"Hang on, this guy's a little too close for comfort," I said, skirting to the shoulder to let the car pass. But instead of passing, the car followed me onto the shoulder. "That's weird." I swerved back off the shoulder and onto the quiet road. Both the late hour and the residential neighborhood meant there was hardly anyone around. I flicked a glance towards the speedometer to double-check I hadn't been crawling, but I was precisely at the speed limit. There was no reason for this driver to be so close, but sure enough, they were back behind me again, with barely any breathing room between them and my rear bumper.

"Conner," I said, trying to keep my voice steady, "can you make out anything about the car behind us?"

Conner spun in his seat. "The asshole's brights are on," he said. "I can barely see anything. I think it's blue? Black, maybe? Jesus Christ, he's right up your ass."

"I know," I said.

Conner turned back to me. "Fuck."

"I think so, yes."

My mind was racing. Who had a blue car? Or a black car? Just about everyone. What color was Stu's car? He didn't have one. He ran to work for fun like some kind of monster. But Ivan had a car, I was sure. Was it black? Or blue? I'd only noticed it a handful of times when it was too cold or hot for Stu to run.

"Can you tell what kind of car it is?"

"Something big," said Conner.

That didn't narrow things down by much. The headlights were blinding. I picked up my speed, but the car matched us. Beads of sweat had bubbled onto my forehead. My grip on the steering wheel tightened as my palms grew damp.

And then I felt it. The impact took me by surprise, though it wasn't much at first. Just a light ram. Or as light as a thousand-pound metal vehicle ramming another can be. I jostled forward, my chest nearly bumping the steering wheel before my seat belt had the chance to lock.

"Shit," I hollered, swerving into the empty oncoming traffic lane to avoid a second hit. "Are you okay?"

"I mean, I'm dead," said Conner. "You?"

"Fine," I lied.

The car had followed us into the other lane and appeared to be gearing up for another attack. My left hand abandoned the steering wheel and fell to the swell of my stomach. I couldn't die. Not now.

"Hold on," I said, stepping on the gas and careening down a side street. It was seconds before the headlights were back in my rearview mirror.

"Fucking hell," Conner said.

"I know," I said. "We're going to get out of this, okay? Just hang in there, kid."

Another hit. This one sent me flying forward even harder. When I pulled back, I realized both of my arms were cradled around my belly. My upper arms stung with the bloom of fresh bruises. I kept driving. I needed a plan. Who the hell plans for this? Okay. I took a deep breath, trying hard to stifle my tears. If you're out walking alone at night and someone follows you, you go somewhere public. This was something ingrained in every woman from birth. Why should someone following you in a car be any different? I swung my car around in a sharp left turn. Once again, the headlights emerged from the darkness within seconds.

"Whatever you're doing, Grim, keep doing it," Conner said. He scrambled through the back of his seat like it wasn't there and emerged on the other side to peer out the back window.

"What the hell are you doing?" I cried. "He'll see you!"

"He obviously knows I'm here or else we wouldn't be playing the world's worst game of bumper cars," said Conner. "I'm going to see who this fucker is."

I sped through the empty streets, passing closed restaurants and sleeping shops, eyes flicking over street signs as we hurtled by. We were getting close.

"Anything?" I asked.

"It's too bright to see a face," said Conner. "But I can make out most of the license plate. GTR 75-something."

The car rammed us again, barely grazing us as I kept my speed impossibly high.

"Get back up here," I ordered. My logical brain knew Conner couldn't be hurt without a body, but the rest of me didn't care.

Conner emerged through the passenger seat. "Whatever your plan is, do it quick," said Conner. We both watched in horror as the car zoomed towards us again. I held my breath and made a sharp turn just before I passed the next corner, my right wheels levitating for a moment as I sped down Magnolia Street, informally known as Club Row. It was just after two a.m. and a few of the clubs were letting out, clusters of people milling around on the sidewalks, the women wobbling in towering heels next to men sporting too much hair gel. The street was flooded with cars, taxis, and Ubers attempting to make their way home; their home or someone else's. The car tailing us turned down Magnolia after me, hovered for a moment, and made a U-turn away from the chaos and back out into the still, unyielding night.

I pulled over and parked by the curb, hands glued to the steering wheel, knuckles aching, body stiff. Neither of us spoke for a long moment as the car cooled down with a few gentle ticks.

"Shit," I said at last.

"Shit," Conner agreed.

"Are you okay?"

"Still dead."

"Right." I sucked in any air my lungs could find. "I wouldn't have let anything happen to you. Whoever that was. Whatever they did or wanted to do. I wouldn't have let them get you."

"Thanks," said Conner.

"I mean it," I promised. "I'm getting to the bottom of this, and no one is going to take any more from you than they already have. Okay?"

"Okay," said Conner.

Once I'd finally stopped trembling, we drove home.

I turned on every light in my apartment. Bolted every lock on the door. Checked inside my closets and behind my shower curtain for good measure. My breathing still hadn't fully steadied.

For a fleeting second I wondered what kind of impact this might be having on the baby. I'd already put it in danger and it wasn't even here yet. I swallowed down the thought in a hard gulp.

Conner had been trailing me as I flitted around from room to room. Whether he was worried about me or himself or simply bored I couldn't tell, but when I finally stopped and landed lead-legged on my couch, he flopped down beside me.

"I'm calling Jo," I said.

"Okay, good," said Conner. "Good. She's got her shit to-gether. She'll know what to do."

I dug my phone out of the purse still slung over my shoulder and hit Jo's number. The monotonous ring was soothing at first, as I imagined the blaring equivalent on the other end rousing Jo from sleep, but it continued for too long, and instead of a groggy "hello," the ringing ended in a click and her voicemail message:

"This is Jo. Do your thing at the beep. Unless this is Donovan calling. Honey, give it a rest."

I hung up before the beep, hit redial twice, and gave up. Jo could sleep through an apocalypse without stirring; it had been too optimistic to think a phone call would do the trick. My eye-lids grew heavy as I leaned back into my couch cushions. I looked behind me to my bedroom door, knowing I should just slink into bed and put this whole night behind me, but I was unable to move. Even my bed didn't feel safe tonight.

"No dice with Jo?"

I'd forgotten for a moment that Conner was beside me. He'd been so still, so quiet, since we got back. For once I wished he was his usual vulgar, talkative self, if only to drown out my own rac-ing thoughts.

I shook my head in reply.

"Do you think you should call the cops? I mean, I know death is kinda your deal, Grim, but it's a bit different when someone's actually trying to kill you, right?"

"I can't go to the police with this," I said. "S.C.Y.T.H.E. operates on the very outer perimeters of the law, both judicially and dimensionally. Besides, it's against company policy to tell anyone outside of the company about what we do. I can't involve just anyone in a situation like this."

"Ah," said Conner. "That sounds lonely as fuck."

I sucked in a breath. "It is."

I could feel the exhaustion of the night grabbing hold of me. My limbs were heavy, my head light.

"Conner," I said blearily, "can I sleep out here tonight?"

"Hey, it's your house, Grim."

"No, yeah, but I know you like your TV at night." I was barely making sense now. "I just, I don't want to be alone. Not tonight. I'm always alone. Just not tonight."

Conner rose from the couch to let me spread out across it, half my face smooshed against an itchy pillow.

"Yeah," said Conner. "Me too. To all of that. You sleep well, okay? I'll be here. I'll just be right here."

Conner's words faded into a haze along with the world around me as I sank into sleep.

22

Twenty-Seven Days to Ghost

It was nearly eleven by the time I woke up, dazed and disoriented, in my living room. Conner was sitting on the narrow windowsill, peering at the pigeons on the other side. My head was throbbing. It felt like I was hungover without having been drunk in the first place.

"Conner," I gurgled.

The soul in question turned from the window.

"You snore," he said.

"Good morning to you too."

"You okay?" He'd moved to sit by the side of the couch.

No, was what I wanted to say. My legs were swollen, my empty stomach was ready to toss any crumbs it could find up my esophagus, and my heart rate was still dialed up at the memory of last night. What I said instead, though, was "I'm good."

Conner let out an airless breath of relief. "Good. I mean, last night was . . . I'm glad you're good, Grim. So, what now?"

I dug between my couch cushions for my phone. "I'm going to try Jo again. We need help. Assassination attempts are above my pay grade."

No answer from Jo again. This wasn't like her. Even when she was off on some wild Jo adventure, she'd still answer the phone when my name showed up.

"Come on," I said, trying to quell a rising panic. "We'll swing by her place. Ten dollars says she's still in bed, and not alone."

"Sick," said Conner, though I couldn't tell if that was a good or a bad thing.

I tried a smile, but my face and my brain were at odds. After last night, all I could think about was death. Which was not something I liked to think about in my off-hours. Whoever tried to run us off the road last night was almost surely from S.C.Y.T.H.E., which meant they knew about Jo and about our friendship. If it was Stu, he also knew her address. Which put her at risk in a way I hadn't considered before.

We hurried down the stairs and into the parking garage. I was panting as I started the car and pulled out onto the street beneath a pale morning sky. Half a block from my complex, my phone began to ring. I scrabbled through my purse with my right hand, trying to keep my eyes on the road and promptly fumbling the phone onto the passenger-side floor.

"It's Jo," Conner said, peering at the caller ID.

"Thank god," I breathed. I pulled to the curb, stuck my hazards on, and retrieved my phone, trying hard not to let my arm slip through Conner's intangible calves.

"Hello? Hello?" I called down the line before the phone was even to my ear.

"Morning, sugar."

"Thank god," I said again. "Jo, hi, we were just on our way to you."

"Ah, well now, I need to tell you something, but first I need you to promise me you're not going to panic."

I swallowed. "What's going on?"

"Nothing to be concerned about," she said.

"Jo," I barked.

"Did I tell you they have salsa nights every Friday at the Black Cat Cafe?"

"Jo," I said again.

"Well, they do. And I was there last night. It was great fun. There was this one young man—"

"Jo!"

"I had a little fall, sugar. It happens from time to time when you've lived long enough."

"Are you okay?" The relief that soared through me was short-lived.

"Well, I'm in the hospital. Did a number on my hip. The doctors think I'll be here for a while yet."

Shit. "On our way."

I hung up and flipped the car around.

"What's going on?" Conner asked.

"Jo danced herself into the hospital."

I PULLED UP TO THE TOWERING REDBRICK BUILDING AND HOPPED out of the car. Ambulances lined the curb by the entranceway, a parade of empty stretchers wheeling by. The automatic doors ushered us into a world of muted green and beige, blue scrubs wafting by at every turn.

A young woman scarcely as old as Gemma sat typing away at the front desk, her long acrylic nails clicking against the keyboard.

"Hi, hey, good morning," I greeted breathlessly.

The woman looked up at me, heavily drawn eyebrows arched. "Can I help you?"

"I'm looking for Jocelyn Smith's room, please."

"Popular lady," said the woman. "Are you a family member?"

Conner shot me a look. "I think you're gonna have to be a family member, Grim," he said.

"I'm a daughter," I said, which was true. I just wasn't her daughter.

The woman nodded and turned back to the computer.

Conner leaned lazily over the counter that rimmed the desk. "Yo, there's somebody in here for Giant Balls Syndrome."

I rolled my eyes. "Stop that."

The woman behind the desk looked up at me.

"Oh, no, sorry, not you," I said quickly.

"Right," she said warily before returning her attention to the computer screen. I glared at Conner, but he was too busy chortling to notice.

"Room 124," said the woman. "Down the hall, on your left."

"Thank you," I said.

"Nice tits," said Conner.

"Enough," I said.

The woman just stared at me. I opened my mouth to give some kind of explanation, thought better of it, and simply walked away.

"This is a hospital," I said as we walked down the seafoam-green hallway. "Be respectful, Conner. People are dying here."

"Well, I'm already dead, so I've got them beat."

I just sighed. He did have a point.

We turned a corner and walked a short way along the corridor before reaching room 124. Jo had the bed nearest the window, which I had no doubt she'd fought valiantly for. The bed nearest the door was empty, and a third bed was shielded from view by sterile white curtains. The room smelled of bleach and poorly cooked meat, but Jo didn't seem to mind. She was propped upright by an entire flock of pillows, wearing a bright yellow floral housedress, one leg elevated, her hands running agilely across a braille book on her lap. Chap, for his part, was snoring soundly at her side.

"Jo!" I hurried to her bedside, but she held a finger up and didn't acknowledge me again until her page was done. She closed the book as I dropped into the swamp-green chair beside her bed.

"You brought my boy with you," she said. Conner beamed at this.

"How are you?" I asked, scooping up her hand.

"That depends, dear. How's my hair?"

I ran an eye over the stiff-set gauzy curls. "Immaculate."

"Then I'm just fine."

I shook my head. "Are you in any pain?"

"Oh yes," said Jo. "But it's nothing I can't handle. They've got me down for surgery this afternoon, which means I'll get the good drugs. But you? Sugar, you're squeezing my hand so hard it might need surgery too. Something tells me, as much as I'd like to believe otherwise, that it isn't just little old me that has you all worked up."

I glanced at the curtained bed across the room. "Something happened last night, Jo," I said as quietly as possible. "Stu showed up at the bar—"

"Stu? At a bar? No wonder you're so shaken up."

"No," I said. "That's not . . . He said something to me. It sounded like a threat. He said I had to stop asking questions about . . . that case . . . and then, on our way home . . ." I lowered my voice even more. "Someone tried to run us off the road."

Jo pulled her hand away and fiddled with the book in her lap, her face tight. "Well, I don't like that," she said. "I don't like that one bit."

"We weren't huge fans either," said Conner, but I didn't bother relaying it. Some things went without saying.

"You both okay?"

"Just a bit shaken," I said, and flashed a reassuring smile at Conner, who had tensed beside me.

"Sounds like that might've been your second warning of the night," said Jo. "Someone wants to keep you in line. If it was Stu, I can't see him giving up so easily."

"No," I agreed. "So what do I do? I need you, Jo. I can't do this alone."

"You're absolutely right about that, sugar. But you've got our Conner."

Conner shrugged. "Like, thanks, but there's not a hell of a lot I can do without a body."

"Conner says he can't do much in his condition," I said. He was right. I needed the help of someone living. I needed Jo. But Jo needed to recover.

"I don't suppose he can," Jo mused. "But there is one person we're all forgetting about in this."

I folded my hands in my lap as a few moments of silence ticked by.

"No one? Really?" Jo tutted. "You have Simon, you silly girl."

I nearly guffawed. "Simon?" The name drew me to my feet. "I do not 'have' Simon."

"You've always had him, you just didn't know what to do with him."

I was pacing now. "Jo, Simon and I are getting a divorce. And besides, he can't know what I do."

"Oh, bullshit."

"It's company policy, Jo."

"So's not murdering clients or mowing down coworkers, but that sure ain't stopping whoever's behind this. If they can play dirty, so can you. You need help, you need support, and that's all that man's ever wanted to be for you."

My mouth gaped open and closed like a guppy's for a moment. This policy of secrecy had kept a wall firmly between Simon and me throughout our whole relationship. In its towering shadow festered tension, disappointment, distance . . . and comfort. Because the truth of it was, as long as I had my walls, I could keep Simon on the other side of them, so all he could see of me were the glimpses I wanted him to. And a job of mandated subterfuge was the perfect excuse to keep him there. Sometimes I wondered if that was why I strove so hard to hold on to it. Because I thought . . . because I *knew* that if I knocked those walls down, the carefully crafted illusions of a competent, lovable woman would be quickly replaced by the messy reality of a person with the opposite of a Midas touch.

"But I . . . But he . . ." I clapped my hands on my thighs in desperation. "Conner, tell her."

Conner's eyes were wide, as though I'd caught him off guard. "Uh, I mean he is a bit of a wet blanket."

"See," I said. "There. A wet—no, that's not what I—"

"Child, sit down," Jo ordered.

"I . . . but . . ." I gave up and did as I was told.

"Why are you divorcing the love of your life and the father of your unborn baby?"

"You know why." I waited a beat. "Because I have to keep things from him."

"No," Jo corrected. "Because you *want* to keep things from him."

That was accurate enough to get my hackles up. "That's rich coming from the queen of divorce herself. How many are you up to now? I've lost count."

"Dude, she's in a hospital bed with a broken hip," Conner said. "Maybe cool it a bit?"

I took a deep breath. "What are you trying to say, Jo?"

Jo tapped the book cover with one red-polished nail. "You want to know why I've been divorced so many times? Because those marriages weren't the real deal. Sure, they were fun, and I don't regret a thing about them, but they were for their time, and when their time was done, so was I. That's how I chose to live my life, and I chose well. For me. But you? Honey, what you and Simon have is the real deal. You're just too scared to let him see all of you, so you push him away instead. Listen, you know my opinion, but forget about whether to stay married to the man. Just let him help you. That's all he wants. That's all he's ever wanted. Let him into your life, your real life, and see what happens. Besides, you need an ally right now. Who else you got?"

Jo was right about one thing. I had no one else. But the thought of turning to Simon of all people, after all the work I'd done to distance myself from him, made my skin crawl. This kind of disaster was what I was divorcing the man to spare him from.

The chaos of this case and my questionable competence throughout was everything I didn't want him to see.

I turned to Conner. "I'm not making this decision alone," I said. "This is about you, too. If I'm bringing someone new into this mess, you need to feel okay about it." I grimaced as I said, "How do you feel about getting Simon involved?"

"I mean, it sounds like we're pretty short on options, Grim, and I'm definitely short on time." Conner shrugged. "Bring on the baby daddy."

23

had already arranged to take the day off of work for my sonogram appointment, which was just as well. There was no way I was ready to face Stu after what had happened at the bar. Even the *thought* of Gemma and her youthful pep, Jesse and his polo shirts, or Caroline and her awkward love felt like too much. I'd spent the rest of my weekend on Google, trying to track down the license plate of the car that had nearly run us off the road, to no avail. Even with Conner's web searching guidance, the only sites that looked remotely promising required special access, leaving us back at square one. With one exception. And he would be here soon.

Hunching over my kitchen sink, I scrubbed an oatmeal-clogged mug so abrasively I barely needed the harsh green sponge. Simon was arriving in half an hour. When I'd asked him over for lunch before the appointment, he'd dropped his phone twice before mustering a "yes" filled with barely contained enthusiasm. It was so sweet I hung up immediately.

My apartment was a disaster that I'd managed to turn into merely an off-putting mess by the late morning. All that was left to do was to actually make us something for lunch. I turned the mug over onto the towel-strewn counter with the rest of the drying dishes and tossed some sliced cheese on bread.

"You didn't tell me you're a gourmet," Conner said as he wafted into the kitchen. I buttered the bread and plopped the sandwiches onto a frying pan on the stove. "Nervous?" he said flippantly, but his dark eyes belied concern.

"Well, let's see," I said. "I'm about to tell my soon-to-be ex-husband that the mother of his unborn child taxis dead people around for a living. So, no. I'm not nervous. 'Nervous' doesn't begin to cover it."

"Could be worse," said Conner, dropping into a dining chair. "At least you're not coming out as a dentist or something. Did you know they have a super high suicide rate because everybody hates them?"

"I didn't know that, but thank you, Conner, that helps immensely."

"Hey," said Conner, kicking his feet onto my table and quickly lowering them again as I swatted at them with my free hand. "This guy's crazy about you, Grim. Seriously. It's disgusting. What you do isn't gonna send him running for the hills if he hasn't run already, all right?"

I gave a small smile. He meant well, I knew he did, but he was just a kid. He didn't get it, couldn't get it, and someone had made it so he'd never have the chance to get it someday. At least he had been spared that, if nothing else.

The truth was, this whole "open and honest" thing felt like a slippery slope; always had. Tell Simon about my impossible job and it would be a green light for him to start poking around into other, less savory parts of my life, and then what? Would I have to tell him about how my longest relationship before him was a three-week fling with my English literature professor who turned out to be a married father of five with really bad taste in nineteenth-century poetry? Or how I was the only one in at least three generations of my family without the brains to go into accounting? Or maybe how I'd been fired from my first handful of jobs for reasons ranging from "lacking the charisma required in a customer-facing role" to "cried from stage fright mid-presentation on two separate occasions, one seemingly brought about by basic math." Simon loved me because he saw me as someone I could never be, and I thought—I knew—that if I let him see the me I actually was, then all that love would shrivel up and wither like the rose he'd given me on our first date, which only left my windowsill a week before our wedding. I needed this wall, and in a matter of minutes I'd be pulling it down brick by brick.

"I appreciate the pep talk," I said, flipping one of the grilled cheese sandwiches with a shaky hand. "You're a good kid, Conner."

"Don't go getting soft on me, Grim." Conner turned his face away, but I thought I caught a hint of red fill his cheeks, and I wondered how often he'd been called a good kid before. Not nearly enough, from what I could tell.

A gentle knock sounded at my door, somehow catching me off guard even though I knew Simon was always right on time. My heart heaved into my throat, a panicked frenzy overtaking me, and in my haste to get the grilled cheese onto plates, I decided my hand was an appropriate spatula substitute. It was not.

"Shit," I hollered as the sharp sting registered across my left fingertips. I dumped the sandwich unceremoniously onto the waiting plate.

"You okay?" Conner asked.

"You okay in there?" Simon called from the other side of the door.

I waved my hand like an eighteenth-century French courtesan with a fan and a nervous tic. "Fine," I shouted to both men. I crossed the kitchen and peeled back the door to find Simon in a green-and-yellow striped button-down shirt and a broad smile. My heart skipped and I realized I was glad to have Conner there as an unwitting chaperone. I needed one.

"I burned my hand on the stupid grilled cheese," I said instead of hello. "Thanks for coming."

"Good heavens, you poor thing." Simon reached for my wrist, and when I didn't pull away, he examined my bright red fingertips. "Let's get these little piggies under some cold water, shall we?"

I nodded, my eyes stuck to the place on my wrist where our skin connected, and let him lead me to my sink. He turned on the faucet and gently held my hand under the water, the freckles on his balding head staring back at me.

"Thanks," I said.

"Better?" He looked up at me through pale, caring eyes.

"Better."

"Jesus Christ," said Conner. "This is like that scene from *Ghost*, except I'm the ghost and I have no choice but to be here."

That broke the spell. I pulled my hand away.

"I made grilled cheese," I said, gathering the murderous sandwiches from the counter and setting the plates on the table. "Sorry. I still can't cook."

"Grilled cheese is fine by me."

Conner barely had a chance to slide out of his chair before Simon was in it. I sat down across the table from him and nibbled at the crust of my sandwich, unable to stomach an actual bite but unwilling to leave my mouth free for talking.

"C'mon, Grim." Conner was behind me now, his hands hovering on either side of the back of my chair, his voice in my ear like a conscience. "Rip that bandage off. He's right there, just chowing down on that bread like a buffalo. Now's your chance."

I turned and gave him a look that I hoped read "stop."

"Don't vagina out of this, Grim."

"There's no need to be a penis about it," I shot back.

Simon choked on his toast.

"What?" he coughed.

Shit.

"Wow, what a way to start the conversation," Conner said, laughing.

I wanted everyone out of my kitchen.

"Simon," I said. My palms were moist. My head felt ready to float away. "I need to talk to you about something."

"About . . . penises?"

"What? No. Seriously?" I steadied myself against the table. "About what I do, Simon. About . . . who I am, I guess."

"Oh," said Simon. He dropped his lunch and folded his hands in his lap. "Okay, then. I . . . the floor is yours."

I didn't want the floor. Not unless I could curl up on it and let the cold tiles calm my nerves.

"I know I told you I work in transportation," I said. "And I do. But it's a little more complex than that. The goods I transport . . . they're . . . unusual."

Simon's eyes grew wide and he said on a riveted whisper, "Drugs?"

"No, Simon, come on!" I took a breath and regrouped. "It's going to sound hard to believe, but I really need you to trust me. I promise you, everything I'm about to tell you is the truth."

"Sweetie . . . Kathy, I always believe you," said Simon. "You tell me so little, there's no room for lies."

"Okay," I said, sucking in air. "Here it is, then. I work for a very old company called S.C.Y.T.H.E., which is an acronym for Secure Collection, Yielding, and Transportation of Human Essences."

"Human essences?"

"Souls," I blurted. "The core of who we are; what's left behind once we shed our bodies. I'm what's called a Collections Agent. My job is to collect the souls of people who have died and transport them to processing. I'm the first person a soul sees who can see them, and the one who makes sure they get to their next stop safely. It's an important job, I think. It's important to me, anyway. And I . . . I . . . I really need you to say something here."

"Right, okay," said Simon. "I can do that." But he stopped saying anything for a long moment. "Souls, Kath? As in ghosts?"

"No," I said, wondering how I could explain this to sound the least insane. "Ghosts are different. A ghost is what a soul becomes if it isn't processed in time." I sighed. "I know I must sound crazy here . . ."

"Not crazy," said Simon. "A bit . . . surprising, maybe, but not crazy. It's all . . ." He waved his hand in a circle. "It's a lot to wrap my head around."

"Yes," I said. "I know. It was for me, too, when they first hired me. But it's not so strange when you think about it. I mean, we need to go somewhere after we die, and I'm someone who helps with the logistics."

Simon was staring at me, his look unreadable.

"I can prove it," I said quickly.

"Look, Kath." Simon scooped my hands into his. I grimaced as he grazed my burnt fingertips but quickly forgot about the pain; his eyes locked on mine so hard I could barely feel anything but their intensity. "I'm just glad you finally told me something."

"Well, then, you're going to love this," I said bleakly. "It turns out one of my clients was killed by someone I work with, and if I don't find out who and how, he can't move on to whatever comes next. But . . . uh . . . someone really doesn't want me finding out. Or at least that's what it seemed like when they tried to run me off the road on Friday night."

Simon sat back in his chair.

"You need time to process. This is a lot to absorb," I said.

"Yes. No. I don't . . . Kathy, do you know what you're telling me here?"

"I have a pretty clear idea, yes," I said, trying to swallow back a rising wave of defensiveness. "If you don't believe me—"

"Someone's trying to—to kill you?"

I gave a weak shrug of acknowledgment.

"This . . . soul they're after, where is it now?"

"Just behind you," I said, tipping my chin at Conner, who was now by the counter on the other side of the table.

"Yo," said Conner.

"It's here?"

"Tell your guy he needs to hike up his pants," said Conner.

"Seeing dinosaur boxers on a dude that old is the worst thing to happen to me since I got murked."

"His name's Conner," I said. "And he says hi. But really, Simon, your dinosaur undies? I thought you threw those out."

Simon whipped around in his seat, adjusting his beige slacks with one hand and steadying himself on the chair back with the other. He sank back down, gave one final look over his shoulder, and returned his attention to me.

"Okay," he said. "Okay. This is a lot."

"Too much?"

Simon shook his head. "No. If you can handle it, so can I. It's just a lot."

"Good," I said, my head suddenly very light. "Because I need . . ." The word jammed in my throat. I didn't want to need anything from him, least of all this. "Help."

"From me?"

I nodded.

"Right, okay," Simon said, eagerness bubbling out of him. "I'm happy to help. I'm here to help. Just tell me how."

"I don't know," I said. "Jo's been helping me through this, but she just broke her hip, and I need someone else to talk it through with. You always used to be my person."

At this, Simon sat a little straighter. "Right. Okay. Of course. I can do that. I'm happy to do that. Beyond happy, really." Then his posture deflated a little. "But you're not going to like what I have to say here, Kath."

I gave him a nod to continue.

"If someone's after you, you're not safe here. I say this with no agenda, but we need to get you back ho—"

"Simon, no," I said before he'd even finished his thought.

"See, I knew you'd say that. But it won't be forever. We'll figure this out, Kath, I promise. Together. But in the meantime, we have to keep you and our little peanut safe."

I rested my forehead in my hands. He was right; the best way to get out of the line of fire right now was to remove myself from the address Stu had on file.

But not like this.

"Simon—"

"You're alone here, Kath. Something could happen to you, to our baby, and there'd be no one to protect you. Unless the soul . . . ?"

I shook my head. Simon had a point. If Stu did show up at my door, Conner couldn't help me or the little human growing in my belly. He likely barely had enough residual energy left to close a door if the occasion called for it. We'd made a good team so far, but we were no match for someone determined to do us harm. Still, I felt raw and vulnerable. I was standing naked on a first date and he hadn't come into the room yet. Soon the sags and bumps would become obvious and the other shoe would drop. "I need you to promise me this isn't some ploy; that you'll let me go without any puppy dog eyes as soon as we've sorted this out."

"You have my word."

"Fine," I said in spite of myself. "Let's get this appointment over with and then we can move my things back to the house. Just for now."

"Just for now," Simon agreed.

24

The hospital gown was too thin. The pale mint fabric, speckled with an offensively inoffensive diamond pattern, left every curve, contour, and roll beneath it exposed in a way that was totally inappropriate with an ex and a teenager in the room. Both man and boy made an obvious, intentional effort to avert their eyes from me as I shuffled onto the parchment-wrapped bed, though somehow their show of decency only made the situation worse. I slung an arm across my chest to keep from inadvertently winking a nipple at anyone.

"I can wait outside, you know," Conner said for the fourth time since we'd arrived at the doctor's office and the sixth since we'd left my apartment.

"No, Conner, I told you. I'm not letting you out of my sight until we figure out who we can trust. I know this is weird for you. It's weird for me too, if that helps."

"It's not that weird," Conner said. "I mean it is, but like, whatever. I've been to one of these before. It's chill."

Simon tried to pinpoint the spot in the room that housed Conner, but he kept missing the mark by a solid foot as he flashed understanding smiles over his shoulder with each sentence I relayed.

"What were you doing at a sonogram appointment?" I asked.

"My mom," said Conner. "When I was like ten, she got knocked up again. The baby didn't end up making it, but that's just as well. One less kid to ignore."

This I didn't relay to Simon. Instead I asked, "Did you want a sibling?"

"I mean, I guess it would've been cool. I think Mom was actually excited about this one, which was super weird."

The ultrasound technician was in the room before I could reply, her fine red hair pulled into a bun at the nape of her neck, her cat-eye glasses clutching the base of her nose bridge.

"Kathy? Hi there, my name is Mary," she greeted over a clipboard. "And this is the father, I presume?" She tossed a nod at Simon.

"I am," Simon enthused, rising from his little plastic chair beside me and giving Mary a body-rattling handshake. "Simon Valence, the father, lovely to meet you."

Mary returned his smile and sat down on a rolling leather stool. "Well, congratulations," she said. "Now, let's have a look at this baby of yours, shall we?"

"Sure," I said.

Mary placed a scratchy blanket over my lower half and lifted my hospital gown up to expose the swell of my stomach. I closed my eyes as a splat of cold, sticky wetness hit my skin, followed by a firm pressure.

"There we are," Mary's soft voice hummed from somewhere above me. "Do you want to have a look at the monitor, Kathy?"

"I'm fine," I said, turning my head to face the wall. When I opened my eyes, Conner was in my line of sight. A small tear escaped down my cheek before I could stop it.

"Come on," Conner said. "Even my mom looked at the ultrasound."

"I can't," I mouthed.

"Why are you even having a kid if you don't want one?" Conner shot back, anger reddening his cheeks.

"Kath, you okay?" Simon pulled his chair up to the bed and took my hand in his, but my eyes stayed on Conner. His own eyes were muddled with a mixture of rage and defeat, the light behind them like a flame. The way he looked at me, it was as if he was watching me become every adult in his life who'd let him down or neglected him. I couldn't be that, not now, not after how hard I'd worked to gain his trust. I held out my other hand to him. Conner looked at it as though it was made of dog shit.

"Please?" I said, my voice strained. Conner huffed but crossed towards me and placed a substance-less hand in mine, his face turned away from me. I squeezed both the hands I was holding, though I could only feel one, and turned to face the screen.

There it was. The source of that whoosh sound filling the room. The source of my nausea and ankle swelling for the past seven-odd months. A blur of black and white on the screen, a steady pulse emanating from the center.

"Okay," said Mary, clearly trying to hide her puzzlement. "If you look here, that's baby's head. And that pulse right there? That's baby's heartbeat. It's very strong; this is exactly what we like to see at this stage."

I followed Mary's fingers across the screen as she shaped the fetus into a baby. It was beautiful. Perfect in every way. And I was terrified. That beautiful, perfect baby in front of me, inside of me, would be born to a mother who could only ever do one thing right in her entire life, and that one thing was now potentially deadly. I closed my eyes as more tears fell. This baby deserved better; so much better than anything I could provide. I wasn't meant to be a mother. I was barely meant to be anything.

When I opened my eyes again, Conner was back in my field of vision, looking uncomfortable. I'd let him down. This, I supposed, was just a taste of what I was in for.

"Would you like to know the sex?" asked Mary.

"No," I said. "I'll be happy with whatever it is."

I only hoped that by some miracle it would be happy with me.

SIMON DROPPED THE CARDBOARD BOX HOLDING MY THINGS ONTO the living room sofa to catch his breath.

"You painted," I said, annoyed. One of the few things Simon and I ever fought about, aside from my secrecy, was how to decorate the drafty Victorian town house we'd shared through the decade of our marriage. I wanted to counter the sparsely windowed darkness with floral walls and pale furniture; Simon wanted blue. Not one tasteful blue wall or a blue couch offset by complementary paint, just blue. When I'd asked him why, he simply said, "I like blue." I'd won in the end, but clearly my hard-earned victory had an expiration date, because I now stood in the belly of a blueberry.

Simon's face couldn't have looked more uneasy if I'd caught him cheating.

"It's . . . nice," I said.

"It looks like that time I drank too much blue Gatorade and vodka and threw up everywhere," Conner said.

"I knew you'd like it if you gave it a chance." Simon beamed. "Just wait till you see what I did with the upstairs."

An involuntary shudder rolled through me at the prospect. The last time I'd been in this house was more than seven months ago, and I'd ended up getting a baby out of the deal. It was strange to be back; mostly because it wasn't strange at all. It felt like coming home. Even if that home was now shockingly cobalt.

Simon scooped my box from the couch and led the way up the creaky narrow staircase. At the top of the stairs, the hallway emerged, looking somehow self-conscious in a dizzying cyan wallpaper.

At the far end of the hall sat the master bedroom, still etched in my mind with visions of Sunday morning cuddles and sweaty, naked acrobatics past. I would be avoiding that room at all costs. In front of me, the guest bedroom's door lay open enough for me to see that the room had somehow managed to escape Simon's blue period. I followed Simon inside to find pink flowers dancing across green-and-white striped wallpaper, just as I'd left it; my grandmother's heavy oak bed frame still taking up half the room. Simon placed the box on the bed and dusted his hands off on his beige slacks.

"I'll go start dinner and let you get settled in," he said.

"Thanks," I said. "Really, Simon. Thank you."

He gave a bashful shrug and shuffled back downstairs. Conner poked his head around the door.

"Holy shit, I almost forgot what other colors looked like."

"Simon likes blue," I said.

"Clearly."

I sat down at the foot of the bed and ran my hand over the floral bedspread. The texture of it, this room, this house, felt very surreal. I was in a daze; in a dream. I could hear Simon banging pots around in the kitchen beneath me, the neighbor kids playing in their backyard outside my window. It was like someone had pressed play on the soundtrack of my old life. I had to remember why I was here. And why I wasn't.

"Think you'll be good here?" I asked Conner.

"Yeah," said Conner. "You?"

"Yeah."

Dinner was spaghetti with homemade tomato sauce and awkwardness. Simon had made sure to turn on every light in the house in order to avoid the merest suggestion of romance, and neither of us could manage to speak more than three words at a time. Conner, for his part, stayed in the living room, scanning Simon's record collection and commentating on it just loud enough for me to hear. Simon's taste in music wasn't faring much better than mine in Conner's estimation so far.

Finally, Simon said what I'd been expecting since that afternoon.

"Kath, I know it isn't my place, but maybe . . . maybe you shouldn't be chasing down a murderer right now."

I slurped a stray noodle from my carefully twisted forkful and said nothing.

"It's just . . . with the baby . . . and it isn't exactly something you have experience with. I don't like this."

"I'm not crazy about it either, Simon," I said. "But what choice do I have? If Conner . . ." I lowered my voice. "If his soul falls into the wrong hands, he could end up trapped here. Or worse. As it is, we're running out of time to get him processed. Am I supposed to just abandon him?"

"Of course not," Simon sighed. "Kathy—"

"Simon."

"Sorry. I just want you safe."

"I know." I rubbed a hand across my belly. I wanted me safe too. I wanted us safe.

"And you really have nothing to go on? About the identity of the killer, I mean."

"Well, there were Stu's threats," I said. "But I have no way of knowing if that was him in the car that night. The brights were on; we couldn't see who was driving. All we got was a partial license plate."

Simon dropped his fork. "You didn't tell me that," he said.

"It didn't seem relevant," I said. "Not much we can do with that."

A little glimmer ignited in Simon's gray eyes. "Oh, I wouldn't be so sure about that."

"What's that supposed to mean?"

"Well," said Simon almost shyly, "you spend a lot of time fiddling with technology when you work in IT. Sometimes it's fun to push it a bit. See what you can do with those skills."

"Okay . . ."

"I . . . I may have hacked into a few databases in my time. Nothing too serious," he added quickly. "And it was mostly when I first started out. But . . . the skills are there."

"Simon!"

"What, you're the only one allowed to have secrets?" His eyes were glowing now, a mischievous smirk on his lips. That burst of confidence and playful roguishness was intoxicating. I could have swept the table clear of plates and thrown him on the tablecloth instead.

"Are you serious?" I asked, still swimming in disbelief.

"What's the license plate?"

I called Conner in from the next room.

"Do you remember the partial license plate number from the other night?" I asked him.

"Sure, why?"

I looked at Simon, trying hard to keep the thrill from my voice. "Simon's going to do some hacking for us."

"That guy?" He jabbed a thumb in Simon's direction.

I glanced across the table at the short, bald man staring back at me through basset hound eyes.

"That guy," I confirmed.

"If you say so," said Conner. "GTR-75. I couldn't make out the rest."

I repeated the number to Simon.

"Leave it with me," said Simon. "I'll see what I can do."

25

Twenty-Three Days to Ghost

There was a bubble in my stomach that trod the delicate line between a gut instinct that I shouldn't have gone into work that morning and gas. It was just after nine a.m. and I was already exhausted. Getting out of the house had involved separate—though at times overlapping—arguments with both Simon and Conner about my decision to go into the office, and I'd only won by promising I'd come home before lunch, which Stu always arrived just after most days for some potentially nefarious or possibly fitness-related reason. As for whoever tried to run Conner and me off the road on Friday (assuming that hadn't also been part of Stu's fitness regimen), I had very little chance of encountering them during such a small window of time as long as I didn't leave my desk. The only cubicles directly surrounding mine were Gemma's and an older man's named Tom who I was pretty sure existed—though I'd only seen him once three years ago when he'd popped his head above his cubicle wall during a fire alarm before shrugging and sinking behind his gray fortress again. Anyone else would have to make a concerted effort to see me there, and, being that I wasn't the type most made a concerted effort to see, I wasn't too worried about being discovered. Besides, I needed to be there. I had left one of Conner's files in my desk, and though it didn't hold any particularly sensitive information, leaving it behind, where his killer worked and lurked, felt like a betrayal somehow.

By the time Gemma showed up at 9:08, coffee in one hand and open phone in the other, I was near doubled over with stomach cramps. It was as if the fetus had scooped my insides into a vise and was turning the lever to entertain itself.

"Oh," Gemma said as she caught sight of me over her phone. "Hey, Kath. You okay? It was so weird seeing your cubicle empty yesterday."

I tossed a thumbs-up in her direction and ran a hand over the swell of my stomach. I knew little about pregnancy, but the wrong feeling I'd had since stepping through the office doors made me uneasy. Was this normal? I popped my laptop open and pulled up Google, beads of sweat sprouting on my forehead in response to the growing stomachache.

"So where were you?" Gemma continued, sidling up to my desk.

I quickly backspaced on my search: "cramps while pregnant—normal?"

"Ultrasound," was the most I could offer.

"Wow, so exciting. It's, like, so real now, huh?"

I nodded mid-grimace.

"Can I feel?" She inched a polished hand towards my increasingly cramping belly and all I could picture was the atomic explosion that would follow. I rolled my chair back, the discomfort now causing me more concern than pain. No, this couldn't be normal.

"I'm not feeling so hot right now," I said, and typed my search back in with a newfound lack of concern for Gemma reading over my shoulder.

Gemma's voice harmonized with my frantic typing now. "I was just going to ask if you wanted to grab a coffee or something after work. I mean, Friday was so fun. And I don't even think I know what neighborhood you live in, which is crazy considering how long we've worked together. Kath?"

But I was only half listening at this point. The first hit on my search stated in no uncertain terms that severe cramping could indicate a miscarriage, and suddenly I was faced with the very real prospect that the little whoosh of heartbeat I'd seen on the ultrasound screen just yesterday might be leaving me.

"Kath?"

I was out of my seat and grabbing my jacket before I had time to think, Conner's file and my laptop squished under my armpit.

"Where are you going?" Gemma's voice trailed after me as I sailed past Stu's empty office, my doctor's speed dial already up on my phone. "I'll text you, then, 'kay?"

IT TURNS OUT THE LINE BETWEEN GUT INSTINCTS AND GAS ISN'T AS delicate as I'd thought. I was halfway through both my ride home and a round of tight small talk with my doctor's receptionist when the true cause of my discomfort emerged. Loudly and on speaker. I hung up, deleted the text I'd drafted to Simon, and swallowed down the trove of emotions this experience had excavated. Baby was fine. I was fine. There were more important things to worry about now. I briefly contemplated going back to work for the rest of the morning, but every time I thought about it, I felt another bout of gas come on as if in direct response to the idea. Instead I drove straight home, explained the situation in as few details as possible to Conner, who still read between the lines enough to grimace and tell me to stop talking, and then promptly went up to my room and fell asleep.

By the time I awoke, Simon was home from work and I had sweat through the Snoopy twinset I'd slept in. I greeted him with a damp wave from the top of the stairs and shuffled off to wash the day away.

I stepped out of the shower, the guest bathroom thick with steam, and wrapped a cornflower-blue towel around me. Wiping a small patch clear on the foggy mirror, I ran a comb through my sopping hair and examined the deepening lines around my eyes and across my forehead. My so-called pregnancy glow was little more than a constant sheen of sweat that prickled my freshly scrubbed skin even now, and my hips somehow seemed to be growing in tandem with my stomach. Whoever said this was a beautiful process had clearly never been through it.

I left the bathroom and went back to the guest room to dress, but just as I began to peel the towel off, Conner wafted into the room.

"He's found—JESUS CHRIST."

"No! No, no!" I screamed.

"Jesus Christ, Jesus Christ," Conner panted back.

Only half a boob and a touch too much thigh were on display, but it was enough to send us both down a horrified spiral. I scrambled to refasten the towel as Conner threw both hands over his eyes.

"No, no," I hollered again.

"Oh my fucking god."

"Why didn't you knock?" I was now shrieking, my voice was so high.

"Because I don't have a fucking flesh hand to knock with!" Conner shouted back.

"Why would you just come in?"

"Because I didn't think you'd be giving a fucking striptease to the wall."

"How much did you see?"

"Too much. I'm never recovering from this."

"What the hell are you even doing in here, Conner?"

At this, a tentative knock sounded on the door.

"Everything okay in there?"

I ran a hand over my face. "Come in, Simon."

Simon appeared in the doorway, face white, a sheet of paper in his hands.

"I heard shouting."

"Can I open my eyes now?" Conner asked.

"Yes, Conner. Sorry, Simon. There was . . . an incident."

"An incident," Conner repeated, mocking my voice. "Fuck's sake, Grim, I feel like I've been murdered all over again."

"All right, enough. Somebody please explain to me what the hell is going on. What's so urgent that everyone needs to be in here while I'm in a towel?"

"Barely," Conner muttered.

Simon held out the piece of paper. "This is a list of everyone in town with a license plate that matches the partial you gave me. I got a little too excited when I found it, and I guess Conner heard me."

Conner nodded in confirmation, still avoiding eye contact.

"Have a look," Simon said gently. "See if you recognize any of the names on there. It might help you narrow things down if nothing else."

"Thank you," I said, taking the paper and sitting on the bed. Simon eased down beside me. Conner kept as far across the room as possible, but his interest was clearly piqued.

I ran my finger over the list of plates and corresponding names. Nothing jumped out at me at first, but as I read over the list a second time, my heart caught.

Two-thirds of the way down was a name I was only peripherally familiar with, so much so I'd missed it the first time and nearly the second time too. But somehow I managed to land on it and make the connection.

Melissa Hare.

I'd met her once at a craft fair last year. She was tall, with copper hair and a warm smile, and was buying the same hand-knit tea cozy as me. Her husband introduced us.

"I know who tried to kill me," I said on a breath. I couldn't believe I'd let myself be blinded by an easy manner and a nice-looking face. But even with the name on the page in front of me, I struggled to come to grips with reality. Jesse Hare was a murderer.

26

I couldn't go back to work. Not after what we'd discovered.

Calling Stu the morning after Simon found the license registration made me queasy. I hadn't called out sick more than twice since I'd started at S.C.Y.T.H.E., and the second time only because Simon insisted I couldn't do my job properly after an emergency appendectomy. Still, it had to be done. Now that I knew who the killer was, I couldn't just continue as if everything was normal. I needed more information. How much did Jesse know about Conner's current location? Was he working with Stu? What was he doing in the woods with all those souls? What did Conner witness that was worth killing him for? There was no way I'd be getting any of those answers over reheated lasagna in the lunchroom. I'd need to be stealthy, and I'd need to be safe.

Stu seemed almost relieved when I called in, though I couldn't decide if that made him more suspect or less. I told him I was pregnant and that I was having difficulties right now, which was true, though almost entirely unrelated to the pregnancy. I'd barely finished talking before he offered me a week off to rest, but before I could thank him, he continued, "And I'm taking over case 507032."

My chest clenched. "That really isn't necessary, sir, I—"

"You have a lot on your plate right now, Valence, and this case is clearly putting your welfare in danger." There was something dark in his voice. He and Jesse were both high up enough to make sure the case was closed with no questions asked, especially with me out of the picture. "This is a most unusual situation, so it'll take a while for the reassignment to be made official," Stu continued, "but you are to relinquish all investigations as of this moment. Are we understood, Kathy? Your involvement in this case is over, and if I find out about any interference on your part, there will be consequences."

He hung up then, leaving me with a heart dejectedly throbbing in rhythm with the stark dial tone.

LIFE SEEMED TO PASS AT A DIFFERENT PACE WITHOUT THE ROUTINE of work. I spent my days behind my laptop as usual, but instead of writing up reports, I was looking into Jesse Hare—every possible combination of search words, on every conceivable social media site, Conner hanging over my shoulder as we scoured each corner of the Internet. The only connection to S.C.Y.T.H.E. I had left was the odd exclamation mark–riddled text from Gemma asking if I needed anything and the occasional company-wide email.

Before I knew it, three days had passed and I'd made next to no progress on the Jesse front. His social media presence was limited to family photos and posts about his favorite sports teams, and Simon's hacking skills turned up nothing out of the ordinary. We were running out of time. I would need to be more hands-on, even if it meant putting my safety at risk. And Stu had made it very clear that it would. It wasn't just my life at stake, it was Conner's future. If I couldn't get him processed before Stu got the authorization required to close the case, Conner would be condemned to ghosthood, or worse. Tucked away in the old Victorian town house, we'd managed to stay enough off the radar to avoid any more run-ins with Jesse. But with the request for Conner's files, Stu could easily have requested mine too, and my old address still sat somewhere inside them.

Nineteen Days to Ghost

A couple of days before I was slated to return to work, Simon, Conner, and I piled into my car for a field trip back to my apartment to pick up a few odds and ends I'd left behind and had begun to miss. When we approached the door, two things quickly became apparent: first, the paint job was worse than I remembered, and second, the door was no longer locked. I pushed it with my index finger and the door opened a sliver with an affronted creak. I looked at Simon.

"That's not good," he said. I couldn't help but agree. "Let . . . let me go in first."

"No," I said. "You take Conner to the car. Keep him safe. I'll go in."

"Kathy, please," Simon said. "You're just as much of a target as he is. You take Conner to the car. I'll go in."

"You don't know what my place looks like as well as I do," I countered. "If anything's been moved or taken, I'll be the only one to know it. You take Conner to the car. I'll go in."

"If someone's still in there, they'll be far more likely to harm you than they would me. As far as they know, I have no part in any of this. Besides, you're carrying our baby, Kath. You take Conner to the car, I'll go in."

"Hey guys," came Conner's voice. "You coming in or what?"

I looked around, but Conner was no longer in the hallway. I pushed the door open the rest of the way, and sure enough, there Conner was, standing in my kitchen.

"What the hell do you think you're doing?" I shouted. "Do you have any idea how much danger you could have just put yourself in?"

"He's in there?" Simon asked. "Conner, really, that was a reckless thing to do."

"You can't just go running off willy-nilly like that."

"Listen to Kathy, she would never be able to live with herself if anything happened to you."

"All right, all right, Jesus," said Conner. "Sorry. But neither of you were coming in, so I figured I may as well be the one to pop that cherry. Nobody's here anyway. But, I mean . . ." He flung open his arms and I looked away from his face for the first time since we'd stepped inside.

My apartment was trashed. Not in its usual untidy way, but in a way that said someone had been here rummaging through my things, making my mess into their own mess. Even the air smelled different; tinted with something light and fruity.

"Shit," I said under my breath. The kitchen drawers had been pulled out, their innards strewn across the floor. My cupboards all stood open, their contents shuffled around. I raced into the living room to find it in a similar state; my bedroom was equally turned over. "Shit."

When I made my way back to the kitchen, Simon was on his hands and knees, replacing my assorted junk into the drawers they'd been evicted from. He wobbled to his feet when he saw me.

"Jeez, Kath," was all he said.

"I know."

"We really can't call the police?"

I shook my head and slumped into a chair at the table.

"Good thing we weren't here," said Conner. I felt sick at the thought. Jesse had been in my home. Touching my things. It all felt so violating.

"He was obviously looking for something," I realized aloud, still dazed. "But what?"

"Conner's case files?" Simon offered, back to tidying now.

"Maybe," I said. "I brought those to your place. But if he really wanted, he could just wait until Stu gained official access. No, it must be something else. Conner, you really can't remember anything else about that night in the woods?"

Conner shook his head. "Sorry, Grim."

"What about what you were wearing?" I asked.

"These jeans, I think," said Conner.

"Was there anything in your pockets? A wallet?"

"Just the weed and my phone."

"Your phone?" I repeated. I'd seen the bag of weed on the bench the day I'd gone looking for Conner, but I recalled now that there was no phone on or near his body when I went to collect him. Ethan had shown us the photo Conner texted the last night of his life. Who knew what else might be on his phone? Something incriminating, maybe. Something that might give us some answers. Jesse clearly thought I had it, and he clearly wanted it, which meant I needed to get to it first.

"Do you know where your phone ended up?" I asked Conner.

"No," said Conner. "But I think I know someone who might."

27

The late September air had already turned crisp with the promise of changing leaves and cooler days ahead. I kept my windows down, letting in a fresh breeze tinged with a hint of smokiness and decay. I used to love the scent of autumn, the fresh earthiness filling me with warmth, but all it did now was fill me with dread. It was a reminder that summer had slipped away, and so had more than half of my time to get Conner safely moved on. I needed this to work. We both did.

"Left at the stop sign," Conner directed from the passenger seat. I turned and drove down a quiet suburban street lined with fat old trees and matching houses, a spattering of young children chalking on the sidewalk.

"Not a bad place to raise a family," Simon mused from the back seat. I said nothing, taking one more left turn at Conner's say-so and pulling into an asphalt parking lot.

We all exited the car as the lot began to fill with groups of teenagers; a sudden sea of bad facial hair and exposed midriffs. I could only barely remember what it was like to be a teenager. Some days I wondered if I'd actually been one at all or if that portion of my life was just a pimply fever dream. I was certainly never a teenager in the way these teenagers were: hair expertly curled, makeup sharp, clothes they clearly bought for themselves instead of something itchy and paisley picked out by their mothers. Everyone was bright-faced and laughing. Everyone was surrounded by friends. It was all very intimidating.

"Which way?" I asked Conner, eager to get away from the throng. For his part, Conner seemed lost in thoughts of a very different nature. He watched each group pass us with a look of dreamy melancholy. He had been one of those teenagers, I realized. Bright-faced and laughing and surrounded by friends. And now he had to stand by and watch as everyone else got the chance to keep being who he used to be.

"Conner," I said gently.

Conner shook himself out of his thoughts. "Yeah?"

"Where do we go?"

"This way," he said. Simon and I fell into step behind him as he trod over the asphalt and onto the freshly cut grass surrounding the high school. The building was an imposingly dark, sprawling testament to 1930s architecture, the two stories marked by narrow rectangular windows, with an arched entryway in the middle topped by an elaborately shaped roof. Conner showed no hint of awe at the haunting structure or beautifully maintained grounds. These were everyday sights for him; just a place he had to go, and likely resented, for the past three years.

"There." Conner stopped walking as we rounded the back of the school, pointing towards the track. A few students were using their lunch hour to get some exercise in; a fact that both deeply confounded me and made me picture Stu as a teenager in spite of myself. Meanwhile, walking directly across the track and interrupting more than one runner was a silhouette I vaguely recognized.

"We'd always cut through here," Conner explained. "There's a pizza place just down the block, and this gets us there faster than going around the school."

I nodded and turned to Simon. "I'll do the talking, all right?"

"Of course," he said, raising his hands as if I'd just smacked them away from a dish I was cooking.

As we approached Ethan, I tried to decide what to do with my face. When we'd met at Conner's funeral, he'd thought I was a detective and I'd let him believe it to make life easier, but now I realized I had no idea how a detective looks. I finally landed on a neutral expression that I hoped appeared confident and authoritative, but somehow gave my left cheek a cramp. Simon, for his part, was smiling warmly in greeting.

"Good afternoon," I said as we cornered Ethan on the grass in the middle of the track.

"Uh," said Ethan. "Wait, I know you."

"We met at Conner's funeral," I said.

"Right," said Ethan. He made scare quotes with his fingers. "The 'tutor.'"

I nodded.

"And who's Napoleon here?" Ethan jabbed a thumb in Simon's direction.

"Simon Valence," Simon said, extending a hand. "Very nice to meet you."

Ethan furrowed his brows at me.

"My partner," I said. "Work partner," I added quickly, before

Simon had the chance to look at me. "Can we talk to you for a minute? We just have a few questions."

"Sure, I guess," said Ethan. "I'm on a bit of a clock here, though. You hungry?"

"He's a dirty liar," Conner said from beside me. "He never goes to calculus after lunch. But the pizza at Charlie's is epic, so just roll with it."

"Lead the way," I said.

Charlie's Pizzeria and Gyros sat on the corner of an otherwise residential street, sandwiched between a convenience store and a vacant unit.

"Get the Chuck Special," Conner said as I walked up to the counter of the narrow little shop. The menu on the screen behind the counter informed me that the Chuck Special was two slices packed with bacon, green pepper, sausages, jalapeño, BBQ chicken, and onion, drizzled with ranch, with a side of fries and a can of soda. Normally the mere thought of something so rich would require a two-hour nap, but my pregnancy hormones decided this was an excellent suggestion. I ordered three specials and brought them to the table by the window where Simon and Ethan were already sitting, apparently swapping stories about Internet forums.

"Ethan," I said after navigating my first unexpectedly delicious bite of pizza. "We still haven't been able to locate Conner's phone and were wondering if you might be able to help us out."

Ethan shrugged. "Sorry, no idea where that would be."

"Bullshit," Conner said. "We made a pact. If one of us dies, the other clears the dead one's browser history and smashes their SIM card. If my phone wasn't on me, it's because he was doing me a solid."

"Are you sure you can't think of what might have happened to it?" I tried again. "We think it would really help us a lot in figuring out what happened to Conner."

"Yeah, but like"—another shrug—"I don't know where it is."

"He's fucking lying," said Conner. "He must not trust you or something. Mention the pact."

I sighed. "I know sometimes people will make an agreement with their friends to erase the content from their devices if one of them dies, or even destroy their SIM card. Since you were Conner's closest friend, I thought he might have had that kind of pact with you."

"Sure," said Ethan. "But I never got the chance. I mean . . ." He absently twirled a fry through a dollop of ketchup on his pizza box. "Like, I didn't even know he was dead right away. His dad called my dad like way late that night. By that point, what was I supposed to do, ask his mom and dad to let me into his room to delete some shit? I just . . . It's fucked up, man."

"Yeah," said Conner.

"Yeah," I agreed. "Well, thank you for your time all the same."

I was about to get up to leave when Simon said, "Were there any girls in his life?"

I shot him a glare over the table. This was hardly the time for guy talk, and besides, I could have asked Conner that myself.

"Sure, yeah, loads," said Ethan. Conner flashed a smug smile.

"Loads, huh?" Simon said, ignoring my "stop talking" eyes. "That must have upset one or two of them. Were there any he had issues with?"

"Nah," said Ethan. "Conner was chill. Even with his ex."

"When did they break up?"

I cocked my head at Simon. He clearly had an angle here, I realized, which caught me off guard. Simon never had angles. But try as I might, I couldn't follow it.

"Like a month before he died," said Ethan. "Oh shit, do you think she killed him?"

Simon shook his head. "I don't," he said. "But I wonder, did they exchange any particularly racy photos, do you know?"

"I mean, yeah," said Ethan as though this was a given.

"Ha, yeah." Conner sat back in his chair and ran a hand over his face. "Good times."

I ignored him. These were mental images I definitely didn't need.

Simon looked at me as if to say, "Anything else we need?" I shook my head, finally hopping aboard his train of thought. If Conner still had explicit photos of someone he'd been dating, she might be worried they wouldn't be so private now that they were broken up, especially if that phone fell into the wrong hands after he died. I could get the rest of the details from Conner at home, but this was definitely something to look into.

Before I had the chance to say so, Conner sat bolt upright in his seat.

"Fuck. She was there that night. Tasha was there."

I just stared at Conner for a long moment, unable to speak. Not only because Ethan was present, but because I didn't know what to say.

"I remember," Conner continued. "It's super hazy, but I remember her. I was on my way home from the park and she jumped out of fucking nowhere and punched me in the gut, grabbed my phone, and ran off. Said something about her sister and revenge porn. But I think . . . there might've been other pictures on there. Like, not of her. From that night. More like the one I texted Ethan. I think I took more."

My chair toppled backwards as I rose to my feet. "We have to go."

"Cool, well, I've got places to be anyway," said Ethan.

"Thanks so much for your help." Simon shook Ethan's hand across the table and shot me a glance glazed in question marks before they both stood and the boy left.

I watched Ethan's back shrink as he walked towards the high school, trying to maintain my composure until he was out of sight. As he disappeared, I said to Simon, "That was good."

"Yeah?" said Simon.

"Yeah," I said. "Though it does make me wonder what you've got on your phone."

Simon laughed. "Nothing to destroy a SIM card over, I assure you. But I was young once. And I work in IT, besides. We get some interesting questions."

"Sounds like it." I smiled before Conner's revelation returned to me. "All right, let's get a move on. Conner, I've got some questions for you. We've got a phone to find."

28

Halfway through the drive home I experienced an unfortunate sequel to the Chuck Special. Simon was forced to take over behind the wheel while I stretched out in the back seat and tried to keep from throwing up all over the back of his head. Two emergency puke pull-overs later, the nausea had evolved into a simmering heartburn. Back home, I hauled myself up the stairs on heavy limbs, leaning on Simon's shoulder. I flopped horizontally across my bed, legs swung over one end and head hanging off the other, waiting for the flames in my chest to extinguish. It looked like I wouldn't be doing much more investigating today.

Simon brought me enough antacids to quell an active volcano and, per my strong request, left me to my suffering.

Conner kicked towards one of my dangling legs. "You okay, Grim?"

I held a thumbs-up over the mattress. The heartburn was beginning to ease ever so slightly, but I was exhausted from the whole ordeal.

Conner hopped onto the bed beside me, throwing his gangly legs over the edge and hanging his head next to mine. The mattress didn't shift beneath him, the blankets remaining un-ruffled. We lay like that for a long moment, staring at the rotating ceiling fan. I had information I knew I needed to get out of Conner, information he might not be too keen to give, but I was barely thinking about that now. Instead I said, "Hey, was it weird for you today? At your school? With Ethan?"

Conner turned his face towards mine. "What do you mean?"

"I don't know," I said. "Was it difficult? Under the circum-stances."

I waited for a smart-aleck quip, something to defuse my earnestness, but it didn't come.

"I mean, I hated school," said Conner. "Like, not just the ac-ademic stuff or the pressure for good grades, but there was so much social politics, you know? I just wanted to hang out with whoever and do whatever, but you can't be like that there. You've gotta play by the school rules. Dress a certain way, have certain friends, that kind of thing. It's stupid, and exhausting. I won't miss that. But"—he looked at the ceiling again—"Ethan, man, he has no idea. He breaks out of that prison next year and gets to go do whatever the hell he wants. No more parents breathing down his neck. No more teachers telling him about the 'real world.' Just life. Big, scary, whatever-you-want-it-to-be life."

Conner's words pricked at me. He was the popular kid—the kind of kid I would have hated and revered when I was his age—and yet his life had been a gilded cage of social expectations while mine was anonymous and free. No one cared what I wore or who my friends were because no one knew I existed, and at the time I would have given anything for the opposite to be true. But now I wasn't so sure. I'd had a chance at limitless opportunities that I never fully recognized, and I squandered it.

"That sounds like a shitty way to live," I said. "All that pressure."

Conner shrugged. "I mean, that's high school, though, right?"

"It wasn't for me," I said. "I was an awkward, quiet nerd, if you can believe it. But that meant I could do whatever I wanted without consequence."

"Must've been nice," Conner mused.

This time I shrugged. "I didn't do much with it. But would you really have wanted it that way?"

"Guess I'll never know," said Conner. "God, fuck, there's so much I'll never know, isn't there?" He sat up on the bed. "Like, who the hell goes and dies at seventeen? Do you know what seventeen-year-olds have done with their lives? Fuck-all. I wasn't finished. There was so much . . ."

I sat up beside him. I wanted to scoop him up in a hug, to tell him I understood, but he had no body to wrap my arms around anymore, and the truth was, I would never really be able to understand. He'd had his future ripped away from him, and nothing I could do would change that.

"What did you do?" I asked softly.

"What?"

"With the time you had. What did you do?"

"Like, nothing."

"Bullshit," I said. "Ever broken a bone?"

"Yeah, sure," said Conner. "Broke my wrist falling off a BMX bike when I was like twelve."

"So you've ridden a BXM bike?"

"BMX," Conner corrected.

"Right. Well, I've been alive for forty-two years and I've never even seen a BMX bike. What else? You've traveled, right?"

"A bit."

"Well?"

"My dad took me hiking in Peru last year," said Conner. "And we went on a family trip to Italy a few years before that, and Germany when I was like eleven. Oh, and we visit my abuela in Mexico every winter, and my Gran in England every other year."

"Keep going," I said. "You're already putting my life to shame. What else have you done? Something you're proud of."

A hint of a smile pulled at Conner's lips. "Well—"

"And let's keep it PG, please," I added quickly.

"I was! Last year I volunteered for this program because my mom thought it would look good on my college applications. Basically, you get paired up with a kid from a rough background and look after them a bit. So my kid, Aidan, he was about thirteen and was already getting into some rough stuff. But we got along pretty alright. I mean, I'd always wanted a little sister or brother and he became kind of like that. Anyway, some of his friends were getting into shoplifting. Which like, yeah, fuck the man and stuff, but they were definitely going to get caught the way they were going. Shit started escalating, right, and these friends decided to rob a store. Like full-out, with guns. Aidan told me about it the day before it was going down and I convinced the kid to stay out of it. Two of his friends got caught; I think one ended up going to juvie, but Aidan was safe watching movies at my place."

"Conner," I said, "that's incredible. You really helped that boy."

"I guess," said Conner. "I think I set him on the right track, anyway. I mean, what do I know? I'm just some rich kid, I have no idea what it's like to have to deal with the shit he does, but at least he was safe that night."

"That's big, Conner," I said. "Stuff like that, it's what keeps you alive long after you've died."

Conner flopped back down across the bed. "So, like, what happens to me now?"

"What do you mean?"

"I mean after we figure out how I was killed, where do I go?"

"To processing," I said.

"No, but like, where do I *go*?" He took a deep breath. "Like, I didn't think . . . I guess I was trying not to think about it before. I mean, coming to terms with being dead is enough of a mind-fuck. But it's hard not to think about, you know? I know I've gotta go somewhere. So is this a heaven or hell situation?"

I lay back down, my eyes on the ceiling fan again. "I don't know," I said. "That information is way above my pay grade."

"Because I mean, my family's Catholic, and I've sinned a bunch," said Conner.

I stifled a smile. "S.C.Y.T.H.E. operates as a secular company," I said. "But I don't know anything more than that."

"I wish I could know," said Conner. "Or that I wasn't so scared not knowing, you know?"

"I know," I said.

"I wish I could have done more," said Conner.

"I know," I said again. "What would you be doing now, if you could?"

"Probably something pointless, like smoking up or finishing *Legacy 5*," said Conner. "Maybe hitting up a new girl."

"What about your old girl?" I said. "The one who might have your phone. Do you . . . Those pictures . . . I . . ."

"Un-clutch your pearls," said Conner. "I don't want to talk about it with you any more than you want to talk about it with me. But there's nothing to talk about anyway. I deleted those pics as soon as we broke up. I'm not a creep. That shit was shared in a specific context, and that context was over."

"You really are a good kid, Conner," I said, eliciting a small smile from the Conner in question. "But does your ex know that you deleted them?"

"I mean, I didn't say anything to her. It would've been kinda weird to be like 'hey Tasha, I know you hate my guts right now but I'm just texting to say I deleted your nudes,' you know? Anyway, I figured she would just assume I did."

"Well, if she was there the night you died, it sounds like maybe she wasn't so sure," I said. "I'll need her information from you."

"Sure," said Conner.

"And as for that other thing? It might not be possible to flirt with anyone or get high, but I think I can arrange something you might enjoy just as much."

29

Seventeen Days to Ghost

Tasha Sinclair's house was more modest than Conner's and Ethan's. Grander than anything I'd ever lived in, to be sure, but there was something about the nostalgic mid-century architecture and subtly overgrown garden that made the walk to the front door less intimidating. My knock was answered by a man in his seventies, wrapped in a gray wool cardigan to ward off the slight chill in the air.

"Hi, good afternoon," I said. "I'm looking for Tasha Sinclair."

"I'm sorry?" said the man at the door.

"Tasha Sinclair," I said again.

"Natasha," said Conner from the stair below me on the front stoop, where he and Simon stood waiting.

"Natasha," I tried.

"I'm afraid I don't know anyone by that name," said the man.

"She lives here," I said, looking back at Conner to confirm. He nodded.

"Sinclair, you say?" said the man. "Yes, I believe that was the family who lived here before us." He looked over his shoulder. "Harriet? Harriet, there's a girl at the door looking for the last homeowners."

A rustling started from somewhere inside the house.

"They moved?" I asked, cursing internally. "When?"

"Oh, about three weeks ago now. Harriet," he called again.

A small woman with sharp bone structure and sharper eyes emerged beside the man at the door.

"Honestly, Ron, you'll scare off the hummingbirds out back. What is it?"

"These young people want to know about the last homeowners," said the man I took to be Ron.

"What do they want that for?" said the woman I took to be Harriet.

"I don't know, I didn't ask," said Ron.

"Well really, why would you call me out here before asking?" said Harriet. "They could be murderers."

"They're not murderers, Harriet."

"How do you know? I bet you didn't ask that either."

"No, Harriet, I didn't."

"For goodness' sake, Ron, why don't you just invite them in and hand them a gun."

"You're not murderers, are you?" Ron asked me.

I was too caught off guard at being addressed to say more than, "No."

"Robbers?" asked Harriet.

"No," I said again.

"Hmm," said Harriet. "Well, what do you want, then?"

Without thinking it through, I decided on a tactic I instantly regretted. Turning behind me, I scooped Simon's arm into mine and dragged him forward beside me.

"I'm Kathy," I said. "And this is my husband, Simon." I rubbed my belly with my free hand for extra emphasis. "We're old friends of the Sinclair family and we're trying to track them down."

I could feel Simon straighten his back a little beside me, his chin raised.

"Well, that's nice," said Harriet. "Isn't that nice, Ron?"

"If you say so, Harriet," said Ron.

"You'll want to know where they're living now, I suppose?" said Harriet.

Simon and I both nodded, neither of us brave enough to risk saying the wrong thing to Harriet.

"Well, I don't know much. The father got a new job a few towns over. Couldn't tell you what job or where, but it was far enough to move the whole family away for it." She leaned in conspiratorially. "Though I heard the little girl's beau died of a drug overdose a month or so back and they wanted to get away from here to spare her reputation. Such recklessness. But mark my words, that type always gets what's coming to them."

"It wasn't an overdose," I snapped. "And even if it had been, 'that type' doesn't deserve any more scorn than gossipy old ladies who don't have their facts straight."

Simon pulled me back a step. "Pregnancy hormones," he said, forcing a laugh.

Harriet glared at me. I could feel my cheeks burning. Ron was looking at me with what appeared to be awe. Simon was still trying to encourage everyone to join his gentle laugh, but no one was following suit.

Finally, Harriet said, "Slam the door on them, Ron," and Ron obeyed.

I deflated against Simon's arm. "What a miserable old bitch," I said.

A laugh rang out from behind me. A real laugh. I turned to find Conner wearing one of his biggest shit-eating grins.

"Hey, thanks," he said.

"I'm not about to let people start rumors about you," I said as we walked back to my car.

"I've had worse," said Conner. "I'm sure everyone at school has a different story about how I kicked it by now."

"Well, still," I said, my jaw tense. I opened my door and slid inside, and Simon followed suit, while Conner melted into the back seat. "You deserve better than that. And anyway, it's not like they were any help. We're back to square one."

"Do you still have this girl's social media details?" Simon asked the general vicinity of Conner.

"Yeah," said Conner.

"He does," I said.

"She may have updated her location. And if not, it still shouldn't be too hard to find."

"Should I be concerned about this hobby?" I asked.

Simon just laughed as I pulled away from the curb.

Fourteen Days to Ghost

Teenagers never failed to confuse me. It seemed as soon as they broke up, Tasha had blocked and deleted Conner on all her social media accounts. I could sympathize well enough with the inclination, despite the fact that I was currently living with my ex-husband. What I didn't understand, though, was why she chose to use an alias online rather than her real name. An alias that had apparently changed since her days with Conner, when she went by the unfortunate username Ta$hMoney.

In fairness to Tasha, my first email address was heathcliff _lvr_1234@hotmail.com, but I'd grown out of that account by the time I was sixteen and had used my own name online ever since. Unfortunately for us, Tasha preferred to go by something entirely unidentifiable, which made tracking her down a headache. Simon assured me he had this under control, but three days later we were still hunting through Conner's friends of friends on social media for anyone remotely resembling his ex.

It was a gray autumn afternoon and I was hanging over one of Simon's sloping shoulders, Conner at the other, watching him type away on his laptop, when my phone rang.

"Hey, sugar," Jo greeted from the other end. Her voice sounded different as it tumbled down the line. Strained, maybe. I had been in to visit her a few days earlier, after her second surgery, but half of me assumed she was calling to chastise me for leaving her alone too long.

"How're you feeling, Jo?" I asked, stepping away from the kitchen table and leaving Simon and Conner to continue sleuthing. I wandered into the living room and stretched out on one of my old couches, my ankles throbbing under the weight of my ever-expanding stomach.

"I'm just fine, honey, but I really think you should get down here."

I wiggled my toes, my feet propped on a stack of pillows. The thought of going anywhere right now didn't particularly appeal to me. "I miss you too, Jo, but I was just there a few days ago. I'll be in again next week, okay? I can pick up some of those fancy donuts you like on my way in."

"That's all well and good," said Jo, "but I'm not calling you because I'm lonely. In fact, I've just had a visitor."

"Brandon or Julio?" I asked through a yawn.

"Couldn't tell you who it was," said Jo, her voice simmering to a whisper. "Alls I can tell you is that my things are strewn around my room like a tornado blew through, and for once I wasn't the cause."

I bolted upright on the couch and was out the door before my thoughts could catch up with my feet enough for me to drag anyone along with me.

30

I stormed into Jo's room in a tangle of wafting autumn layers and anxiety. A nurse was still stooped over the linoleum floor at Jo's bedside, cleaning up the last pieces of debris. Jo was in a private room now, the comforts of home—assorted house-dresses, a few thick braille books, and some makeup—stashed in a bedside table and a closet by the door. The patient herself was sitting up against some pillows as I walked in.

"Did anyone see anything?" I demanded of the nurse as well as Jo.

"Sit down, sugar," Jo directed, indicating the chair by her bedside with a wave of her hand.

"But I just—"

"Sit down."

I sat down.

"Jo, I need some details here," I said. "Did anyone see who was in your room?"

"We're good just now, darlin', thank you," Jo said to the nurse on the floor. He rose and took his leave, saying someone would be by with dinner soon.

"What the hell is going on?" I was getting impatient now, my left leg bouncing unbidden, my hands clasped tightly in my lap.

"You still sitting, sugar?"

"Yes, Jo."

"Good. All right, then. Take a breath for me. Are you breathing?"

I sighed. "Yes, Jo."

"Let me hear you, honey."

I drew in an exaggerated breath and let it out loud enough for the next room to hear.

"Good. Very good. Now, where were we? Ah yes. They have me on some pretty strong pain meds these days. I've been known to get a bit groggy after a dose. As luck would have it, I was out cold for most of the break-in, and just as well, too. I woke up to someone with their hands under my pillow. At first I thought it was a nurse, but my day nurse is Angela and she smells like lavender. This person, they smelled like sweat and lemon, and they were being far too rough for a nurse, jostling me about. I guess they figured I was too knocked out to be woken up. When I realized what was going on, I started hollering for help, and that's when things got dicey."

"Dicier than someone breaking into your room?" I asked breathlessly. Had Jo not made me take a deep breath before she'd started speaking, I'd have passed out by now.

"Well, see now, whoever was in here didn't want anyone else to find them, it seems, because as soon as I began shouting and Chap started getting riled up, they pulled the pillow out from under my head and stuffed it right over my face. Likely messed up my lipstick, but I've been too bent out of shape to ask."

I was on my feet in a heartbeat. "Jesus Christ, Jo, are you okay?"

"You're not sitting now, are you?" Jo sighed. "You should sit. You'll upset the baby with your pacing. Your shoes are squeaking like horny mice."

I tried to pace more quietly. "Jo, you could have been killed."

"Coulda, shoulda, woulda, honey," she said. "I'm made of tougher stuff than a pillow. Sit."

I sat. "So what happened?"

"I fought, naturally," Jo said. "Kicked and scratched and all of it. I keep these nails manicured for a reason. But this little pecker was strong, and I like my air without cotton as much as possible. So I did what any patient does when they have something to complain about. I pulled that handy little cord that calls for a nurse. And sure enough, as soon as I did, a whole host of footsteps started coming my way, the pillow lifted, and whoever it was left the room before my nurse army entered. When the nurses got here, I said the mess was because I couldn't find my vibrator and needed some help. Got a nice lecture about when it is and isn't appropriate to call for a nurse. Still, I figured it was better than anyone calling the authorities, who definitely don't cover S.C.Y.T.H.E.'s jurisdiction."

"I'm so sorry I got you into this, Jo." I deflated against the back of the chair, tears biting at my eyes. My Sadim touch was out in full force, and it could have cost Jo her life.

"Oh please, you got me into nothing," said Jo. "Now, you want to fill me in on what's important enough for someone to dang near kill me over?"

"Conner's phone," I said. "Someone broke into my place a

few days back. We think that's what they'd been looking for." A shudder ran through me as I imagined what might have happened to me if I'd been home that day. Or if Jesse found out where I'm living now.

"And you were going to tell me this when, exactly?" Jo asked.

"You have enough going on here," I said. "I haven't wanted to worry you."

"And what else haven't you wanted to worry me about?" Jo's tone dripped with annoyance. I relented and told her about the license plate leading to Jesse's wife, about moving back in with Simon, about Conner's ex and the pictures on his phone.

Jo was silent for a long moment, letting these revelations sink in. "Jesse Hare," she said finally. "He's always been something of a dark horse. Never could get a proper read on the boy, though I heard rumors back in the day that he'd been involved in a few nefarious dealings before coming to S.C.Y.T.H.E. But I suppose it does take a certain type to head up Murder. And you still think our Stu's involved?"

"Stu and Jesse are both managers," I said. "They both have access to things the rest of us don't. Information about Conner, and about me. Stu knows you and I are good friends; that I'd trust you with something important. Jesse wouldn't know to come here on his own."

"Hmm," Jo mused. "Well, I did ask around, and no one recalls seeing anyone but my usual visitors stop in today. Not even the girls at the front desk. But you always did say Jesse was handsome in a nondescript sort of way. I suppose if it was him, he could blend well enough. That is very on brand for someone from S.C.Y.T.H.E. It's only too bad he didn't find what he was looking for."

"Why's that?"

"Because he might be tempted to have another look."

I OPENED THE FRONT DOOR OF THE LITTLE VICTORIAN TOWN HOUSE with such force that the navy-blue hallway paint chipped.

"We need to find that phone," I called into the darkness. The sun had set during my drive home, and it seemed no one in this household knew how to turn a light on. My hands were still tingling from stress, and the darkness of the house only made my foggy head feel lighter.

Before leaving the hospital, I had insisted on strict monitoring of both Jo and her visitors, concocting a ridiculous story about a rogue son with violent tendencies who was set to inherit Jo's nonexistent fortune. After twenty minutes of protest from Jo, I also decided to halt my visits in case my presence was the reason she had a target on her back. But my stomach acid still burned with fear that it wouldn't be enough.

Jo had nearly been killed today for no other reason than because she was in my life. I had nearly gotten Jo killed. Who next? Simon? My baby? This had gone too far.

"Do you hear me? We need to find that girl," I shouted down the hallway.

A single set of footfalls from the kitchen yielded Simon and Conner, both looking red-faced and giddy.

"We found her," said Simon.

"What?"

"We found Natasha Sinclair," said Simon. "Or should I say 'Tay_Tay_Sinz'?"

"You absolutely should not," I said.

"She hasn't updated her location on social media," said Simon. "But I was able to track her family down to a town about two and a half hours from here."

"The man's a wizard," Conner said. "It was intense. He found the office where Tasha's dad works and everything."

"She goes by her mom's maiden name, so it wasn't easy to find her father," said Simon, "but I finally did. He was some bigwig finance guy who got laid off for dipping into company funds five years ago; I guess she wanted to duck the bad press."

"He always seemed skeezy," said Conner.

"I have their home address and her new school in case you need to track her down there," said Simon.

"Your man's thorough," said Conner, crossing his arms approvingly.

I put my hands up. "Everybody stop talking." Simon gave a puzzled look, then turned to glance behind him.

"Is he . . . ?" He jabbed a thumb over his shoulder.

"Beside you," I said, rubbing my temples. "So we've got her?"

"We've got her." Simon beamed.

My heart rate began to ease. Tomorrow we would get that goddamn phone and use whatever was on it to take Jesse and Stu down, figure out what happened to Conner, and help him move on. No more cars trying to run me off the road. No more break-ins. I could almost see the end of this. I planted a hearty kiss on Simon's shiny forehead.

"Any idea what time Tasha's new school gets out?"

"Uh, two forty-five," he replied, looking at the scribbles on a notebook in his hands.

I turned to Conner, my head switching from too light to too heavy without warning. "We're leaving the house at noon."

"Aye, aye, captain." Conner gave a salute.

"Simon, we'll fill you in on what we find when you're home from work. I think I can handle one more teenager by myself. Now, please entertain Conner. I'm going to bed."

"How do you feel about magic tricks?" Simon asked the opposite end of the room from Conner.

I climbed the stairs and shut the guest room door on Conner's disgruntled groan.

AFTER AN HOUR OF GRAY AND GRIDLOCK, THE CITY FELL AWAY. Conner and I sailed through open roads lined by trees aflame with fall colors and fields of swaying crops ready for harvest. The air was as crisp and biting as mouthwash as it streamed in through open windows, playing roughly with my mop of hair. Conner's own dark waves remained undisturbed.

"Feeling okay about seeing Tasha again?" I asked, disrupting the flow of Conner-assigned song choices.

"Yeah, completely," said Conner. "I think we just outgrew each other, you know? She was really into partying and shit, which was fine when I was about that life too, but I got more into just chilling with friends and shooting the shit and she'd get all pissy about it."

"So you broke up with her?"

"Nah, she dumped me when I said 'no' one too many times."

I turned down a road with grazing cows on either side. "Said no?"

Conner shrugged. "Drugs," he said. "Like, the hard stuff. The real stuff. I don't fuck around with that shit. Never did."

"But Tasha did?"

"Sure," said Conner. "Most kids at my school did, honestly. Like, what else is a rich kid gonna do on a Friday night when they're too young to get into a club, I guess. That shit was everywhere on campus."

"And you were never tempted?" In that moment I realized how sheltered I was. I was sure there'd been drugs around my school too, but I'd never been the type to be offered, much less try them.

"My parents are defense attorneys, man. Do you know how many of their clients got to where they were for doing stupid shit on drugs? More than half, for sure. Sorry, I'm not down to get arrested for swimming naked in a public water fountain because I got so high I thought Santa Claus set my dick on fire for forgetting to leave out cookies. That was a weird fucking Christmas, but I was like eight, so I didn't get the full story until a few years back."

I snorted a laugh. "You don't seem to have anything against marijuana, though," I said.

"Grim, it's a plant. It's no big. I just . . . It makes me calm, you know? Like, things could get too much sometimes. My parents expected awesome grades so I could get into one of the best schools in the country, and Tasha was always throwing a fit about something, and I'd always come home to an empty house 'cause my parents were still working. I hate an empty house. It just stressed me out. So I smoked up, and it helped."

"I'm sure an empty house isn't as stressful as living with Simon and me," I said lightly, trying for humor.

Conner turned to look at me. "Nah, you guys are all right. Kinda nutty, but I don't think I'd need weed with you, even if I still had lungs to smoke it."

"Oh," I said, surprised. "Well, thanks."

Conner shrugged. "It's cool you're around a lot. Your baby will like that."

I rubbed a hand over my belly. "You're not bad to have around the house either, you know."

"Sure," said Conner. "I don't eat anything or leave the bathroom a mess. An ideal son."

"I mean it, Conner."

Conner rolled his eyes. "Don't go soft on me, Grim." But there was a smile on his lips all the same.

We coasted through a bustling town and crossed to the outskirts, where rows of newly built homes stood like beige tombstones marking the graves of overtaken farmland. I pulled up in front of the address on my sticky note; a tan house with a pale pink two-car garage that looked almost identical to every other tan house with a pale pink two-car garage on the block. It was just after three p.m., and with any luck, Tasha would be home from school and her parents still at work. I wasn't entirely sure which story I would be going with yet, but something told me whatever I chose would be easier to make convincing if it was only Tasha I had to convince.

"Ready?" I unbuckled my seat belt.

"Why not."

I wobbled out of the car and up to the pale pink front door, where I rang the bell. A moment later, the door opened and a teenaged girl stood in its wake. Tasha, I assumed. She had chestnut hair flowing in iron-straight curtains down to her armpits, her dark blue eyes framed by lash extensions. She wore black sweatpants and a cropped white sweater with a peach emoji on it draped over her slight frame, a steaming Starbucks cup in her hand.

"Can I help you?" she asked, tone disinterested.

I snuck a look at Conner, but he seemed as disinterested as her voice. "Hi," I said, already thrown off-kilter by Tasha's inherent teenaged-ness. "Are you Natasha Sinclair?"

"Yeah," said Tasha, taking a swig from her cup.

I scratched at the back of my head, running through the scenarios I'd made up in the shower before leaving this afternoon and finally landing on one. "This may be a bit of a sensitive topic," I said, "but I'm looking into the death of Conner Ortiz."

"Why would that be sensitive?" Tasha took another sip of her Starbucks.

"I understand you two dated for a while."

"That was forever ago," said Tasha.

"Two months ago," Conner muttered under his breath.

"So what, you're like a detective or something?" Tasha continued.

"Something like that," I said. "I'm looking for his phone. It's crucial, and I have reason to believe you have it."

Tasha sucked her teeth. "You got a warrant?"

"N-no," I said.

"Can't help you, sorry." Tasha went to close the door, but I wedged my foot in the frame. I *needed* that phone. The safety of everyone I cared about depended on it.

"You do have it, though?" I asked.

"What the hell would I want with Conner's phone?" Tasha spat through the sliver of door that was still open.

"To retrieve any explicit pictures of you that may be on it," I said.

Tasha opened the door a crack further, pushed her head through, and hissed, "Who says?"

"That's . . . confidential," I said.

She straightened her back a little and regained her composure. "Why would I care if that pig kept my nudes to jerk over? If anything, it's a compliment to me and a sign that he was too big of a loser to find anyone else who'd fuck him."

"Tell that gross bitch I deleted them all as soon as I could. I can find ten times better for free."

I shot a warning glance at Conner.

"But surely you wouldn't want that kind of content spread around, which is always a risk after a breakup," I said.

Tasha's eyes darted to the floor.

"She has it, I know she does," said Conner.

"Tasha, do you have the phone or not? I promise you won't be in any trouble if you do. I just need it for this investigation. To help Conner . . . 's family."

No response.

"From what I understand, he deleted the photos anyway," I tried. "So maybe he wasn't as bad as all that? Maybe he deserves a bit of kindness in return?"

The look on Tasha's face quickly told me this was the wrong tactic. Her eyes narrowed to slits.

"Fuck you," she shouted, and slammed the door in my face.

I rang the bell again, but that only served to elicit another "fuck you" from the other side.

I huffed a hard exhale through my nose. I wasn't leaving without that phone. For the sake of everyone in my life, I had to get to it before anyone else at S.C.Y.T.H.E. did.

"Conner," I said. "Get in there."

"What?" said Conner, who had been aggressively flipping the bird at the closed door.

"Do your non-bodied-sliding-through thing and get in there. Figure out where the hell that godforsaken phone of yours is and I'll get it out."

"What, like break in?"

"Everybody else seems to be doing it," I sighed.

"I really don't want to go into Tasha's fucking house," said Conner.

I rubbed my temples, which were suddenly throbbing. "Conner, I thought you said you guys outgrew each other. That girl clearly hates you. What the hell happened?"

"I may have . . . okay, told her parents about the drug thing. But only after she tried heroin. I didn't want her messing around with that shit. But I didn't expect her to get into so much trouble."

I couldn't even be mad. Of all the things Conner could have done to anger Tasha, that was among the more noble.

"Her parents sent her off to a rehab thing," Conner continued. "That's when she deleted me off of everything and changed her username."

"Well, she clearly isn't thrilled with her newfound sobriety," I said. "Nor its cause. But we have to get that phone."

"I know," said Conner. "Not my first choice of someone to haunt, but I guess I could ghost through there for a bit."

"Thank you, Conner," I said.

Conner gave a half smile and crossed through the pale pink front door as if it wasn't even there.

31

I was half hanging out of the passenger side of my car when Conner returned. My S.C.Y.T.H.E. name badge wouldn't get me into Tasha's place—it only granted access to homes I was collecting from—but its ability to render my presence unnoticeable would keep me from getting caught. It had gotten me out of some close calls in the past, preventing EMTs and distraught family members from wondering exactly what a random middle-aged woman in business casual slacks was doing beside the dead body. If it could help me then, surely it could help me now.

I found my badge wedged between a pack of gum and a pair of broken sunglasses at the back of my glove compartment.

"You good, Grim?" Conner's voice came from behind me. I wiggled the badge to freedom and wobbled uneasily out of my hunched position, pinning the badge to my collar as I stood.

"Did you find it?" I asked, assessing the boy in front of me. His hands were tucked in his sweatshirt pockets, sparkling eyes glued to the badge at my neck, tracing the same logo he had seen before he died.

"Yeah," he said, pulling his eyes away. "The dumbass left the phone sitting on her bedside table. She's on her bed Face-Timing her friend, though, so you're gonna have to be stealthy about it."

I tapped my badge. "I'll be fine," I said. "Which room is hers?"

Conner guided me around the house to the backyard, a covered, kidney-shaped pool taking up most of the lot.

"That one." He pointed to a window on the second floor. There was no way I'd be able to scale the wall that led to that window, which meant I'd need another way in. I tried the back doors but found them locked. As were the side and front doors. But as we rounded the house a second time, I caught sight of an open window, the curtains inside billowing gently in the autumn breeze.

"Right," I said, striding down the driveway and dragging an empty recycling bin back up with me. "Here we go." I took a deep breath, placed the bin just beneath the window, and stepped onto it. Now eye level with the window, I grabbed onto the inner sill and heaved myself up. Or at least, attempted to heave. The last time I had done something like this, I was a child without wide hips or a pregnant belly in the way.

"I'd offer to help, but . . ." Conner shrugged unhelpfully from behind me, holding up his incorporeal hands. By this point my boobs were squished against the sill, feet dangling just above the recycling bin, ass everywhere.

"I'm fine," I wheezed. This was like the reverse of giving birth, I thought, and shuddered. There were no community center classes or breathing exercises for this. I pushed off the sill and hauled my torso into the house, stopping myself just before I tumbled into the kitchen sink. With one final push, I slithered through the rest of the way, the sink faucet tearing my sweater as

I skidded past and landed in a heap on the adjoining marble countertop. I dropped to my feet on the floor. My boobs hurt, I'd almost certainly bruised my shin, and I couldn't even bring myself to look at the state of my tattered sweater.

Your birth won't have much more dignity than this, I warned the fetus in my belly. *But I'll do my best.*

Conner wafted easily through the wall beside the sink as I dusted myself off.

"Show-off," I said.

"What? Not my fault you have the grace of a drunken hippo."

"Hey, you try getting around while growing an entire human."

"Pass," said Conner. "Phone's this way."

Conner led me down a hallway and through a dining room to a white-carpeted staircase lined with family portraits. A step creaked beneath me as we climbed, which should have been perfectly fine thanks to the cloaking abilities of my name badge, but then I heard Tasha's muffled voice above us say, "Hang on, Kylie, I just heard another noise."

I stopped walking. Stopped moving. Stopped breathing.

"I'm gonna check it out," Tasha's voice said.

This didn't make sense. She shouldn't have heard anything. I was as good as invisible as long as I had my badge.

"Uh, Grim?" I looked up at Conner on the step above me. He was looking at me with wide eyes, finger pointing at my sweater. I followed the line of his finger with my eyes until I saw it. A gaping hole at the top of my sweater, right where my badge should have been. It must have caught on the windowsill and ripped off. Shit, shit, shit. I was standing out in the open in the middle of a house I had broken into, with nothing for protection.

A door somewhere above us opened and closed. Footsteps walked slowly towards us.

"Do you want me to call the police or something?" came a voice on the other end of the phone.

"Shh," Tasha hissed. "I'm recording this for YouTube."

I stared up at the ceiling, my body frozen as Tasha's steps drew closer.

Conner grabbed my shoulders. I felt nothing, but his eyes grabbed mine with a fierce gleam.

"Run," he said simply.

I nodded dumbly and padded back down the stairs as silently as I could. I was determined to be the most graceful drunken hippo the world had ever seen. The stairs creaked behind me, but I didn't have time to turn around. I darted into the dining room as Tasha's hushed voice followed behind me.

"I told my parents this place is haunted as fuck, you guys," she said into her phone. "Write in the comments if you think this is a ghost or a robber, and don't forget to like and subscribe."

"She went into the living room." Conner appeared in the doorway. "Go get your fucking badge, Grim."

I nodded and turned to take off towards the kitchen, but as I spun around, I smacked hard into a full china cabinet by the kitchen door, sending me to the floor and the delicate dishes inside chattering.

"Fucking hell," Conner swore for both of us. He glanced over his shoulder. "She's coming!"

I scrambled to my feet, my hip bone throbbing where the heavy wood had hit it, and limp-ran through the doorway to the kitchen. Where the hell was the badge? The hardwood floor below the sink was empty. I dove for the counter as footsteps grew louder behind me. Aside from a basket of overripe bananas, there was nothing there. My heart thundered in my ears. I could barely suck in a breath as my eyes scanned wildly across the room, those footsteps growing ever nearer.

Something silver caught the corner of my eye. I flew to the sink. Sure enough, straddling the drain and half wrapped in forest-green sweater wool was the badge. I grabbed it with shaking hands as Tasha's voice seeped into the room.

". . . coming from the kitchen."

I yanked the badge from the sink, pinned it to the other side of my sweater, and held my breath as Tasha's lean silhouette emerged from the doorway. She scanned the room with narrow eyes, holding her phone up in front of her. Conner was on her heels. He careened over to where I stood unmoving by the sink, his face twisted with concern.

Tasha froze as her gaze landed on me. My teeth had begun to chatter, my hands shaking so hard I thought they might pull free of my wrists. Tasha stared at me, her expression shifting unreadably. I opened my mouth to say something, though I didn't for the life of me know what, but she turned her phone back to face herself.

"Guys, my mom left the fucking window open. It must have been that fucking squirrel again. God. Anyway, don't forget to smash that subscribe button for me and join Team Tasha for more crazy shit." She left the room, still talking to her phone.

I exhaled.

"Holy shit," said Conner.

I slunk down to the cold floor, my legs refusing to hold me up a moment longer. "Holy shit," I echoed.

32

"You would not believe the day I've had." Simon plopped his laptop bag on the kitchen table next to where my forehead was resting. I sat upright in my chair and glared.

"It was like I'd angered Murphy somehow," Simon continued, oblivious to my narrowed glower of death. "You know, the one with the law? First I was stuck in an hour of traffic driving in to work." He grabbed a brick of cheese from the fridge and ripped off a hunk. "Then when I got there, everything was in an uproar because one of the servers was down. Then Mo—remember Mo? You met him at that awful work camping thing Jerry's still convinced was a good idea—anyway, Mo was on a tirade because he—" Simon finally looked up from his cheese and caught sight of me glaring with my arms crossed. He cleared his throat. "Anyway. How was your day, Kath?"

I uncrossed my arms and pulled Conner's phone from my pants pocket, sliding it across the table towards him.

"You got it. Amazing, Kath."

My lip wobbled.

"Hey, you okay? You look a little . . . tired, maybe?"

I sniffed but said nothing. Goddammit, his kindness always did me in.

"Kathy?"

I burst into tears. Loud, snotty, unceremonious tears. Simon rushed around the table and knelt down beside me, his hands smothering mine. At least Conner didn't have to witness this again. He was up in my room taking some space after everything that had happened that day.

"Kath?" Simon said more softly, a hand now cupping my soggy cheek.

"I had to break into Tasha's house and she almost caught me and I bruised my everywhere and then we opened the phone and it was empty. It was empty, Simon. Everything on it has been wiped!" I was wailing by this point.

Simon took a beat to make sense of everything I'd just sobbed at him. He chewed his lip absently for a moment and then said, "Let me have a look at that phone." He dragged it back across the table from where I'd slid it and fiddled with the screen while I hastily attempted to wipe the tears and snot from my face with my sleeve.

"No." Simon answered a question I hadn't asked, heavy-voiced, placing the phone back on the table. "This is beyond me, I'm afraid. I'm not much of a phone guy."

I swallowed back a second wave of sobs.

"But I might know someone who can help," Simon added, a note of hope in his voice. "One of the guys at work used to do phone repairs. He's on vacation right now, but I'll show it to him when he gets back. Okay, Kath? How does that sound?"

I squeezed my eyes shut. Stu would have access to Conner's case any day now. Conner himself only had a few weeks left before it would be too late to get him to processing. We were running out of time, and fast. I looked down at Simon, his face alight with optimism. I had no choice. Even if I had to wait, this was the best chance I had. He was the best chance I had. He always had been. "You'd really do that for me?" I whimpered, feeling too many emotions all at once.

Simon sat back on his haunches, his face as puzzled as if I'd asked him the secrets of the universe. "Of course I would, Kath. Of course I would. All I've ever wanted was to be part of your world. I know you're not letting me in by choice, but I won't lie and say I don't appreciate it; don't take more pleasure in it than I should. If things go back to the way they were when all this is over, then so be it, but I'm going to enjoy it while it lasts, and do whatever I can to help. Okay?"

I blinked hard, trying to keep both the tears and the cartoon hearts out of my eyes. "Okay."

He stroked my hand. "Good. Now, have you eaten dinner? You must be starved from your ordeal today."

We ordered pizza; half pepperoni and mushrooms, half onion, anchovies, and pesto, for reasons I had once promised myself not to question for the sake of our marriage. By the time I had four and a half slices in me, I'd calmed down and regained a small sense of optimism. The now-empty pizza box lay in the center of the table like the bones of an elephant that had been picked over by a pride of lions; a trophy of the hunting prowess required to phone for delivery. We both sat at the table in familiar silence, the top button on Simon's pants undone, the elastic at my waistband engaging in the fight of its life. Eventually Simon rose, stacked my plate under his, and made his way to the sink. I followed suit, the movement a reflex. He turned the faucet on, and as a veil of steam began to rise around him, he started to hum. It wasn't any song in particular, at least none that existed outside of Simon's imagination, but it was the same tune he always hummed while doing the dishes. I grabbed a towel from its usual drawer and swirled it around the glass he handed to me as I fell into harmony with his disjointed humming. He squeaked out a high note, I matched it. He swooped down into an unnatural bass, I forced my voice low to follow. In recent years, he'd started adding words between hums, now uttering the odd "scrub-a-dub" or "squeaky clean like a lima bean" in the same places as always, though he'd added the line "this foody crud may be invasive, but my sponge sure is abrasive," which I felt could use some workshopping. Still, I sang along as best as I could, our mediocre voices filling the kitchen with a song that lived only in that space, only for us.

Our singing came to an end as I put the last dish in its cupboard. We weren't exactly the von Trapp family, but it was a little ritual that had always brought an unexpected joy to such a mundane task. Simon smiled at me as he dried his hands, and I reveled in that joy for a moment longer, wondering what level of embarrassment the whole affair would have elicited from Conner if he'd been there to witness it.

Shit. Conner.

I left Simon in the kitchen and climbed the stairs to give a gentle rap on the guest room door.

"What?"

I cracked the door open and stepped inside. Presumably a soul couldn't get up to much that required privacy, but I figured it was better to knock than find out the hard way. Conner was flopped over the bed, watching the ceiling fan turn above him, hands resting on his stomach.

"How's it going in here?" I asked.

"Fucking great."

"Conner." The bed squeaked as I lowered myself down. "What happened back there, it might not be for nothing. Simon thinks he knows someone who can help. We might get some answers yet."

"I'm just sick of it, you know?"

"Sick of what?"

He sat up. "Like, some asshole offs me and we have to jump through all these fucking hoops just to know who, or why. It's bullshit. Why can't I remember anything? Why would someone want to kill me? It's bullshit."

"It is bullshit," I agreed. "And none of it's your fault. Whatever happened that night, whatever reason you can't remember it, it's not your fault."

"But I should be able to remember. Fuck, I can remember my first dentist appointment, why can't I remember this?"

"I don't know," I said. "But we're going to find out. I promise." I tweaked one of his toes, the feel of his running shoe like air between my fingers. "And in the meantime, I have a surprise for you."

I rose from the bed and rummaged through my underwear drawer, retrieving a box from under a ripped pair of beige tummy control panties.

Conner looked at the box, then up at me, then back to the box one more time. "No way."

"Interested?" I presented the box like a model showing off a prize on a TV game show.

"Are *you* interested?" Conner asked in disbelief.

"You got me curious. Besides, you have to find out how it

ends, don't you?" I dug a nail into the plastic seal hugging the *Legacy 5* box. "Simon has a gaming system around here somewhere. What do you think?"

Conner slid off the bed. "I think you're gonna need all the help you can get."

Conner, Simon, and I piled onto the cobalt living room sofa. As it turned out, Simon had already played *Legacies* one through four and had been meaning to give five a try for a while now. Still, he insisted I take the first turn at the controller. Video games had always been something from his world; a world I didn't travel in as much as I should have. I decided it was time to start.

To my delighted surprise, I wasn't half bad, though I did have Conner's veteran advice in one ear and Simon's educated guesses in the other. The game told an unexpectedly beautiful story about two young siblings separated after their kingdom was usurped by an evil sorcerer, and Stella, the sister, was abducted by their family's killer. Throughout the game, her brother, Owen, travels through a gritty, war-torn kingdom in order to track her down. This wasn't the Donkey Kong experience I'd always associated with video games. This was . . . enjoyable. By three a.m. we'd made it to the second-to-last chapter and I would have happily kept playing had Simon not fallen asleep beside me. I paused the game, suddenly feeling the weight of exhaustion seeping over me.

"How much of this part have you played?" I whispered to Conner.

"I think this was about where I stopped last time," he said. "So?" He looked almost bashful somehow in the flickering light of the TV. "What do you think?"

"I like it," I said. "I really like it."

"For real?"

"For real."

"Cool."

THE NEXT THING I REMEMBER WAS WAKING UP TO THE SOUND OF MY phone shrieking from my purse in the front hall. I pried my eyes apart, dazed and disoriented. Cold, veiled sunlight streamed in through the window, Simon's steady breath coming in waves from beside me on the couch. I was still in the living room, more tired than I'd realized once I finally put the controller down. Conner poked his head in from the kitchen.

"You gonna get that?" he asked, hitching a thumb in the direction of the hall and my still-ringing phone. I nodded blearily and rose to my feet, shuffling zombie-like across the main floor. I slid my phone open with a clumsy finger.

"Hello?" I murmured.

"Kathy?" Stu's voice instantly shocked me back to my senses.

"Mr. Calhoun," I said, my professional tone fully activated. I pulled my phone away from my head just long enough to check the time: 7:04 a.m. He was already running to work; I could hear his slightly elevated breathing. Was this about Conner's case? Did he finally have access to it, and all the information that access entailed? "Really looking forward to returning to work soon," I tried weakly.

"No need," Stu said. My heart jerked. Was I being fired? Just like that? My whole life snatched away in the span of an early-morning phone call? "I've given it some thought, and I've come to a conclusion." I held my breath as he continued. "I've made the hard but necessary decision to suspend you until further notice. You will not be welcome in or around S.C.Y.T.H.E. facilities. And if I hear you still have anything to do with case 507032 . . ." He paused, cleared his throat, and added, "Some of the digital files for this case have been . . . corrupted. I require your hard copies. Which will require a home visit, Valence."

My mind fired in a million different directions at once. I couldn't tell Stu where I was living without putting Conner at risk. And I couldn't find out about Stu and Jesse if I didn't have access to the office. Until I could gain some insight into whatever might be on Conner's phone, I had no other leads.

"I could just drop the files to you at the office," I said quickly; desperately. "Or bring them to Gemma to give to you. She keeps asking me to . . . uh . . . 'grab some bevvies' with her, which I assume means seeing each other outside of work."

"That's out of the question," said Stu. "I told you, Kathy, you're suspended. That means no coming into the office. And I ask that you refrain from getting your colleagues involved here. I would like to keep this between you and me. Besides, when it comes to this boy," he added darkly, "you've done enough. Understood?"

"Understood," I replied, even though I understood none of it.

"Good," Stu puffed. "You're still at the Paradise Apartments, number 704, correct?"

"Y-yes," I lied. He did know my apartment address, then. Of course he did. Shit. So that could have been him rummaging through my things the day of the break-in. Or he could easily have given my address to Jesse. I would meet him there with Simon as backup, and keep as many crucial documents back as I could. No way was I telling him where I was living now. Where Conner was. I just hoped he hadn't found out already.

Stu gave a noncommittal goodbye grunt and hung up. I held

my phone to my chest, my heart drumming wildly beneath it. What the hell did this all mean? I was almost too afraid to know the answer to that question. But the strangest part of it all, I realized, pulse still roaring in my ears as Stu's words faded around me, was that my fear was no longer that I might be losing my job. No, for once, that didn't matter, the traces of its initial sting fading like a healing bruise. For once, that prospect was so far down my list of concerns it was scribbled on the other side of the paper. For once, I didn't much care that I might have the only important thing in my life taken away from me. Because for once, there were other things that had become even more important.

"Kath?" came a groggy voice from behind me. Simon staggered into the hallway, looking as exhausted as I felt. "I thought I heard your voice. Is everything all right?"

"I've been suspended," I said to both him and Conner, who stood watching from the kitchen doorway. "Stu doesn't want me in the office."

"So he's getting rid of you. Getting you off his tail. This is bad, isn't it?" said Conner.

"I think so," I said.

"What do we do?" Simon watched me with concern.

"I don't know," I said. "I need to get into the office. I need to know what Stu and Jesse are up to. I can't find anything out from here."

"What if I go?"

"Into my work?" I blinked at Simon.

"Well," said Simon slowly, formulating a plan as he spoke, "I'm an IT guy. What if they had a tech problem at your office? I could go in without anyone batting an eye. We're more or less interchangeable to most office drones. I'm assuming no one at your company actually knows the folks who work in tech. As long as I can flash an IT badge, no one should bat an eye. If this problem affected one of your guys, it would give me access to his computer. People keep a lot of things on their computer."

"Simon, no," I said. "That could be dangerous."

"Kath," said Simon, "you were nearly driven off the road, your apartment was broken into, and your best friend was almost murdered. I think that's just where life's at right now. I'll be careful, I promise. And you'll be with me the whole time."

"What, like in spirit?"

Both Simon and Conner snorted a laugh at that, but presumably for different reasons.

"No, silly, by phone. I'll keep my phone on speaker in my pocket and have you on mute. You can listen in on everything that happens so you know I'm safe."

I put my hands on Simon's rounded shoulders, fighting hard not to kiss him. "Thank you," I said.

He gave a bright smile. "I'll set it up for the end of the week. Work's been slow anyway. They won't be bothered if I call in sick. Meanwhile, you should go get some proper sleep. You look like you're about to topple over."

"Okay," I said. I gave a nod at Conner in the corner as Simon shuffled upstairs to shower and dress for work. "And you? You all right?"

"Not super crazy about this Stu guy getting my files," said Conner.

"He won't," I said. "Not the important ones, anyway."

Conner's eyebrows lifted. "Grim, this is your job you're fucking with."

"Yeah, well, this is your soul he's fucking with. I'm not help-ing him fuck with it any more than he has."

Conner's eyes dropped to his shoes. "Jesus Christ, Grim. Like, your job is already on the line by the sounds of that phone call. I know how much it matters to you or whatever. You sure you know what you're doing?"

"Yes," I said. "I'm doing something that matters more."

33

Twelve Days to Ghost

All it took was the name of S.C.Y.T.H.E.'s Internet provider and Simon was off. Apparently, someone at the company owed him a favor—one big enough to get the Wi-Fi turned off on the third floor—though he didn't tell me what kind of favor that was. Which, in combination with Simon's hacking skills, made me wonder if I hadn't been the only one hiding a more interesting life throughout our marriage.

It was just before the lunch hour when Simon got the call that the Wi-Fi was down. He tossed his IT lanyard around his neck, popped his phone into the breast pocket of his yellow shirt, and gave me a confident wink on his way out the door. Now all I could do was wait.

I made myself a cup of chamomile tea to calm my nerves and sat down beside Conner at the kitchen table.

"You think he's got it in him?" Conner asked.

"I honestly don't know," I said. "I'm not sure what he has in him anymore. But it's the best chance we've got. He just needs to keep from getting caught."

My phone rang at 12:37. I put it on speaker, the muffled sounds from the complex world of Simon's shirt pocket filling the kitchen. He had one wireless headphone in his ear in case I needed to speak to him, but we'd agreed that would be used for emergencies only. After the past month with Conner, I knew that having a covert conversation with someone no one else could see wasn't the most productive way to blend in.

A few polite greetings and the echo of footsteps crept through the phone as Simon made his way across the nondescript office building to the third floor. I crossed my fingers under the table, my leg bouncing rapidly. If Jesse truly was a killer, and he realized who Simon was and why he was really there, things could end very badly. I swallowed hard, a hand fluttering to my belly.

"You good, Grim?"

"I just want this over with," I whispered back to Conner.

The sound of knocking on the line.

"IT." Simon's voice. "I understand there's a problem up here?"

I held my breath.

The creak of a door peeling open. "Yeah, the Wi-Fi's down." Jesse's voice this time, deeper and more self-assured.

"Let me see what I can do about that," said Simon. The sound of footsteps. Keystrokes.

"Ah." Simon again. "I think I know what's going on here, but it'll take a bit for me to fix."

"How long's a bit, man? I need this thing up and running by one."

Simon cleared his throat. "Hmm, not a problem. Fifteen minutes should be plenty of time."

The sound of leather squeaking.

"Oh," Simon said, "you're certainly welcome to stay, but this might be a good time to grab lunch if you haven't already. It always feels longer when you're waiting. A watched pot and all that."

A pause. I closed my eyes.

"Yeah, sure," Jesse said. "I'll pop by the cafeteria. You want a coffee or anything?"

"That's very kind, but I'm okay. I'll just buckle down and get this working for you."

"Thanks, pal."

The sound of a door closing. I exhaled for the first time in decidedly too long.

"All right," Simon said, to me this time. "I'll get you up on video so you can see what's going on. Does that work?"

"Yes," I said breathlessly. "Simon, you were amazing. Cool as a cucumber."

Simon's face appeared on my phone screen, his smile taking up half his face.

"You really think so?"

"Uh, well. Conner does," I added quickly to a raised brow from the soul in question.

"Right, well." Simon repositioned the phone so it faced Jesse's desk, the laptop in full view. "Let's jump in."

Simon opened Jesse's folders and dug through photos of his family, of flashy cars in a file entitled "Someday," of various amateur sports teams with Jesse front and center. The documents on the computer were all work-related: reports and a few old case write-ups from when he was still a Collections Agent. Even his browser history—aside from a few casino sites and searches for "silverfish in bathroom," "toe fungus treatments," and "how much cheese is too much cheese"—was offensively inoffensive. I slumped back in my chair. Either Jesse was more adept at hiding his involvement than we'd given him credit for, or he wasn't our killer. Which didn't explain why it was his wife's car trying to run me off the road that night after the bar, but nothing about Conner's case made sense, so why should that detail?

It was five minutes to one. Simon had just texted his contact at the Internet provider to tell them to turn the Wi-Fi back on when he stopped, phone facing the ceiling.

"Let me have a quick look at his emails before I go," said Simon.

"Okay," I said reluctantly, my hope already evaporated. "But be quick. He'll be back any minute."

Simon faced the phone back to the computer and pulled up the email account, still logged in. He clicked on the inbox and scrolled through. It seemed pretty standard for the most part—Collections Agents from the Murder department emailing with various questions or grievances—but one name kept popping up that I didn't recognize: Dr. Alfonso Russi. While it was entirely possible Jesse's toe fungus was serious enough to require frequent correspondence with a medical professional, something in my gut made me say, "Click on one of Dr. Russi's emails."

Simon clicked on the most recent email. There wasn't much in the message:

Dear Mr. Hare,

I thank you and your partner once again for your assistance. Confirming transfer for 8th October at 9:30 p.m. at the usual location. Please contact me directly once you are able to ac-quire the requisite materials.

Sincerely,
Alfonso Russi

Core Labs

The office door swung open behind the laptop screen. I jumped. Simon's phone jostled. Jesse strode in, a coffee cup in hand.

"Done?" Jesse asked, rounding the desk.

Simon fumbled with the mouse, his hands visibly shaking. The email was still up on the screen.

"Just, uh," he muttered as Jesse neared him. I could hear the footsteps getting closer. The little cursor arrow sat mockingly still on the screen. Simon must have frozen under pressure. I couldn't breathe. One glimpse of that email and Jesse would know Simon wasn't who he'd said he was. I wanted to scream.

In one swift move, Simon hit the back button twice to return to the inbox and minimized the browser. The phone shifted again, so I was once again looking at the office ceiling, followed quickly by the yellow innards of Simon's shirt pocket. "Should be up and running for you," Simon said, his footsteps padding fast beneath him. I'd barely managed an exhale when there was more shuffling from somewhere behind Simon.

"Wait a minute." Jesse's voice.

"Yes?"

"There's still no Wi-Fi. I thought you said you'd fixed it?"

"I . . . I did," Simon's voice nearly pleaded.

"Yeah, I don't think so, buddy." A pause. "Wait, isn't Paulo our usual guy? I don't know you."

"I'm new."

"Don't remember seeing any hiring notices."

"I . . . um . . . I'm a cousin of one of the department heads. He got me in."

"Hmm." The sound hissed skeptically from Jesse's nose. "Which department head, exactly?"

"Uh . . ."

There was a long pause. I could have sworn I heard Simon's racing heart through the phone, but perhaps it was my own.

"Oh, wait, there she goes."

"What?" Simon's voice and my whisper sputtered in tandem.

"The Internet. It's up and running now."

Thank god.

"Get the hell out of there," I ordered into Simon's ear.

"Have a good one, then," said Simon briskly, the sound of his footsteps increasing in speed with each word, a door clicking shut. In a minute I could hear the elevator ding. He was safe. He had done it and he was safe. The elevator dinged again.

"Afternoon," said a voice I knew. This time my heart stopped beating altogether. That was Stu's voice. I could hear the elevator door close. "I know you," Stu continued. Shit.

"N-n—" Simon began.

"You're Kathy's husband. I've seen your face on her screen saver."

Shit, shit, shit.

"What are you doing here?"

"I—"

"Because this is a private company that is not open to

outsiders. And besides, I explicitly told Kathy she was not to come in here right now."

"She—"

"When you see her, remind her that actions have consequences, and that hidden things always come to light in the end. Sometimes at a grave cost to those doing the hiding."

The elevator dinged again and the tap of dress-shoed footsteps fell into the distance. I could hear Simon give a heavy exhale, but try as I might I still couldn't breathe.

34

One Week to Ghost

October rolled in like an aging diva making the most of her last night on the stage; melodramatic and heavy-handed. The sky had been smothered in billowing gray for the better part of a week now, threatening rain but in the same way a soft-touch parent threatens to take away their child's favorite toy. The sky and I both knew it wasn't going to happen, but we regarded each other warily all the same.

I tossed an umbrella into the back seat of my car and squeezed behind the wheel. I needed to move my seat back. Again. At this rate, I was seriously wondering whether maternity cars were available in the same way maternity clothes were. Maybe with a nice elasticated steering wheel and something on my seat cushion for the hemorrhoids.

I didn't say any of this aloud to Conner, though. After he overheard me on the phone discussing nipple discharge last week and subsequently shriveled up like a repulsed raisin for half a day, I decided to give him a break. Besides, he had enough on his mind. We'd both been keeping track of the calendar. It had been thirty-eight days since his death. We were almost out of time.

I checked the clock on the dashboard. At least here we still had time. The hospital was only a fifteen-minute drive away and Jo wouldn't be released for another half an hour yet.

By some miracle, the rest of Jo's stay had been mostly without murder attempts, though she argued that hospital food could be considered manslaughter. Still, she was about to go home, and I wasn't sure who was happier about it. I needed this. I needed something good. I needed Jo.

Even with the information gleaned from Simon's incursion into Jesse's office last week, we'd hit a roadblock. Core Laboratories didn't exist; at least not as far as the Internet was concerned. We'd used every possible search engine and scoured every available social media platform but came up empty-handed. It made no sense. Everything was online these days. Even my sister's budgies had their own Instagram account, except Sheila, who was remarkably private for a bird. Dr. Alfonso Russi had a few hits, but nothing notable besides a few research papers published in the late 1990s about a field he was developing called "New Biology," though the papers themselves were unavailable. Based on the only citation I could find on the subject, it appeared this line of research led Dr. Russi to be ostracized by the rest of the scientific community, though any details beyond that were vague at best.

This meant we would have to get our answers another way. If we couldn't learn about this laboratory online, then we'd have to do what we did in the days before the Internet; we'd have to leave our house. I wasn't thrilled at the prospect, but we didn't have time to make any more mistakes. Stu had most of Conner's case files now, after I'd left them for him on my apartment doorstep, and any day now he was sure to figure out where I was keeping Conner. Conner himself was only a week from going ghost. I wasn't about to let that happen. If Jesse was meeting this doctor guy on October 8, then so was I.

We pulled up to the hospital at the tail end of a song I'd tuned out but Conner was swaying to. He always came alive when we had the radio on: eyes alight, hood off, face bright with excitement. I watched him return to earth as the song finished and I turned off the car. "Who was that?"

"Starfish House Party," Conner replied, the band's trivia already primed on his tongue. This had become our driving rhythm; I would flip through the stations until Conner yelled at me to stop, we'd listen to the song in its entirety, and then he'd tell me everything he knew about the people behind it. Sometimes I was genuinely interested, most of the time I wasn't, but watching Conner drop his teenaged snark and bubble over with enthusiasm was worth it every time.

When he was finally done talking, it was time to get Jo. We walked side by side through pale, tangled hallways, the buzz of the overhead fluorescent lights and the ever-present scent of bleach guiding us to our final destination. Jo was already in a wheelchair at the reception desk when we arrived, Chap at her feet, regaling the man behind the counter with—by the look on his face—one of the bawdier stories in her repertoire.

"Jo," I called, hoping to spare the man behind the counter. Jo's head swiveled towards us as we neared.

"Hey, sugar." She flashed a warm smile. "And you brought our boy."

Conner gave a sheepish grin beside me.

"How are you feeling?" I asked.

"Ready to get the hell out of here," said Jo. I took the handles of her wheelchair and guided us back through the hospital to the parking lot.

"You two get into any trouble since you were here last?" Jo asked as I helped her into the passenger seat of my car.

"Nothing as fun as the trouble you get into," I said. And in truth, she was up to speed on the case, which only served to highlight my lack of progress even further.

I played Ouija board for most of the ride to Jo's house as she and Conner bantered back and forth about failed dates and music concerts.

"Kids today have too many expectations on them," Jo tutted as we sailed down a cheery street framed by plots of daffodils and black-eyed Susans. "All that 'college' this and 'career' that. At seventeen I was living with three other girls above a diner and waiting tables downstairs for pocket money. It was the summer before I came of age and started nude modeling for a French exchange student."

"You did art modeling?" Conner asked through me.

"Oh, he wasn't an artist, but he was French and that was close enough for me."

But as we pulled up to the little pale yellow house with the overflowing garden at the corner of the street, I stopped paying attention to the conversation. Something twisted in my gut, and this time it wasn't the future Cirque du Soleil acrobat growing inside me. I eased to the curb and ran my eyes over the house. It was the same compact clapboard building it always had been, but something was off.

"Wait here," I said, unbuckling my seat belt. Conner gave me a look, but I ignored it and left the car. I was less than halfway up the front walk when I saw it. The front door. Buttercup yellow with an oval window taking up most of the top two-thirds. Except the window was smashed, and the door stood slightly ajar. Shit.

I turned, intending to hurry back to the car, when from the corner of my eye I caught sight of a figure beside me. A man. I gasped, whipping to face my would-be assailant.

"Fuck," I shouted in spite of myself. My heart was seconds away from a full-blown escape through my esophagus. "Conner!" I could have throttled him.

"I came to make sure everything was chill," said Conner, his tone defensive. "Which clearly it is not."

I steadied myself, my pulse calming. "I appreciate the sentiment," I said, "but could you not go creeping around like a . . ."

"Ghost?" Conner said, a hint of sadness in his voice.

"Conner," I said, my voice lowered, my tone serious. "Someone was here. Likely the same someone who killed you, and who tried to kill me and Jo. It's not safe for you here."

"Not safe for you here either," he countered. I couldn't argue with that.

"No," I agreed, closing the door. "So let's get going."

We ran back to the car and I started the engine.

"What's going on?" Jo asked as I peeled away from the curb.

"You got a home visit," I said.

"I expected as much," Jo said calmly. "Stu or Jesse, whoever it is, he'd surely have started there before making his way to the hospital. But it should be safe now, honey. I'm sure he's long gone."

"I'm not taking that chance," I said, speeding through a yellow light.

"Just where exactly do you expect me to go?"

I knew I'd regret it even as I said the words. "My house."

35

peeled the fitted sheet from the guest room bed and tossed it onto the pile of bedding in the corner. *I'm an idiot.* The clean sheets were waiting, patient and crisp, by my feet. I swept them up and over the mattress, tucking in the edges. *I'm a goddamn idiot.* I flung the rose-strewn comforter across the bed, straightening the corners and flattening any creases with my palms. *The biggest goddamn idiot in all of Idiotsville.*

"Jo?" I called down the stairs like an idiot. "Your room's ready."

"Thanks, sugar," came the shouted reply.

Gathering the discarded sheets into a heap, I tottered awkwardly to the laundry hamper in the master bedroom. The room still smelled the same, in the way every house has its own scent that says "I'm someone's home." This had been mine. The plush white curtains were pulled back, streetlights and headlights tossing their beams carelessly through the windows on either side of the bed. Simon hadn't gotten around to painting in here. There was no jarring blue on the walls. Only the same muted floral wallpaper from when we had slept in this room together. I put the sheets into the hamper and ran a hand over the bed. My side of the bed. It was hard to breathe all of a sudden. I sucked in a few gulps of air and turned my back on the bedroom.

A moment later, Jo crested the top of the stairs with Simon at her arm, a cane in her hand, and Chap a few paces in front of her. I rushed to Jo's Simon-free side and we eased her onto the guest room bed together.

"Can I get you anything?"

"I'm fine for now, honey."

"We'll let you know when dinner's ready," I said. We left Jo to get acquainted with the room and went downstairs, where Conner was waiting in the kitchen.

"She good?" Conner asked from the table.

"Jo's always good," I said, and tossed him a wink. He'd been more tense than I'd expected on the ride home, asking over and over if we should even stay in town at this rate if it meant Jo or I could end up dead, but I knew where his true concern lay. His love for Jo had been evident from their first exchange over a month ago, and his insistence on tagging along to each of my hospital visits only confirmed it. I couldn't blame him; it was hard not to love Jo.

"What are we feeling like tonight?" Simon rubbed his hands together like a cricket, a dish towel already flung over his shoulder.

We landed on chicken and vegetables; a tame meal for a chaotic day. I turned some music on at Conner's insistence and sat beside him at the table chopping carrots and onions while Simon prepared the meat. I could look at dead bodies in whatever state they came to me, but raw meat always made my stomach turn.

Simon was behind me humming along to the folksy, banjo-heavy song floating up from my open laptop. Conner had already given me a full discography of the band before I was through with my first carrot. I reached back into the bag for another when I felt Simon's hands wrap gently around my wrists from behind, his voice still lifted in a hum.

"Dance with me?"

I turned around and gave him a warning look. Even if it were under different marriage-related circumstances, I was barely able to muster an elegant waddle these days, which was a subtle downgrade from my usual dancing abilities. I peered over his shoulder to the thick night sky, any stars in that swirling blackness devoured by a blanket of gusting clouds. The light of the kitchen was soft and warm, the air still against the hammering winds beyond the windowpane. That night was like a bowl of soup; warm and familiar and soothing in contrast to the world's chill. I relented.

The banjos were gone, replaced by an airy voice and a mournful fiddle. Simon scooped my elephantine waist into his hands and swayed with me around the kitchen as the music swelled and the chicken crackled in oil on the stove.

"Dip her," Conner hollered, as though we were a pair of mediocre street performers primed for heckling.

"He wants you to dip me," I said to Simon.

"I think we can manage that."

We swooped around the table and Simon gently eased me back so my head dangled beside Conner's shoulder. Despite the upside-down angle, I could see a smile grow on Conner's face, a mixture of delight and embarrassment wrapped within it. I stood upright again and grinned a conniving grin before forcing Simon over in a dip of his own. By this point Conner's smile had erupted into surprised laughter, quickly met with Simon's and my own.

We turned one more round across the cool beige tiles and landed back in front of Conner. I gave a curtsy, Simon a bow, before he sniffed the air, said, "Oh no, my chicken," and raced back over to the stove.

It was late before I was ready for it to be. We had all eaten together—one strange, dysfunctional family around the dinner table—Conner's place mat empty, Jo's at risk of being swept away by her hand gestures as she regaled us with tales from her hospital stay. Apparently three nurses on her floor were all sleeping with the same doctor, and none knew about the others. But Jo, who collected gossip the way others collect stamps or action figures, knew the whole scenario within four days.

"The whole thing was absurd," Jo said. "I met the doctor in question once or twice and his bedside manner was fine, but how he managed to stock up a whole harem, I'll never know. No charisma. Cold hands, too.

"Now, the doctor I was with in '96 was worth fighting over. He stitched me up after I had that fall off a camel while visiting some Bedouin friends in Egypt and suddenly we were shacked up in his Cairo apartment. I swear they knew us at every dance club in the city by the end of that two-month fling. And his hands were always warm."

After dinner was eaten and the dishes done, we played two games of Scrabble as the clock streaked forward. Jo was the first to crack, yawning just after ten p.m. I'd been able to hold in the yawn I'd had brewing for the past half hour, but it was no use. Jo rose from the table and I helped her to her room. When I got back to the kitchen, Simon was on his feet.

"I think that does it for me, too," he said, his arms raised in an exaggerated stretch.

"Oh," I said. I looked desperately to Conner, as if he could somehow rescue me. "How about you?"

"Simon's leaving a Fast and Furious marathon on overnight," said Conner, my Brutus. "I'm good."

"Right," I said, trying and failing to come up with a reason to stay awake. "I guess I'm heading to bed as well, then."

The march back upstairs felt like a climb up Everest. I swore I could even feel the air thinning. When we reached the summit, Simon and I both moved for the master bathroom without thinking.

"Oh, you go ahead," said Simon.

"I just need to brush my teeth," I said.

"Me too," he said.

"Well, I guess we can share the bathroom"—I gestured to the door—"since we'll both have our pants up."

Simon tried to stifle a smile, but his eyes betrayed him, their corners wrinkling. I forced myself to look away. A moment later his toothbrush was buzzing. He'd upgraded to a newer model since the last time we got ready for bed together, I noticed. It was one of the few new things about him I'd seen in all the years we'd known each other. That was one of the things I loved most about him, I think. The way Simon was always Simon. Someone you knew even before you knew him. He was as warm, as familiar, as a summer day. For all the walls I'd built up around me over the years, he was an open field of wildflowers. One you could frolic in for hours without ever getting lost. I scraped at my own teeth with the brush I'd gotten in my dentist goody bag at the last checkup and tried to keep my focus on my reflection in the shell-bordered mirror above the sink, but I couldn't keep my eyes from sliding his way. By this point his mouth was frothing with toothpaste in a way that made him appear remarkably like a balding, rabid opossum. My balding, rabid opossum. I forced my gaze away.

After Simon spat, I shoved him out of the bathroom so I could have some privacy for my first pee of the night. I was up to an average of seven at this point. The baby had begun using my bladder as one of those little fitness trampolines everyone bought for home workouts during the '90s. One night I could have sworn I felt it land a backflip just as I was dozing off.

Simon was already in bed when I left the bathroom. He was tucked snugly under the blanket, glasses slid halfway down the bridge of his nose, a book propped on his lap, his round face warm and comforting in the familiar glow of the bedside lamp. Revolting. I slid in beside him, pulling my side of the comforter up past my shoulders. He was close. So close. Too close. I could feel his warmth, smell his soap. I swallowed hard and threw the covers off, leaping out of bed.

I tottered down the hall, my ratty Mickey Mouse pajama bottoms hiked up around the watermelon protruding from my midsection, and threw open the linen closet door. My arms were full when I returned to the bedroom.

"What are you doing?" Simon asked over his book as I lined up the pillows I'd gathered along the middle of the mattress.

"Making a barrier," I said.

"Okay," said Simon. "Why?"

"For safety purposes."

"Sweetie—" He caught himself. "Kath, you know I'm not going to try anything."

"It's not you I'm worried about," was what I wanted to say, but all I could muster was, "I know."

"Okay," Simon said again. "Whatever makes you comfortable."

I climbed back into bed, my fortress fortified, and curled onto my side. The lumpy mattress pressed its springs into my love handles and hips, the way it always had. The steady sound of Simon's breathing, pages turning, the ceiling fan spinning; before I could do anything to stop it, I was asleep.

BY MORNING, MY FORTRESS WAS IN RUINS. I AWOKE ABRUPTLY TO the familiar sensation that I was about to wet the bed, the blue-filtered light of early sunrise daring a tentative crawl across our room through the cracks between curtains. I blinked hard, trying to get my bearings before flinging myself towards the bathroom, but it was harder than I'd anticipated. I wasn't in Simon's guest room bed, that much I sensed, and wherever I was, the mattress was moving. I forced my eyes open wide until they'd adjusted to the dim lighting. Shit.

My impenetrable wall of bedding was scattered across my side of the bed, where I should have been. Instead, I was latched onto Simon's gently snoring form like a spider monkey, my head and arm resting across his chest, my leg flung across his bottom half. It was how I'd woken up too many times to count, and usually preceded a kiss on the forehead as I'd reach for my phone to check the day's weather, followed by a lively debate about who should take the good umbrella to work, with each of us insisting the other should stay dry under the polka-dot rayon. Or, if I was very lucky, my weather report would be interrupted by Simon's soft hands, and all thoughts about the world beyond this bed would be forgotten. But I didn't have time to check for rainfall today, much less succumb to any other old marriage rituals. If I waited any longer, I'd end up peeing on my ex-husband, and that wasn't of interest even before the divorce.

I untangled myself from Simon and shuffled uncomfortably to the bathroom, beseeching the pee gods to keep me dry for another five steps. I blamed the baby for this. For all of this. For the frequent bathroom emergencies, to be sure, but it was also the baby's fault I had cling-wrapped myself to Simon, I decided. It wanted its dad, that's all that was. I dropped to the toilet and nearly cried with relief.

SIMON TEXTED FROM WORK THAT MORNING TO SAY HIS PHONE EX-pert colleague was back from vacation and willing to look at Conner's cell. This was the most headway we'd made in days. I'd tried messaging Gemma for details on Stu's progress with Conner's case, but, as so often when I actually needed her, I had yet to hear back. Which meant Stu could have been closing in on us. He was no idiot. It was only a matter of time until he figured out where I'd been staying, and where I'd been keeping Conner. Even though he knew Simon and I were in the middle of a divorce, he had seen Simon at the office that day.

Jo, Conner, and I gathered around the kitchen table, my open laptop in front of us.

"All right," I said, my fingers hovering above the keyboard. "What haven't we searched? How else can we find this goddamn lab?"

"Have you tried the dark web, sugar?" Jo asked. "I hear they have all kinds of oddities on there."

"Sure," said Conner. "If you want to buy a human arm or get

the FBI over for a visit. But I doubt these guys are hanging out on the dark web. Maybe they go by a different name online?"

"Any thoughts on what that other name might be?" I asked. Conner shrugged.

I re-typed the same searches I'd been trying while my crack team threw ideas at me. The best we had by noon was a cosmetics company in Utah called Core Beauty Supplies and an obscure YouTube cartoon series about an anthropomorphic apple scientist called Dr. Core. I slammed my laptop shut and rested my forehead in my hands.

"This is useless," I mumbled into my computer.

"I thought you were going to follow up on that clandestine meeting with the fellow from Core Labs anyway?" Jo said. I pulled my head up.

"I am," I said. "But I can't just sit around and wait until then. Conner died at the end of August. That leaves less than a week before . . ."

"Ghostville," Conner finished for me, his voice a monotone. I cringed.

"Well," said Jo, "why not get out there and do things the old-fashioned way?"

"What, I should follow Jesse around and see if he leads me to some answers?" I said, my tone more sarcastic than I'd meant it to be. I stopped talking and lurched to my feet. "Jo! I could follow Jesse around and see if he leads me to some answers."

"Now you're cooking with gas," said Jo.

"Uh, guys," Conner interjected, "no offense and stuff, but are we sure it's the best idea for a super pregnant lady and a senior citizen with a bum hip to be chasing around a murderer? Like, not to kill the vibe, but . . ."

I sat back down and reached my hand across the table to where his own rested. He was right. But that didn't matter. Not now. "Conner," I said, "I promised you I wasn't going to let anything more happen to you, didn't I? This could help me keep that promise. If there's even the slightest chance this could help you, I'm going to take the risk. You deserve that. Okay?"

Conner looked down at his hands, my own half an inch away, and said nothing.

"So how do we find his address?" I asked, changing the subject before anyone could protest. "I can't ask Simon. I'd never hear the end of what a bad idea this is if he knew about it."

"There might be a reason for that," said Conner.

"Come on," I said. "Where did your sense of adventure go?"

"Where did yours come from?" Jo countered.

"I don't have one," I assured her, my gaze falling over Conner. "But sometimes there are more important things than staying in your comfort zone."

"Great," said Conner. "And what the fuck am I supposed to do while you're off playing hide-and-seek with my killer? Sit here and twiddle my thumbs?"

"Yes," I said. "And keep your eye on Simon when he gets home. Make sure he doesn't figure out what's going on."

"And I'm supposed to do that how?"

"You'll figure it out," I said, though even I wasn't entirely sure what I meant by that. I just wanted Conner occupied. "Now," I continued, "we don't even need Jesse's address, we can just follow him straight from work. See where he goes from there. Don't you think?"

"Whatever you say, sugar," Jo said.

"All right!" I was breathless as I grabbed my keys. "Conner, be good."

"Kinda hard *not* to be good in my condition," Conner shot back.

I went to ruffle his hair, but my hand hit air instead. We both grimaced slightly in reflexive response, though likely for different reasons. I scrunched my nose and waved my goodbye instead. "See you in a few hours."

I hoped.

36

The S.C.Y.T.H.E. parking lot was still full when I pulled into a spot at the back. There was an hour left in the workday; this was going to be more of a stakeout than a chase. I retrieved a cloth grocery bag from the back seat. I'd come prepared.

"Goldfish cracker?" I asked Jo as I dumped the bag of snacks on my lap, trying to remember what I'd already gotten into while packing the bag. Single-serve potato chip bags squeaked as they brushed past one another on their way over my belly hump. I dug through the pile. "Oreos?"

"You got any of those sour cream and onion chips?" Jo asked from the passenger seat. I pulled an open bag from the bottom of the heap and placed it between our seats.

"Get comfy," I said. "It looks like we might be here for a while."

And we were. It was half past the fourth bag of chips when the parking lot slowly began to empty, cars slipping away onto the gloomy, mist-blanketed road. I caught Gemma's lithe form swaying into the lot, already decked out in workout gear, and slunk down in my seat on the off chance anyone I knew decided to scrutinize the one car in the barren row at the back of the lot. Finally, at twenty past five, Jesse emerged from the tall glass doors at the back of the building, a toothpick in his mouth, the collar of his long-sleeved polo shirt fastened to protect his neck from the cold. He walked with the ease of a man who knew he was getting away with something, laptop case tucked under his arm, eyes focused on the sleek red hybrid fifty-odd feet away.

"That's him," I hissed at Jo, who had nodded off beside me.

"Which him?" she asked blearily, forcing herself awake.

"Jesse him," I replied.

"Ah," said Jo. "What's he doing?"

"He just got into his car," I said. "He's starting it. Okay, now he's pulling out. Turning . . . left. We'll give him to the count of three."

I counted down in my head, then pulled my own car out after him, allowing a few other vehicles between us in case he got suspicious or recognized my car from the night he tried to run it off the road.

"He's getting on the highway," I said, turning to follow him.

"Oh dear," said Jo.

"What?"

"Nothing, sugar."

"Jo, what?"

"Well, honey, you and I both know you're not the fastest driver in the world. And that's fine. Safety first and all that. But keeping up with Jesse on the highway with all those other cars racing by . . ."

"Hey," I said as we careened onto the highway. "I've . . . I've got this."

Jesse's red car was still in sight, though it had already

managed to pull five more cars into its wake. I stepped on the gas, determined to close the gap. An eighteen-wheeler trotted up beside me. I ignored it and pressed on, trying to keep from becoming sucked into its orbit. My heart was already racing. We were going fourteen miles per hour above the speed limit and I hated every second of it, but I was losing Jesse's car, and I couldn't afford that. I sped up, jumping into the next lane to get a better view of the compact red car. Jesse changed lanes too, this time moving towards an exit. Cars kept screaming by me, leaving me no room to get over. Jesse pulled off the highway. Shit.

"Jo, hold on."

I swallowed hard, accelerated again, and forced my way into a narrow gap between cars in the next lane before pulling off altogether. We sailed to a stoplight on red, now only two cars behind Jesse. I opened my door, angled my head towards the road, and puked.

"You okay, sugar?"

I closed the door, wiped my mouth, and waited for the light to change with my head pressed against the headrest. "Great," I said.

When Jesse finally parked his car, we were in the lot of a supermarket across town from Simon's house. "This doesn't exactly scream 'suspicious'," I said, my head and arms resting on the steering wheel.

"That depends on what he's buying," said Jo. "I never trust a man who buys pears, myself."

Half an hour later, Jesse was back in his car, his trunk loaded with four grocery bags. We followed him down a few blocks, a few turns, and around one roundabout before he pulled into the driveway of a comfortable-looking brick house, the wizened oak trees and front yard strewn with bikes and toys. I pulled to the curb a few houses down and watched him through my rearview mirror as he got out of his car, the four bags stacked on his wrists, and walked towards the house. He fished a key from the back pocket of his dark-wash jeans and unlocked the door, stepping inside.

"I think we're at his house," I said to Jo, trying to keep the disappointment from my voice and failing miserably.

"Who's to say he's sticking around?" said Jo, her own voice brimming with forced optimism. "Maybe he's just stopping in for dinner."

Hours passed and no one emerged from the pale wooden door at the front of the house. It was late; the already gray day now an unrelenting black. I'd peed in the neighbor's bushes twice and finished the Oreos. This made it only a slight downgrade from my first date with Simon. After dinner at Papa Giuseppe's, he took me to the drive-in on the outskirts of town and bought us both extra-large sodas from the disinterested teenager at the concession stand. By the time our movie's hero was on the verge of unraveling the villain's schemes, I was on the verge of turning Simon's front seat into a Slip 'N Slide. Unfortunately the bathroom was in the midst of being cleaned, and I knew that if I waited until the single stall was finally back to smelling like artificial lemon, I would have already succumbed to the whims of the fifty-plus ounces of Dr Pepper in my bladder. Relaying that information to Simon wasn't exactly the romantic chitchat I'd been hoping for on our first date, but instead of being put off, he responded by scooping my hand in his, rushing me to a small wooded patch at the end of the lot, and standing guard while I unleashed a soda tsunami on a cluster of dandelions. When I'd sheepishly made my way back to him, already prepared to apologize for ruining the date, he kissed me and said I was awfully cute for a public urinater. And I wondered, for the first time and definitely not the last, if I'd actually met someone immune to my Sadim touch. But that was before work, and my walls, became an issue. I sighed and pushed the memories back down. My toes were cold without the car engine on, and the baby was using my uterus as bongo drums.

"What time is it?" Jo asked.

"Nearly ten thirty."

"Are any of the lights still on in the house?"

I looked back at the warm brick building behind us, now half eaten by shadow.

"No," I said.

Jo patted my knee. "We can try again another day."

I could taste a lump of desperation growing under my tongue. We didn't have another day.

"Jo," I said, so quietly even I could barely hear it, "what if I'm wrong? What if Jesse has nothing to do with any of this? What if I'm on the wrong track, and I'm no closer to finding out who killed Conner and why? What if he's stuck here and it's . . . it's all my fault?" I was crying again. Goddamn these pregnancy hormones hijacking my tear ducts. I sounded like a wounded seal. But the truth was, I cared. I cared in a way I had never cared about any client. If I failed, if Conner ended up trapped here, or if whoever did this to him got their hands on him, I knew a part of me would be as dead as he was. And more than that, it would prove to me what I'd always feared: that I wasn't capable of giving a child what they needed most. I rested a hand over the little human growing inside me and sobbed harder.

"Oh, what if, what if, what if," said Jo. "You'll get no answers from asking that question."

"Then how the hell *do* I get answers?"

"By doing exactly what you're doing. And if Jesse doesn't pan out, then you just find someone else."

"But I'm running out of time. Conner's running out of time. Have you ever encountered a ghost, Jo? Because I have, and she was miserable. I can't let that happen to Conner. I won't let it happen to him."

"I know you won't, sugar."

"So what do I do?"

"What you do is you don't give up. You go home and you sit down with all your evidence and your suspects and your ideas and you puzzle it together."

"And if I can't?"

Jo opened her mouth to say something but couldn't seem to find the words. Instead she patted my hand and gave me a look that did nothing to hide her own sadness, my last cry still hanging in the cold air.

BY THE TIME WE GOT HOME IT WAS AFTER ELEVEN AND I WAS exhausted. The sort of heavy, full-body exhaustion that seeps into your limbs, turning them to lead. Between the adrenaline and disappointment of the day, I was ready to slip into bed and stay there until the mattress itself evicted me.

Jo and I kept our voices hushed as we walked up the front steps of the creaky Victorian town house. Simon would be asleep already, and I wasn't about to wake him and explain where we'd been. I unlocked the door and guided Jo inside. We'd barely made it two steps into the narrow front hallway when a shadow-cloaked figure emerged from the stomach of the darkened house. I yelped in spite of myself and smacked the hallway light switch with my palm. A soft golden glow filled the hall, illuminating the shiny head of my ex-husband.

"Simon," I hissed on a hitched breath.

Conner appeared behind him, slinking out of the kitchen with his head slumped like a dog caught eating the pillows. I looked between his face and Simon's and gulped. The air was suddenly thick with tension.

"Why aren't you asleep?" I asked feebly.

"Can I have a word with you in the other room, please, Kathy?" Simon's voice was flat.

I turned back to Jo, who stood a pace behind me taking in the drama with a composed expression, as if she wasn't eating this up.

"Let me just help Jo up to bed," I said.

"Kathy," Simon said, more firmly this time.

"It's fine, honey," said Jo. "I've got my Conner to keep me company."

I squeezed her hand and followed Simon into the kitchen, feeling like a prisoner marching to the chopping block, though not entirely sure what my crime was. We sat down across from each other at the table. Simon stared at his hands for a long moment, sighed deeply, then began.

"You were gone when I got home."

"I know," I said.

"You didn't text me or leave a message telling me where you were going."

"We aren't married anymore, Simon," I said, sharp and defensive. "You don't need to know where I am all the time."

Simon nibbled his upper lip. "No," he said tightly. "Not that I ever knew where you were before, and I would agree I'm not entitled to that information now. Not under normal circumstances. But these are not normal circumstances, Kathy, do you see that? There's someone out there, someone in your life, who wants you dead. Who's tried to kill you. If you won't keep me in the loop for your own sake, I at least request . . ." He took a breath. "I *demand* to know what's going on for the sake of my child. I've been worried sick about the two of you all night. You're my family, Kath, whether you want to be or not. You don't have to be my wife anymore, but you'll always be my family. You and that baby in there.

"If you never want to tell me anything about your life again after this is all over, I-I'll accept that. But while there's still a murderer after you, I need to know you're not in harm's way, or at least to know what you're doing if you are. Come on, Kath. You have to give me that."

I could feel my shoulders ease from where they'd hunched reflexively around my ears, my jaw loosening. We'd had this disagreement, this fight, so many times, my body knew how to respond. Tighten up. Hold my position. Yield nothing. My life is my life. My world is my world. My secrets are my secrets. Where I went and what I did was my business. That was what kept me safe from being seen in a way I wasn't ready for. But he was right; I couldn't afford that mentality right now. He needed to know where I was if he was going to help me, help protect our baby. I needed him. And what was worse, I wanted him. I always had. And that terrified me. He hadn't run from my messy truths yet, but if I let him see them fully, if I continued to strip them naked and let every roll, every jiggly and dangly bit into the harsh light of day, would he still want to be there? It seemed too good to be true. It felt like only a matter of time until my old Sadim touch returned and this all fell apart the way everything always had. That I'd say or do something wrong and this time, instead of a flirty kiss, he'd be really and truly gone.

"We were following Jesse," I said.

"You were following—" He ran a hand down his face. "You were following the man you think murdered Conner. Have I got that right?"

"See, I knew you'd be mad." I was tightening again.

"I'm not mad, Kathy, I'm worried. I'm terrified. What if he'd spotted you?"

"He didn't," I said quickly.

"But what if he had? I don't know what's gotten into you, I really don't. You've always been so practical, always thought everything through. Now you're out there chasing murderers?"

"I—" My voice broke. "I don't know either. But I know if I don't do this, no one else will. And Conner—"

"I know," said Simon. "But I told you, you don't have to do this alone."

"That's the only way I know how to do things."

"Yeah, I figured that one out a while ago," said Simon. "But since you're on this new daredevil kick, why not take a risk and let me in? Fully this time. No more sneaking off and doing things because you're not sure how I'll react. Let me show you how I'll react and you can decide my level of involvement from there, okay?"

My stomach knotted. I was scared, I realized. So incredibly, inescapably scared. Even more than when I had been tailing Jesse on the highway. Letting Simon in meant letting him see what a mess I was, and what a mess I always made of everything.

"Why do . . . did you love me?"

Simon sat back in his chair at that, his hands coming to rest on his stomach. He looked at me for a long moment, as if I'd asked him to explain the formation of the universe. Perhaps loving me was just as puzzling.

Finally, he leaned across the table and took my hand. "Because, Kathy Valence, you are worthy of love."

37

onner cornered me in the hallway as soon as I was out of the kitchen. His hood was up, eyes searching my face uneasily. "Well? Did you find anything?"

I could feel my heart drop to my knees as I shook my head.

"Fuck," said Conner, echoing my own thoughts.

"But we aren't giving up, okay?"

"Yeah," said Conner, clearly unconvinced. "Sure, Grim. I know."

"We're trying again tomorrow. We'll find something. I promise," I lied.

But Conner could see through me as if I were the one without a body. He looked down, his voice small. "How long do I have?"

"It's . . . It's not an exact science," I said. "The average time an essence has to be processed is roughly forty-five days, give or take."

"And I kicked it, like . . . fuck."

I swallowed but said nothing. I couldn't. There was nothing to say.

"Does it hurt?" Conner asked, his expression tight. "Going ghost, I mean."

"I don't know," I said, and quickly added, "but it's not going to come to that. I won't let it."

We both let my impossible promises hang in the air for a long moment, clinging to them like a fraying rope.

"We never finished *Legacy 5*," Conner said at last.

"What?" I said, still half lost in thought.

"We have one chapter left to go. If everything else is gonna go to shit, can we at least see how that ends?"

"Okay," I said. "Of course. If that's what you want to do. But please don't throw in the towel yet, all right?"

Conner just shrugged. I padded down the hall to the living room and dug for the game in the pile behind the TV with a lump in my throat. I'd failed him. Even if, by some miracle, I managed to get Conner to processing in time, I'd failed him. He no longer believed I could help him, and that, that was an unforgivable failure. I paused my rummaging to stroke my belly. Shit. I couldn't even do one thing for this boy; how the hell was I supposed to raise a kid for a lifetime? I sniffed back the dampening snot in my nose and smeared my tears across the sleeve of my sweater before turning back into the hallway with a smile forced across my face.

"Here we go," I said. "*Legacy 5*. Let's see how this wraps up."

```
Owen walks through the mist-
shrouded tunnel, jagged-cut stone
walls illuminated only by the small
rings of light blossoming from
torches suspended just above his
```

```
head. The wizard had said she'd be
here somewhere. He turns right.
Rusted bars mark the remnants of
cages imbedded in the walls. The old
dungeon. A rat skitters by,
squealing as its tail snakes into
the distance. From across the
dungeon a figure appears, cloaked in
a hood.
    "You have reached the end of your
journey," a voice echoes from
somewhere; everywhere. "Your final
battle."
```

"Kill it!"

I turned to Jo, her hands balled into fists, ready for a fight. "Are you sure?" I asked, reading over my options on the screen.

"Use his father's sword," Simon chimed in. "It was made for this moment. Think of the poetic justice. This guy slays Owen's family, and then his family sword is what he uses to get revenge? Beautiful!"

I turned to Conner. "Want me to stab him?"

Conner's eyes were glued to the screen. He shook his head. "No. Tell him to surrender."

"You're sure?" I asked.

"Yeah."

I selected "Surrender" and the game carried on.

```
    Owen sinks to a knee, his
father's sword flung to the ground.
```

It will not vanquish this foe. The
hooded figure steps into the light.
The figure Owen has been trailing for
days since it killed his family and
abducted his beloved sister.

"This will be your greatest fight,
Owen of Farfire."

The figure lowers the hood,
revealing the angelic face of Owen's
sister, Stella.

"Holy shit," said Conner.

"Stella," says Owen, his voice
choked. "It was you all along. But
why?"

"For generations, our family has
achieved its wealth by taking from
those with less to ensure they stay
beneath us. Our people are starving
because of us. I had to do something, Owen. For the greater good."

Owen bows his head.

"Are you going to kill me?"
Stella asks, her tone more a
challenge than a plea.

"Well?" I looked over at Conner as another option screen appeared.

"No," said Conner, shaking his head. "Like, she's clearly

fucked-up for killing her family, but Owen wouldn't off his own sister. Go with 'Alternative Justice.'"

I made the selection before Jo had time to protest.

Owen rises, collecting his
father's sword from the stone floor.
He holds it up to Stella's throat
for a brief, fleeting moment before
lowering it again, his face pained.

"Your hardest fight," Stella says,
but she isn't taunting. She seems
almost sympathetic to Owen's inner
conflict.

"I can't just let you go,
Stella," Owen says. "You must know
that."

"I do," says Stella.

Owen pushes his hair back. "Leave
this kingdom," he says. "Where you
go from here is not my concern. But
if you ever return, I will do what I
could not today."

"I always knew you were a good
man," says Stella.

"And I never knew you at all,"
says Owen. "I have seen much in my
journey to rescue you, but never
someone so sweet and so beautiful
harboring such a bitter ugliness.
There are other roads than the one

```
you have taken, sister, that can
lead to the destination you desired.
But you never gave them a glance.
Now go. Begone. And stay gone."
    Stella lowers her glowing silver
head and backs into the shadows,
vanishing from sight. Owen turns
around and begins his long journey
home. The screen fades to black as
credits begin to roll.
```

I put the controller down and stretched my arms over my head. My left leg had fallen asleep from having it tucked under my bum for so long. The clock on the DVD player read 1:09 a.m. I looked around the room. Despite the hour, everyone was still alert. Simon was the first to speak.

"Wow," he said, pulling at the tufts of hair on the sides of his head. "Wow! This franchise just does not disappoint."

"I still think we should have killed her," said Jo.

"What about you?" I looked at Conner, perched on the arm of the couch we'd all squeezed onto. "Was it everything you'd been hoping for?"

"It was cool, I guess. Having Stella be the bad guy seems a bit dumb to me, but like, I definitely didn't see it coming. I liked it. Yeah, I think I liked it. It was definitely better than the end of *L4* with that weird nymph storyline." His gaze rose to mine but then quickly darted away. "Thanks. For playing it, I mean. I know it's not really your vibe, but like, it means a lot and shit. When I died I just kinda assumed I'd never get to see how it ends."

I smiled. "You know, I actually enjoyed it. You've got good taste. And I'm . . . I'm happy I could give you that."

"Cool," said Conner, his gaze now fully sunk to the floor.

"Yes," I said. "Cool."

Jo squeezed out of the huddle on the couch and rose to her feet.

"Well, I don't know about you kids, but I'm beat. Is the boy happy?"

"I think so," I said.

"Good. Then Chap and I are off to bed. Being a sexy aristocratic renegade is exhausting work." Chap stood up from the floor and stretched as the two walked off to a chorus of "good night, Jo."

"I'm going to head up too if that's all right," said Simon. "I have to be up for work sooner than I'd like."

"Of course," I said, about to add that I'd be following him, but when I looked over at Conner, I immediately changed my mind. "I'll be there in a bit," I said instead. When Simon was out of the living room, I slid one cushion over so I was directly beside Conner. His hood was up, his face down.

"What's up?" I asked.

Conner barely looked at me before dropping his head again. "Nothing."

"'Nothing' my ass."

"Wow, okay, language," he tried lightly, but his heart was clearly not in it.

I rested my arms across my belly. "Why the hood? I'm the grim reaper here."

"It's just . . ." he began. "It's stupid."

"Try me."

Conner sighed. "Okay, so like, you know how in movies and shit ghosts always stick around because of unfinished business or whatever? And like, I know I'm not a ghost, not yet anyway, but how fucking lame is it that finishing a video game was my, like, big unfinished business? What kind of dumb life did I have? Maybe I deserved to die. I mean, it's not like I was using my life for anything anyway."

"Hey." I wanted to pull that stupid hood from his head and run a hand over his hair. Cup his cheek until he looked at me enough to really hear my words. "You did not deserve to die, Conner, you hear me? What about your music? Your DJ career?"

"I mean, that's just some dumb thing I was thinking about. It's not some lifelong dream or something the way other people know they're gonna be a doctor or whatever. And even if it was, it's just dumb. Like, oh, I like music, big fucking whoop. All I did with my life was listen to music and play video games and smoke up. Even my parents knew I was useless."

"You're not useless," I said.

"Oh yeah? Name one fucking thing I've done of any use to anyone."

"This," I said.

Conner looked at me blankly. I waved my arms like a pregnant Vanna White with bad hair. "This. All of this. You brought us together; Simon, Jo, and me. You got me out of my rotten little apartment and back into the home I love with the man I . . . with the father of my child. You've helped me through some of the hardest moments of the past few weeks. If your parents couldn't see your worth, then fuck them. I see it every time I look at you. Every time you prove how thoughtful and smart and caring you are. This is your essence, who you truly are, and you're amazing, Conner. Any parent would be lucky to have you. And you know what? If your big Make a Death Wish was to finish that video game? So what? It was a damn good video game. That doesn't make your life worth any less."

Conner's face was so retreated into his hood by this point I could only see his nose. "Fuck off," he said lightly. "I mean, there's more I wanted than that dumb video game, but . . . you really mean all that sappy bullshit?"

"Every sappy word," I said.

"You should sleep," said Conner, slowly emerging from his hood. "Old people need sleep."

"You're crying, so I'll let you get away with that," I said.

"I am not crying."

"No, no, it's fine, they're manly tears."

"Piss off and get your old lady sleep."

"They bring out your eyes."

"I said piss off."

Without the hood I could see his eyes sparkling, his face broken by a smile in spite of himself.

"Good night, Conner."

"Night, Grim."

I hobbled up the stairs and made a beeline for the master bedroom, throwing back the door loudly enough to startle Simon, who was already curled up with his book.

"I'm going to find his killer."

"I know you are," he said, and I knew he meant it.

When I climbed into bed beside him, I pushed aside the remnants of my pillow fortress and squished close to Simon, resting my head on his chest while conscious this time.

"Kath?" He lowered his book.

"Don't say anything," I said.

"Not saying anything," said Simon.

I breathed in his scent for a moment, listening to the soothing rhythm of his heartbeat.

"I can't give up on him."

"Conner?"

I nodded against his chest.

"I would never expect you to." Simon eased his book onto his bedside table, careful not to jostle me lest I panic and scamper away. He wrapped an arm around my shoulder, still not drawing attention to our closeness.

"So what do I do?"

"Why don't I come along?"

I tilted my head up, surprised. "Come along? As in, you think we should follow Jesse again?"

"I don't know," said Simon. "If that's the best lead you have right now, then you may as well pursue it as far as you can. Safely."

"Right, and you're the one to keep me safe in this scenario?"

"Well . . ."

"I don't know, Simon."

"Hmm."

I could feel the disappointment ripple through him. I was still keeping him at arm's length. It was a hard habit to break.

"What if I let you know when we're going and where we are this time? I can text you every step of the way."

"Or what if . . ." He stopped himself, took a deep breath, and tried again. "What if Jo stays with Conner tomorrow and I go with you instead? I know I work a little later than your crew, but you know this guy's address now, right? Maybe we could start there when I get home. And look, I know I'm not your first choice, but I want to be there with you. For you."

"Okay," I said, before I could talk myself out of it.

"Really okay?" asked Simon.

"Really okay," I said. "And Simon?"

"Yeah, Kath?"

"You've always been my first choice."

Simon's voice cracked slightly on an enthusiastic, "Good night, Kath."

"Good night, Simon," I said into his chest.

He turned the bedside lamp off, leaving us holding tight in the darkness.

38

Five Days to Ghost

woke up the next morning feeling hungover despite not having had a drink in more than eight months. My stomach was balled up somewhere just below my mouth, ready to dump its contents at the slightest hint of prompting. The bathroom door was open just enough to see Simon standing in front of the mirror, the bottom half of his face masked in shaving cream. I swallowed down the bile climbing my throat. This certainly wasn't a hangover, and it wasn't baby nausea either. No, this tasted like the physical manifestation of the last few days; of the past few weeks. I had planned to spend my day reassessing any previous leads and looking more into Stu's background, but all I wanted to do now was curl up in the same fetal position as the baby pressed against my bladder and sleep.

"Simon," I moaned, pulling the covers up to my ears. Simon peeled the door open the rest of the way and poked his half-shaved face out. I continued my whine. "How am I going to do this?"

Simon held a finger up, disappeared into the bathroom for a moment, and re-emerged free of shaving cream, the night's stubble still darkening one cheek. He eased himself down to the bed by my feet and started rubbing one absently.

"Why not sleep in?" he said. "You can't do much until that Jesse guy's off work anyway. And hey, my colleague texted a few minutes ago to say he'll have Conner's phone back to me today. That could be the key to all this, right? But until I have it, why don't you rest? You should rest. This is taking such a toll on you."

"I can't just rest," I said. "How does that help anything? We have days now, Simon. Days. And then that's it, Conner's stuck here, there's no going back."

"I know. But there's nothing else you can do right now. So the best thing you *can* do is look after yourself. That way, when we do have a lead to go on, you'll feel well enough to follow it up. Okay?"

"Damn it," I said.

"What?"

"You're right."

Simon chuckled. "Stranger things have happened." He looked at his watch. "Shoot. I have to get off to work. Are you okay here?"

"Sure," I said. "I'll just be resting. You can't get much okay-er than that."

Simon gave my foot a squeeze and stood up. "I'll call you as soon as I have Conner's phone back. Hang tight, all right? And enjoy your rest."

With that, Simon and his half-shaved face left the room. I stared at the ceiling for a moment, trying to will myself to at least get out of bed, but before the ceiling fan had finished more than a few rotations, I was back in the forgiving embrace of sleep.

* * *

BY THE TIME MY EYES DECIDED TO OPEN AGAIN, THE BEDSIDE CLOCK informed me in blinking neon judgment that it was after two p.m. I threw my covers off and trotted downstairs as fast as my heavily inhabited body would allow. Conner and Jo were watching TV in the living room. One of Jo's soap operas, by the sounds of it. I quickly poured myself a bowl of Simon's fiber-forward cereal to quell my roaring stomach and squeezed in between them on the couch.

"Sorry, I didn't mean to sleep that late," I said to the room, but mostly to Conner.

"You all right, sugar?" Jo asked before I'd had the chance to shovel in a bite. "You just sucked all the energy clean out of here."

"Completely fine," I lied, watching my bowl of sad brown flakes succumb to their milky fate.

"Hmm," Jo hmm-ed, unconvinced. I remained silent. The last thing I had any intention of doing was upsetting Conner more than I needed to.

"You nearly slept all day," Conner said, disappointment in his voice.

"Yeah," I agreed, then quickly changed the subject. "What are we watching?"

"I don't know," Conner said. "But it's nuts. Like, that guy right there with the eyebrows is fucking the blonde behind him, but she's married to his twin brother and doesn't know it's a different dude. Also, everyone thought she was dead for a while for some reason, but then she came back to life. Which is offensive to my people, the Actually Dead."

I let out a breath. With any luck, Conner was too wrapped up in the convoluted plotlines of the show to notice I wasn't working on his case. "Oh, I know that guy," I said. "Didn't he father his stepmother's baby?"

"Oh honey," Jo tsked. "That was three years ago."

"Ah."

Conner pulled his focus from the TV. "So what's the plan for the day?"

"Uh, well . . ." And there it was. That nausea again. That feeling from deep within my guts that everything would all come to nothing in the end. "Good news, actually. That guy Simon works with who's fixing your phone? Apparently he's done and handing it off to Simon today."

"Okay, cool," said Conner. "But like, what are *we* doing?"

"Ah," I said again. Then, cautiously, "I thought we'd just take the day to rest up a bit until Simon has the phone and we have a better idea of what we're working with."

Conner bolted to his feet. "You're joking, right? I'm, like, seconds away from going full ghost and you want a chill day? As if you didn't just spend most of it sleeping in like a teenager. What if there's nothing useful on my phone? Or Simon's work guy couldn't fix it? Do we just keep waiting for something else to fall into our laps?" He was pacing now. "Do you know what I did while the rest of you were off sleeping last night and I didn't have my own fucking body to sleep in? I imagined what it would be like to be stuck haunting this stupid fucking planet, and do you know what I realized? It would really fucking suck. Like, do I even get to choose where I haunt?"

"No," I said, mouth dry. "You haunt where you lived or where you died."

"Great. Fan-fucking-tastic. I get to spend the rest of eternity in my parents' house, but this time I'm even more invisible to them than when I was alive."

"Conner, I told you, I'm not letting that happen—"

"But you are," said Conner. "You're sitting around watching daytime TV without any clue who my killer is."

I swallowed, willing myself not to puke. Not now. This was not the time.

"What can I do, Conner? What do you want me to do?"

"I don't know. Fucking something."

I THREW ON A LOPSIDED SCARF I'D KNITTED IN MY TWENTIES AND sent a quick text to Simon to tell him where I was going. He'd hate me for this. I hated me for this. I was finally ready to let Simon be there alongside me, got his hopes up, and now I was letting him down. Again. But thanks to my inaction, I'd spent the day watching Conner lose whatever hope he had left. I couldn't wait for Simon to be done with work. Not today. For Conner's sake. Besides, anything could happen between the office and Jesse's house. I needed to be there just in case.

I left Jo in charge of Conner and slid out the door.

The sky was already shifting pink when I arrived at the S.C.Y.T.H.E. parking lot, the sun giving up earlier and earlier with each passing day. I pulled towards the back of the lot, nerves wracked, biting my thumbnail lower than I had during final exams, but before I had time to draw blood, Jesse was already out the door. I followed his car onto the road, pulse raging in my ears. As I trailed him to a pizza place around the corner from his house, I could feel my own hope dissipating. I didn't know what I'd expected, really. Even a murderer has mostly normal days, so the odds of me catching him out were slim to begin with. And that was if he actually was the murderer. But this was all I had. Conner was right; his phone could easily prove to be another dead end, and we'd be all the way back where we started, only with significantly less time.

We drove to Jesse's street and he emerged from his car with two cardboard pizza boxes. His young daughters were still outside despite the blackening sky and the bite in the air, chasing each other around the front lawn. I watched from my car across the road as they raced to greet their father, plant a kiss on his cheek, and snatch their carby prize before running into the house ahead of him, pizza boxes wobbling.

My vision blurred, fat tears tumbling down my cheeks unbidden. So this was it, then. Jesse was the family man he'd always presented himself to be. Anything more nefarious was either well hidden or only existed in my own desperate imagination. Maybe it was even a coincidence that the partial plate of the car that tried to run me down matched his wife's. Maybe that toothpick left behind in Stu's office had never seen the inside of Jesse's mouth. Maybe everything I ever thought or did to help Conner was wrong.

When my tears finally cleared, I saw that Jesse hadn't gone into the house at all. The lithe figure of a woman appeared in the doorway, a silhouette against the bright yellow light from inside the house. She waved at him, shouted something that could have been "good luck with your meeting," and retreated into the warmth of the house. Jesse, meanwhile, walked back to his car. I wiped at my snotty upper lip. This was odd.

I followed him away from his quaint, cozy street to a livelier part of town. Pubs of early drinkers and restaurants of early diners dotted the wide streets. As I looked around, I realized we weren't far from the bar we'd all met at the night I was nearly run off the road.

Jesse pulled up to a strip of newly built town houses and parked by the curb. I watched as he pulled a small stack of papers from his back seat.

My phone buzzed. Shit.

I scrambled for my purse and dug out my phone, pressing it to my ear as Jesse trotted up the front steps to one of the town house units.

"Hello?"

"Kath? Hey." It was Simon, but his voice sounded strained.

"Simon," I said, a wave of guilt nearly drowning me. "Simon, I'm sorry, I—"

"I have Conner's phone."

"Oh," I said as Jesse rapped on the front door.

"I hope you don't mind, but I had a peek. I wanted to make sure everything was restored okay."

"Sure, of course," I said. The front door of the town house opened.

"It's the weirdest thing, though, Kath. You'll never guess who there's a picture of on there."

My breath caught as a figure appeared in the doorway. "Gemma."

39

"How did you know?"

How did I know? I was looking right at her as she planted a kiss on Jesse's face and dragged him into the house by the polo collar. Gemma. Fucking Gemma. Perfect Gemma. Perfect fucking Gemma. All this time, sitting in the cubicle beside me, and I'd never even given her a second thought beyond envy. I'd let my own assumptions about a pretty face keep me from suspecting her of anything more sinister than the odd makeup splurge. I'd underestimated her the same way I'd been underestimated all my life, but for the opposite reason, and in doing so I'd let her get away with harming those closest to me.

She'd murdered Conner. I knew that now.

Simon described the picture on Conner's phone to me. Gemma in the woods the night before Conner's death, Jesse an oversized shadow behind her, her badge missing, her face twisted as she raced towards the camera and the person holding it. Conner. My Conner. That bitch killed my Conner. I didn't need to know why or how, not in that moment. All I knew was that I hated Gemma Burke in a searing, blinding way I had never hated anyone before. She took away Conner's life, his future, and for what?

I drove until I found an empty Wendy's parking lot and screamed, long and loud, until my throat gave out. Even in my rage I knew better than to approach a killer's home alone, which meant it was necessary to remove myself from the temptation, but if it weren't for the baby in my womb, I'd have throttled them both. I sat there for a while in that empty parking lot, the dying echoes of my screams still ricocheting off me. How could I not have seen this sooner? Why didn't I do anything to stop it? How could I let this happen?

My screams turned to sobs and then flipped back to screams again before settling on a hybrid of both. A child was dead and I'd sat right beside his killer. Or at least one of his killers. The other was too busy sitting in a fancy managerial office, with enough know-how and privileged access to change Conner's cause of death and send his case to another department.

I smacked the steering wheel until my palms were raw, then wiped my face. I needed to compose myself. I needed to go home. To tell Conner what I'd learned. See if that picture brought back any memories for him. Simon had been called off to a last-minute job, but I'd made him send me that photo from Conner's phone. I just couldn't bring myself to look at it.

The drive home passed like a dream; everything shapes and colors without substance or reality. I pulled up to my own town house and turned off the car, letting the soft ticks of the cooling engine fill the air until I had the strength to haul myself out into the world again.

I walked on leaden legs across the lawn and up to the door,

but when I pushed my key into the lock, the door swung open without prompting. My knees went weak.

"Hello?" I called as I ran into the pitch-black hallway.

"Conner? Jo?"

Nothing. I hit every light as I raced through the narrow house. "Hello?"

All that screaming, all that crying, my throat raw, but I was ready to do it all over again. They were gone. How could they be gone? The living room was empty, the kitchen too. I took the stairs two at a time but was barely at the landing before I heard a whimper and the sound of nails tapping frantically on wood. I followed the noises to the guest room and flung the door back.

Chap bounded at me, his years of training washed away for a brief, relief-filled moment before he raced away to the side of the bed by the lace-curtained window. I followed slowly, cautiously. I should have had a weapon. Why the hell didn't I have a weapon?

There, in the narrow space between the bed and the wall, lay Jo, crumpled on her side. Her face was slick with blood. She wasn't moving.

"Shit, shit." I dove to her side, pushing Chap away so I could feel for her pulse, but I only barely knew how to search. I was used to dealing with the dead, and I prayed that wasn't the case here. "Jo?" I said, fumbling around her thick neck and wrists. "Jo, can you hear me?"

A small, almost inaudible moan.

"Jo!" I cried again. "Jo, what happened?"

"She took him," Jo rasped. And then she stopped talking.

40

The fluorescent lights hung low; the hospital hallway like the tunnel of a catacomb. When Simon arrived, I made it half-way towards him before collapsing to my knees on the cold linoleum floor. I couldn't see anything through the wall of tears coating my eyes, but I could hear frantic footsteps that ended just in front of me, feel warm arms wrap around me, smell a hint of soap.

I cried on Simon's shoulder there in the middle of the hallway until I could breathe again. Nurses stopped to make sure I was okay, that I wasn't the one in need of care, but Simon or I brushed them off each time. When my sobs finally eased, Simon helped me to a chair pushed against the wall and propped me, scarecrow-like, on the stiff, cushionless seat. He crouched down in front of me, his touch never leaving me. He said nothing, just squatted there, watching me with worried eyes and waiting for words to return to me.

"It's a concussion," I said at last, my voice hoarse and foreign to my own ears. "She'll be okay. They're keeping her overnight for observation, but she'll be okay."

"Thank god," said Simon. "And Conner?"

This kicked off another round of sobs. "Gone."

Simon kissed the back of my hand, ignoring the hot tears I'd just wiped there.

"Did Jo say anything? Anything that could help?"

I nodded. "Maybe. I don't know. This is my fault, Simon."

"No, Kath—"

"No, it is. I should have waited for you. I promised I'd wait and I didn't. If I had, this never would have happened."

"Kathy . . ."

"In the ambulance, Jo said Gemma had just left not long before I arrived. Sh-she broke into our house, Simon. Jo said she knew it was Gemma right away because of her citrus perfume. I'd never noticed. All this time I thought it was Jesse and his citrus laundry detergent, but Jo said she recognized the scent right away; it was the same one she'd smelled that day at the hospital. Only this time she recognized the voice attached.

"I saw Gemma when I was trailing Jesse. She was right there in front of me. I never thought . . . but I pulled over to gather myself. Ten, fifteen minutes. Not long, but long enough for her and Jesse to have a head start. I should have gone straight home. She must have spotted my car by her place and gotten desperate. Or maybe Jesse caught me following him. But how did she know where I was staying? It has to be Stu pulling the strings. He's the only one who recognized you that day at the office. He must have told Gemma we were working together and given her your address—my old address."

"Why would he wait until now?"

"I don't know." I jumped to my feet, but a sudden head rush quickly sent me back to the chair. "Jo said . . . I don't really understand it. She said Gemma sprayed something at Conner. She could hear the squeak of a spray bottle, feel a light mist. And then his energy just . . . stopped. Jo heard someone else walk in. It must have been Jesse, he must have taken Conner away. She . . . she said she tried to fight them off, she tried to follow them, but someone struck her with something hard. They could have killed her. She could have died."

"Kath." Simon's warm, worried eyes bored into mine from behind his glasses. "I need you to breathe for me, okay?"

"Where could they have taken him?" I said, ignoring Simon's request. "Where could he be?"

"I don't know," said Simon. "But we'll find him."

"How?"

Simon was quiet for a long moment. "That meeting with the doctor from Core Labs in Jesse's emails, that's coming up soon, isn't it?"

I pinched the bridge of my nose. "It's on October 8."

"Only three days from now," said Simon.

"Conner may not have that long." I swallowed the thought in a loud gulp. "And we don't even know where they're meeting."

"The email said something about 'the usual location.' If this is what we're looking for, if this meeting, this doctor, is the key to why Conner died, then we know where that usual spot is."

"Blazing Meadows?"

"That would be my guess."

I sniffed. "And what if he's not there? Simon, we're almost out of time."

"We have to try."

I nodded. "Will you come with me?"

Simon was quiet for a moment. "Is that what you really want, Kath? Because today—"

"I know," I said. "I'm sorry. For a lot of things, Simon, for so many things, but today's at the top of the pile. I . . . I'm used to doing everything alone. But I don't want to anymore. I don't want to keep shutting you out. You deserve better than that."

Simon gave my hand a squeeze. "So do you."

I shrugged this comment off and said instead, voice weak, "What would they want him for?"

"I don't know," said Simon. "Can a soul be hurt?"

"Oh god, we have to find him."

41

Day One without Conner

The house was still. Even the normal creaks and squeaks of a settling structure seemed absent that morning. I had to force myself out of bed. Jo was still at the hospital; she wouldn't be released until the afternoon. Simon was at work, at my insistence, despite saying eight separate times that he could call in sick and stay with me. He needed normalcy. Familiarity. One of us should have it if both of us couldn't.

Conner was gone. I was alone.

I padded down the stairs, the wood cold on my feet. The sky outside was heavy, mist coating the ground and hiding the bases of the few spindly, near-naked trees in the yard. I could hear my breath. The beating of my heart. And if I really listened, I thought I could hear the beat of the baby's heart too, but I might have been fooling myself. Desperate for company.

I made myself some tea and sat on the couch in the living room. I'd forgotten about the oppressive blue walls until now. When everyone was here—when Conner was here—the house seemed brighter, somehow. Everything seemed . . . alive. I startled myself with a bitter laugh at that. In truth, though, Conner—dead and buried—was the most alive person I'd ever met.

Simon's question from the night before still loomed over me. Could a soul be hurt? I knew it could be trapped, and there were ways, albeit beyond my understanding, of destroying it so there was nothing left of the energy that had once held a person. Hurt, though? Not physically. But this whole experience had made me realize how little I understood about the human essence. I'd always viewed my job as a glorified taxi driver. My clients were just passengers for me to ferry from one destination to the next. And then what? It wasn't my business, so I never questioned it. And what about the souls themselves? What did they want out of all this? I always thought it was simply to move on, but really that was what *I* wanted from them. That was my job. But those essences—stripped and vulnerable, as Jo once said—what did they want?

I had never questioned the process. Get the file, collect the soul, deliver the soul. That was all I needed to know. But now it didn't seem remotely close to enough. Why the month and a half holding period between essence and ghost? We always rushed our clients through to processing on day one, so why was there such a long grace period? And what happened to a soul once it was processed? Was I taking these essences who put their trust in me to somewhere safe? Somewhere better than the alternative?

My head was spinning. None of that even mattered right now. No, all that mattered now was finding Conner. Sweet, sarcastic Conner, who wore his snark and apathy like armor. Armor that broke too easily for him to be out there on his own with the people who stole his life from him. He must have felt so terrified. So abandoned. A theme from his life that followed him even into death.

I walked back to the kitchen and dumped my tea down the sink. I couldn't bring myself to drink it.

When the afternoon finally rolled around, I didn't bother to change out of my maternity pajamas. The drive to the hospital was silent. Achingly silent. I didn't have it in me to turn on the radio; not without Conner there to tell me about each song we listened to. He would have wanted to be there when I picked up Jo. He would have insisted on it.

I parked and paid and went inside, trying hard to ignore the spot where I'd broken down last night as I passed it. Trying hard to ignore the familiar faces of concern on the nurses who'd asked after me while I wept in Simon's arms.

Jo and I walked out in silence as Chap led the way to the car. For once, neither of us had anything to say.

Sometime after we got home, we ate dinner. I can't remember what. Everything tasted the same. I went up to bed not long after, curled into Simon's arms, and didn't sleep at all.

Day Two without Conner

I watched the shadows pull away from the single dark swath of night and crawl slowly along the bedroom floor as rays of weak sunlight began creeping in through gaps in the drapes. Elongated versions of the sparse trees outside the windows fell across the covers like giant, spindly hands grasping for me, trying to pull me from bed and drag me away. I was tempted to let them.

Simon woke up sometime later. He propped his pillows up behind him and sat there beside me on the bed, saying nothing. After a while he got up and left the room. When he returned a short while later, he was carrying a mug of something steaming and a plate with scrambled eggs and two pieces of toast. He placed the dishes on my bedside table and climbed back into bed beside me, still saying nothing.

We stayed like that until noon, the food and drink untouched, the air empty of words. Finally, I swung my blanket off me, the effort like lifting a car off an accident victim by hand. Another five minutes passed before I was able to drag myself to the edge of the bed, and another few minutes more before I could bring myself to my feet. Simon followed my lead, marching over to my side of the bed and looping an arm through mine.

"Shouldn't you be at work?" I said.

"Sweetie, it's Saturday."

"Oh." I leaned my weight against him and didn't attempt to rely on my own strength until we were down the stairs. As soon as my feet hit the bottom step, I could feel a rush of panic take over me. "Where's Jo?" I said, staring into the empty living room. "Where the hell is Jo?" I'd known it was a mistake coming back here, to this house, where we were all sitting ducks without the benefit of flight. Even with alarms now on around the clock and doors fixed with new dead bolts, I knew it wouldn't be enough. I'd let down someone else I cared about.

"I'm in here, sugar." From the kitchen, Jo's voice cut through my panicked thoughts. I closed my eyes and tried to steady myself with a breath, but despite my best efforts, Simon was back beneath the bulk of my weight again. He helped me to the kitchen and sat me gently beside Jo at the table. Jo reached a hand towards me as soon as she heard me sit down. I met it halfway with my own.

"How're you feeling, honey?" Jo gave my hand a squeeze.

"I'm not the one with a concussion," I said weakly. "How are you?"

"Ah, you lost more than consciousness and a bit of blood, sugar. I'll be right as rain in a few days. But you? How are you without our boy?"

I glanced off towards the sink, where Simon was leaning, listening, waiting for a chance to help. But I couldn't look at him, either. I swiveled my head forward again and sank my gaze to where my hand met Jo's. "Jo, what have I done? Why did I think I could handle any of this?"

"Because you have been," said Jo. "As well as anyone could."

"But they've got him."

"They do now," said Jo. "But they'd have had him much sooner if it weren't for you."

"Fat lot of good that did in the end," I said.

"Sugar, this is not the end."

BY EVENING I'D ONLY MANAGED TO STOMACH A PIECE OF DRY BREAD, and only at Simon and Jo's insistence. I was back in bed again not long after the sun went down. Six weeks ago, I had thought my life was in tatters: pregnant, nearly divorced, living in a shitty apartment, with only my job to keep me sane. Now I was fairly certain my job was as good as gone, but right then I couldn't work up the energy to care. It just didn't seem to matter in the same way any longer. It didn't fill my emptiness the way it once had. No, this emptiness ran too deep for office cubicles and Excel spreadsheets. This was the emptiness of a body without a soul.

Despite my best efforts I managed to slip into a fitful sleep once Simon came to bed, scooping me like an overinflated rag doll into his arms. It was strange. This was the most open I'd ever been with him in our ten years of history, but somehow he hadn't pulled away yet. He'd only pulled me closer. I didn't understand it, but I didn't have the energy to question it that night. I was just grateful for the warmth.

Day Three without Conner

When I woke again, I wasn't fully convinced I was awake. My sleep had been plagued by the sort of dreams that left me unable to distinguish imagination from reality, and for a few seconds I lay there, blinking at the ceiling fan, waiting for it to open some hidden mouth and swallow me whole. When it didn't, I dragged myself out of bed and forced myself into the shower.

Tonight was the night of the clandestine meeting mentioned in Jesse's emails. The thought of going felt as surreal as anything I'd dreamed about the night before. I had tried to cling on to hope in the same way Jo and Simon seemed to, but my grip was too weak, and I'd let it go. Conner was gone. I'd lost him. First to Gemma, and then to whatever force would compel him to haunt his childhood home for eternity. It was something I'd have to find a way to live with. And perhaps I would, someday, before I too was nothing more than a lost soul. Though I had my doubts.

Still, I went through the motions. Brushed my mound of frizzy curls. Changed from pajamas to less comfortable but more socially acceptable clothing. Ate the oatmeal Simon placed in front of me. I felt like I was getting ready for a funeral.

The day ticked by slowly. I could almost hear the analog clock of time tease out each aching second with a rhythmic click. When evening finally came, I stepped into my boots and slipped a wind-breaker over my shoulders, leaving my stakeout snack bag in the hall. I had no appetite tonight. We dropped Jo off at my mother-in-law's on our way across town. She was still too injured to join us at Blazing Meadows, but I was not about to leave her alone again. Simon's mom wasn't much of a conversationalist, but she had a good heart, and at least her small retirement home unit promised safety for a few hours.

Once we'd dropped Jo, we headed north. We drove in silence for a while, Simon behind the wheel, me nursing some light cramps in the passenger seat. I couldn't handle it. The silence was too sharp, too stark. I sat my reclined seat upright and switched on the radio. Simon gave me a sideways glance but said nothing as I flipped aimlessly through the stations. I stopped. I knew this song. The car filled with a somber violin layered beneath crisp, rapping vocals. I swallowed.

"Kath?" Simon didn't take his eyes from the road, but I could feel his focus on me.

"This is Dead Sparrow," I said quietly.

"Huh?"

"The band. They're called Dead Sparrow. They're an alternative band from . . . I think Michigan? Maine? Some 'M' state. They're Conner's favorite, but nobody's heard of them. Hang on . . . this is a top 40 station. They actually did it. They've made it." I was almost giddy as I spoke, the words bubbling out of me. Conner would be so excited! He wanted them to make it big. I wanted to turn around in my seat, see him in the back, and share this moment of joy with him. But when I looked behind me, he wasn't there.

42

We parked a few blocks from Blazing Meadows, on a street lined with houses big enough to eat our Victorian town house as an appetizer. The sun was gone, a biting chill in the air as a breeze picked up fallen leaves and herded them across the road. I pulled at my windbreaker, though it could no longer close over my stomach.

We still had time. According to Jesse's email, his meeting with the doctor from Core Labs was set for nine thirty, and it was only eight forty-five. Still, I couldn't stop myself from peering over my shoulder every few steps. Simon didn't seem to notice. He was busy rubbing his hands together to fight off the cold.

We reached the park in a matter of minutes and I quickly led the way across the floodlit open field to the woods, slipping in between trees as quietly as possible, my phone flashlight on but dimmed by the knit of my sweater sleeve just in case.

"This way," I hissed over my shoulder as I guided Simon towards the cliff's edge, where the bench that once held a baggie of Conner's weed looked out over the descending trees. "It must be somewhere around here," I whispered. "This is where Conner used to come smoke. This is where he saw them that night. The night he . . ."

Simon nodded and gave the top of my arm a squeeze. "Where should we set up?"

"I don't know," I said. "Everything is so much sparser than it was when I was here in the summer. There aren't many places to hide."

We crunched over the brown, curled leaves that coated the trail like a carpet woven of decay.

"There." I pointed at a boulder jutting out from the cliffside, just off the path, and we tottered uneasily over tree roots and wet soil towards it. We rounded the side of it and sank into its shadow, crouching to keep out of sight. Within moments my legs were cramping, and my back ached even more than it had in the car, but I said nothing. Minutes passed. My mind was racing. What if they'd changed the location of the meeting? What if this wasn't the right spot to begin with? What if that email had nothing to do with Conner and it was just another red herring? I had felt so numb, so defeated all day, but dropping onto my bum on the cold dirt of the woods, my heart rate started to pick up. Not in excitement, or even anticipation, but in concern that I might discover confirmation of my deepest fear. That this really was the end for Conner. The end *of* Conner.

I saw a light flash beside me. Simon's watch.

"What time is it?"

"Nine twenty-eight," said Simon.

"Shit." Was this the confirmation I feared already? Aside from a few squirrels gathering last-minute winter supplies in the undergrowth, the forest had been still since we'd arrived. No distant footsteps, no approaching voices signaling that this was the right place at the right time. "Shit shit shit."

"Maybe they're running late?" Simon offered. I nuzzled my head onto his shoulder as a wordless thanks for trying. He meant well. He always did. But a secret meeting with a discredited scientist didn't seem like the sort of thing one would be late to.

"We'll give it another ten," I said, though I had no idea what a few extra minutes would do. We fell back into a steady silence as nine thirty happened without ceremony, a small gust apathetically rustling the few remaining leaves in the treetops above us. I stretched a leg out over Simon's lap before it had a chance to fall asleep, my hand pressing into the small of my back as it ached from sitting on the hard ground. And then I heard it.

Bang. A gunshot? No. A car door slamming. But it couldn't have been from the parking lot; we were too far into the woods to hear that. And then I remembered when, so many days ago, I'd dragged Jo and Conner over here to investigate the woods. At the base of the cliff, down a narrow, hidden trail off the main path, there'd been a deserted road next to an abandoned building development. A quiet, little-known, and little-used location perfect for secret meetings.

I struggled to my feet and took off running.

"Kath?" Simon whisper-yelled after me.

"Come on," I called back. "I know where they are."

I followed what I could see of the main trail to the gap in the trees Conner had pointed out, the path more visible now without the benefit of summer's leafy barricade. It was a steep journey. I grabbed on to tree trunks as I made my way down. When Simon caught up with me—which wasn't hard to do when trailing a very pregnant person—I grabbed on to him instead. We clung to each other as the leaves beneath our feet slipped and slid. Between the weak rays of the headlights below and my cloaked phone flashlight, I was able to see far enough in front of me to spot a tuft of evergreens near the base of the hillside.

I tossed Simon a meaningful look and tipped my head to the lush trees. He nodded and we scrambled arm in arm towards them. We slid down the last bit of incline and came to a stop behind the evergreens, tucked just away from the road. The air was heavy with their fresh, earthy scent. I pried a few branches apart and peeked through.

On the road, two vehicles were parked single file by the development; one sleek and silver, the other a S.C.Y.T.H.E. transport van. In the shadows stood the silhouettes of two men, their words mostly muffled by the distance.

". . . too sparse to go that route now," said a voice I recognized as Jesse's. ". . . to find a more discreet . . ."

". . . worked out for the best," said the other man, an Italian accent distinguishing his voice. ". . . many this time?"

". . . for yourself," said Jesse, waving an arm at the van. The passenger-side door opened and a lean, Pilates-toned figure stepped out. Gemma. Without thinking, I turned to run out of the trees at her, my hands already curled into fists, but Simon caught me by the back of my windbreaker.

"No," he whispered.

"But she took my . . ."

"I know. But this isn't how you get him back. If you give us away, everything we've been working for is over. Would you rather avenge Conner or find him?"

I gave a weak nod and moved back behind the evergreen trees.

Gemma rounded the van and opened the back door as Jesse escorted the Italian, presumably Dr. Russi from Core Labs.

"Very good," he declared loudly. ". . . eight or nine?"

". . . than last time," said Gemma.

". . . don't mind . . . journey?"

Gemma said something else in reply to the scientist and closed the van door. Dr. Russi walked back to his car and Jesse and Gemma got into the van.

"We need the car," I said.

"What?"

"We need the car. Now!"

Simon looked back out at the road. Dr. Russi had pulled away, but Gemma and Jesse lingered a moment, the company van idling and waiting to go. Simon gave a nod of understanding and quickly stumbled back up the hill. I lowered myself to the ground, the pain in my back somehow stronger now, and kept my eyes locked on the van. A few moments later, it turned around on the empty road and followed the same direction Dr. Russi's silver car had gone. I trailed it with my gaze as far as I could until it vanished into the distance and all I could do was wait.

What felt like hours later, Simon's blue Ford Focus puttered into my line of sight. I darted down the rest of the hill with no regard for safety and dove into the passenger seat.

"That way," I said, indicating the direction the van had gone. "And Simon? I'm going to need you to speed."

The road turned into a rural highway, empty but for the odd eighteen-wheeler, and we pulled off at the first exit. The next one led too far out of town to make a meeting at Blazing Meadows logical. Crop fields grew up on either side of us, most already harvested for the season, acres of land now bald but for the buzzed remnants of stalks. The farther out we drove, the less there was around us. Most farms fell away to open, untended land dotted with a few buildings here and there. We'd lost them, if we ever had them at all. For all I knew, they'd stayed on that highway and driven to kingdom come.

Something white caught the corner of my eye. "Wait," I said, but that's not a direction you can easily give a car.

"What is it?" Simon asked, but I didn't respond. Instead I hauled myself up in my seat and readjusted the rearview mirror.

"The van," I gasped. On a patch of gravel in front of a low-roofed outbuilding. *The* van, S.C.Y.T.H.E. logo emblazoned across the side.

"Hang on," said Simon, and I did. He swung the car around into a U-turn and doubled back.

"Stop here," I said, "here" being a grassy field just off the road. I wasn't sure what we were walking into, but I knew I didn't want our headlights leading the way. Simon pulled off the road and onto the grass, bringing the car to a gentle stop. I grabbed my purse from the back seat and bolted out.

"Kathy," Simon called after me. "Please. Don't do this alone."

"I'm not," I said, and I meant it.

I swallowed my anxiety as Simon put the car in park and climbed out of it. As soon as he was close enough, I grabbed him by the hand and took off.

The outbuilding was squat and brown, a single yellow light beaming down from its roof. The windows had thick, frosted panels shielded by metal mesh. We crept carefully across the gravel where the van was parked, staying low to avoid being seen. I dropped Simon's hand to slink up to one of the outbuilding windows, flattening my back against the wall next to it and turning my head just enough to peer inside.

The interior differed from the outside in every way. Stark, white, sterile. A metal desk sat beneath a wall of framed certificates, the small room illuminated by blinding fluorescent lights. Dr. Russi, sixty-something and bearing an upsetting moustache beneath a pair of thick black glasses, stood behind the desk, his hands resting on it as though he were preparing to pounce. Gemma and Jesse stood before him, their backs to me.

Dr. Russi bent into his desk for a moment and reappeared with a handful of crisp cash. He was speaking animatedly as he counted out the bills and handed them to Gemma before shaking her hand with both of his. He shook Jesse's next, saying something that caused Gemma to giggle demurely, then sat down and reached for the landline at the corner of his desk. He poked in numbers as Jesse and Gemma walked out.

I grabbed Simon by the arm and dragged him around the corner of the building with me as my colleagues stepped out into the night.

"All right, get them out, then," said Gemma. "I'll go meet Drew at the gate."

Cloaked in the shadowy world beyond the single light of the outbuilding, I popped my head around the corner of the wall. Simon poked his head beneath mine, and I rested my chin on top of it as Jesse opened the back of the van.

I didn't know what was happening at first. The van was parked facing us, its open back hidden from view. But it quickly became apparent what was inside. Nine souls filtered out in single file, lining up beside the van with stilted movements. The last to appear was a tall, lithe silhouette, head covered by the hood of a sweatshirt.

My calm shattered at the sight of him, but before I could even think about abandoning my post, Simon had barricaded me in, his body blocking me from anything beyond the safety of our hiding spot, arms wrapped backwards around my waist. I couldn't breathe. He was there. Right there. Why was he there? It had taken me ages to keep Conner from running away from me at the slightest upset, but there he stood in front of one of his killers, without even the hint of an inclination to escape.

It took everything inside of me not to call out. But Simon was right. We couldn't ruin this. I had to wait.

Gemma returned a short while later with a man in scrubs who wore the same clunky glasses as Dr. Russi. He and Jesse exchanged some pleasantries and then something bizarre happened.

"Cool," said the man in scrubs. "Let's get them in." He snapped his fingers and the line of souls turned in unison and followed him like well-trained dogs. It didn't make any sense. I'd worked with essences for years and they were never this cooperative. Like Jo always said, they were frightened and vulnerable. They had questions to ask and grievances to share. This was . . . this was wrong.

"You can let me go now," I said to Simon when they were out of earshot. "Come on, let's find out where they're going."

I could see the concern in Simon's eyes, but he said nothing as we padded along after the group, careful to keep to the shadows. We followed the souls and their leaders through a gate and down a long driveway that ended at a lavish country home. Two grand stone staircases arched up from the driveway and met in a middle landing at the base of towering oak double doors. Through the light from the house and two lanterns by the stairs, I could just make out salmon brick loosely veiled in artful garlands of climbing ivy, crisp white trim and shutters framing high windows. It was the kind of home someone into dressage would occupy. I gaped, appalled at the prospect of what must be going on inside. Nothing so self-consciously elegant could be trustworthy.

The front doors opened as the soul parade neared, golden light spilling out from the house. A man in a lab coat stepped outside to greet Gemma. He gave her hand a kiss and I winced at the excess of gallantry. She, in turn, retracted her hand and waved it at the essences to much beaming and cooing from the man in the lab coat.

"I'm not the only one who thinks this is weird, right?" Simon asked from the well-manicured shrub we were hiding behind.

"It doesn't make sense," I agreed. "What the hell could anyone want with so many souls?"

Once everyone, living and dead, had filed inside, the front doors closed again.

"We need to get in there," I said.

"Should we not just call the police?"

"And say what?" I asked. "'I'd like to report illegal soul farming?' Besides, I'm not waiting around. They've got Conner, and god only knows what they want him for. But, Simon, if this is too much—"

"Let's get in there," said Simon.

"Thank you," I said.

Once again, we crept up to a low window and peered inside. Instead of the tastefully appointed interior I'd expected, the room was another symphony of stainless steel. Two more men in lab coats and thick glasses stood chatting over a metal table, clipboards in their hands. Through the open door on the far side of the room came a man in all black with a rifle over his shoulder.

"Two guys in lab coats and a third with a gun," I reported to Simon, who was helping prop me up so I could see through the window. "What the hell is going on here?"

"A gun? Kath—"

"We'll need to get in another way," I continued, ignoring him. This wouldn't be easy. Not with armed guards in the mix. But I'd broken into a house before; Conner's ex-girlfriend's house, to be precise. I whipped around to face Simon. "I know what to do."

I dug through the purse on my shoulder and plucked my name badge from the bottom. It wouldn't keep another S.C.Y.T.H.E. employee from seeing me, but it would make me invisible to the workers of Core Labs. I pinned the badge to my windbreaker, making sure to thread it through the shirt underneath as well for extra security.

"Kath?" Simon said fearfully, immediately losing sight of me. Shit, I'd forgotten to mention this. I pulled the badge off for a second and reappeared to him.

"Sorry," I said, holding up the name tag. "Perk of the job. I think I may have forgotten to tell you about it. It wasn't intentional, I promise, there was just a lot to say."

"Okay," Simon said, staring at me in bewilderment. "So . . . what is it?"

"I don't know, really," I said. "So much of the science behind what we do is off-limits to me. But it . . . it keeps me from being seen. So I'm thinking I get in there, find a door that isn't guarded, and get you in too. All right?"

"Yeah, I think so. I'm still stuck on the invisibility thing, but—"

"Not strictly invisible, just not noticeable," I said. I turned to walk away, but something deep inside stopped me. I looked back at Simon and let myself see him. Really see him. See all the goodness and the kindness and the love. It was something I'd deprived us both of for too long. "Simon, I owe you an apology. For . . . so much. You deserve better than the way I've been treating you. I was . . . scared, I guess. But that's not an excuse. I was afraid to let you in, so I built all these walls, walls with big spikes, and you kept letting yourself be stabbed by them. And I'll never understand why, but I know I don't want them there anymore. I think I'm ready to build something else now, something we build together." I held my breath, then added a weak, "Okay?"

Simon pulled me into him and kissed me hard on the mouth, sending a rush of vibrations through me.

"Okay," he said when we'd pulled apart.

"Okay," I said, face warm. "Now get out of sight and keep your eyes peeled for an open door."

Simon gave a nod as I slipped the badge back on and headed up the steps. I took the badge off one more time, just long enough to knock on the door after my first, badged attempt yielded nothing. A few moments later, the lab coat–wearing hand-kisser opened the door, looking around for the source of the knocking. As he did, I snuck in under his arm.

The entranceway was the ornate, old-world postcard I had expected based on the exterior of the house. A turn-of-the-century checkerboard floor guided the way to a grand staircase of lush wood and rich carpeting, all topped off by a glowing chandelier suspended from an elaborately molded ceiling. I passed through quickly, barely taking any of it in, my focus glued to finding a door for Simon. The rooms that led off the entrance were locked behind thick wooden doors, none of the handles turning beneath my increasingly sweaty grasp. From behind one of those doors, I could hear muffled voices. Voices I recognized. I pressed my ear to the door.

"There's really no need to trouble him again." Gemma's voice wafted out through the door. "He already gave his approval at the drop site. I know what a busy man he is."

"I'm sure he'll want to see you off," said an unfamiliar voice, more firmly than the words required. "Let me go give Russi another call." The squeak of leather. The padding of footsteps.

I pressed myself against the wall as the door swung open. Yet another man in yet another lab coat emerged. He took a few steps down the hall and rapped on a door. One of the men from the room I'd looked into through the window came out.

"What's up?" said the new lab coat to the one who'd been with Gemma.

"We just got results back from the preliminary scan. One of the cores Ms. Burke delivered is on the verge of expiring. We can't work with it; the risks are too high. I've been trying to reach Russi, but he's not answering."

"Shit," said the new lab coat. "All right, I'll go find Drew and get him to run down to the office. Keep Burke here as long as you can. Russi might want some money back. Hey, is that guy with her again? The one who follows her around like a lost puppy?"

"Naturally," said Gemma's Lab Coat. "He's the muscle. I'm just hoping he doesn't kick up a fuss about this. We can't work with spoiled specimens."

"Good luck." New Lab Coat disappeared back into his room, leaving the door open as it had been when I'd looked in from outside. Gemma's Lab Coat returned to the room he'd come from.

Since the door was open, I slipped into the room with New Lab Coat. Wherever the armed guard was, he wasn't here now, but there were no outside doors here either. The other man in the room was in the process of laying out some sort of tool kit on one of the stainless steel tables. I hadn't noticed it from the window, but in the far corner of the room was a machine of some kind. I had never seen anything like it; it towered to just below the high ceiling and emitted a soft glow from the cracks of what looked like a metal door.

"Hey, I've gotta go track down Drew. You good here for a sec?" New Lab Coat said to his colleague.

I pried my eyes away from the machine and followed New Lab Coat from the room, still determined to find Simon an entrance. He walked through the hall and towards the grand staircase. I followed him up until we reached a carpeted hallway lined with dark wood paneling. We stopped at the furthest end of the hall and he fished in his lab coat pocket for a moment until his hand re-emerged with a key. He slotted the key into the lock of a weathered wooden door and twisted until he heard a click. As soon as the door opened, I felt my stomach drop.

Inside the room, which was wallpapered innocuously with little white flowers on a forest-green background, stood the nine souls from the van. The man in scrubs I'd seen outside was in front of them with a clipboard.

"Which one's the dud?" New Lab Coat asked.

"The kid," said the man in scrubs, pointing at Conner with a pen.

"Ah, that's a shame. We haven't had many young ones to work with. Anyway, Drew, I need you to run down and grab Russi for me. Everyone else in order?"

"Yeah, the rest are fresh. What do you want me to do with the expiring one?"

New Lab Coat looked Conner up and down and sighed. "Give him the reversal and let nature take its course. He hasn't got time to do any damage anyway, if your readings are right."

"They always are," said Drew, putting his clipboard down on a desk.

New Lab Coat bobbed his head. "I'll leave you to it, then." And he did.

But I couldn't move. Couldn't breathe. Conner was right there, but it was like he wasn't there at all. What had they done to him?

Drew pushed aside a few vials and bottles on his desk until he came to what appeared to be a spray bottle. He walked up to Conner and stopped within a foot of him, raised the bottle, and sprayed. I held my breath, nausea rising. He could be hurting Conner, and I was just standing by watching it happen.

The spray settled and Conner blinked.

"There now, how's it going, buddy?" Drew asked as Conner blinked harder.

"Where the fuck am I?" said Conner. "Who the fuck are you?"

I had to swallow a sob. That was Conner. That was my Conner.

Drew gave a light laugh as Conner's sparkling eyes scanned the room.

Shit.

They landed on me and widened. My own eyes widened too

as I realized what was about to happen. Conner was about to give me away.

I put my finger to my lips and pointed at my badge. "He can't know I'm here," I said, my voice filled with sorrow even to my own ears. I just wanted to get Conner out of here, but I couldn't. Not yet.

Without missing a beat, Conner turned back to Drew, ignoring me completely.

"Well?" Conner demanded, terrified and fearless.

Drew just laughed again. "That doesn't matter now. Why don't you run off, okay? You're free to go."

Conner gave me a sidelong glance. I nodded.

"Fine," said Conner. "I'm out of here."

He gave a wary look at the essences collected beside him before racing out the door. I followed him down the hall to the staircase.

"What the ever-loving fuck is going on?" Conner whispered furiously as we scurried back downstairs.

"I'm not entirely sure," I said. My head was light, buzzing. Could it really be this easy? Did I really have him back, just like that? "Jesse and Gemma brought you here. Wherever here is. You really don't remember?"

Conner shook his head as we bounced off the last step and back onto the checkerboard tiles just in time for me to careen straight into Gemma, my shoulder bouncing off hers with a hard smack. Jesse stood beside her, the only other person in the houseful of lab-coated men and armed guards who could see me. I froze. Jesse and Gemma froze.

"Kathy?" said Gemma.

"Shit," I said.

Conner said nothing. When I turned to look at him, he seemed paler somehow.

"You," he said, his voice as tight as I'd ever heard it, his finger pointed square at Gemma. "It was you. You did this to me. You fucking bitch. I . . . I remember. You said you'd give me better weed if I deleted all the photos off my phone. Shit. Fucking shit. I remember. That brownie you gave me back at Meadows. There was something else in it, something other than weed. That's what did me in, isn't it?"

I looked back at Gemma, swallowing hard, waiting for her to plead that she'd barely had anything to do with it, that it was actually Jesse who murdered Conner. But she didn't. She couldn't.

"Cyanide," she said instead, her girlish voice eerily matter-of-fact. "I always keep some on me just in case. It was just a lucky coincidence that you turned out to already have a seizure condition, considering its effects. You must understand that with any great progress come unfortunate casualties." With that, my thoughts stopped. The aching in my back stopped. The sounds in the hallway evaporated into nothingness as I lunged forward, grabbing Gemma hard by the throat.

"What the hell is happening?" I heard a man mumble through the echo in my ears. "How can I get a clear shot if I can't see anyone?" I squeezed harder, watching as Gemma's eyes grew wide, her hands grabbing at my wrists.

"Grim," Conner's voice cut through my fog. "Remember *L5*. She isn't worth it. This isn't you. You're better than this bitch could ever be. Select 'Alternative Justice' from the option screen and let's get the fuck out of here."

I closed my eyes and exhaled hard through my nose, loosening my grip as my senses returned. Gemma sputtered a cough, her eyes watering. But before I could re-sync my thoughts to my actions, Gemma reached her hand at me. I braced for a punch, a slap, a scratch, but it never came. When she pulled away again, I stared at her, befuddled. It was only when I caught the glimmer of silver in her hand that I realized what she had done. My name badge, my protective shield, lay in her open palm. And I stood exposed, a rifle pointed at me.

"Who the hell is this?" the man with the gun muttered at Gemma.

"A colleague," said Gemma.

"One you didn't think was worth mentioning to me?" came an Italian accent from the front door. Dr. Russi pushed through the small crowd at the base of the stairs and landed square in front of me. I couldn't see his eyes behind those thick black glasses everyone here decided were on trend, but I could feel them scrutinizing me all the same.

"No," said Gemma. "I didn't. I didn't think she'd be a problem."

"You were mistaken, dear," Dr. Russi said, "and this puts me in a difficult position." He turned to me. "You'd better come along until I've decided what to do with you."

The man with the gun pressed in closer. "Move," he said. I fell in behind Dr. Russi as he led me away from the staircase.

"What about the boy?" Gemma called, hurrying after us.

Dr. Russi stopped for a moment. "His death was your doing, was it? What a disappointment. I thought our methods were more aligned. Well, we can't use the specimen at such a late stage. Under these unusual circumstances, the core will have to be destroyed, I suppose. Such a pity."

"Nooo!" The sound that came out of me was barely human.

A ripple of pain tore through my lower stomach. "No," I wailed again, unable to muster anything else. "Run," I groaned at Conner across the hallway.

He opened his mouth to protest, but I gave him a look so stern even the guard flinched. With a quick nod, Conner bolted through the crowd of lab coats—literally through them—slipping through the wall by the front door.

"Get the spray," one of them called to the others as they all dispersed.

Another wave of pain ripped through me. I didn't care. They were still after Conner. With his attention distracted by the commotion at the front door, I swung an elbow at the guard's face. My arm hit his nose with an unpleasant crunch, followed by an even less pleasant shower of blood. Dr. Russi rushed at me, but I hurled myself at him with my full body weight, knocking us both to the floor. I landed on the doctor's spindly body and eased my way back to my feet as quickly as I could manage, charging for the front door, lab coats on my heels.

Just as I reached the door handle, a bang sounded, rich and metallic. A bullet lodged in the wood just beside my head. I pried the door open as another gunshot rang out, and pain like I'd never felt before erupted within me. As I flung myself into the cool night air and down the concrete steps, I ran my hands down my body to check for blood.

My hands came away damp from between my legs. Shit. It was even worse than I had thought.

My water had broken. I was in labor.

43

Where the hell was Simon? I couldn't spot him as I darted away from the house, wobbling and in pain. I had told him to stay out of sight, and I hoped to god that was what he was doing now. That he was safe. I needed him to be safe.

I stopped for a moment behind one of the rectangular hedges lining the endless driveway, scanning the darkness for Simon or Conner or anyone who wasn't out to kill me. Footsteps pounded towards me. I swallowed through another contraction and took off again, heading into the sprawling back property of the house.

The lawn stretched out to the horizon, an old stone barn about a quarter mile in the distance. I tottered towards it at full speed. As I closed the gap, I had to fall to my hands and knees, my abdomen in a sudden burst of agony. I staggered the last few feet and sat down hard against the barn door, gasping for breath. I closed my eyes and pressed my head back against the door. When I opened my eyes again, Conner was standing over me.

"Jesus Christ," I yelped.

"Sorry. I was hiding over there." Conner pointed to the other side of the barn. "I heard weird sounds and figured it was you."

"Don't be sorry." I raised myself to my feet, still panting. "I'm just so goddamn happy to see you. Come on, we'd better get inside. If nothing else, there could be some old farm equipment I can use as a weapon."

"You really don't wanna go in there, Grim," Conner said.

"We're on a flat lawn, Conner. They'll see us anywhere else." I grabbed the round, rusty handle of the barn door and pulled, sliding the door to the side. We stepped in and I hurriedly closed the door behind me.

"There's got to be a light or something," I said, feeling along the wall in the blackness. Finally, my fingertips ran over a switch. I flipped it, flooding the building with light. Like the house, the barn's interior was nothing like the outside suggested. The rustic exterior gave way to walls and floors as white and as sterile as that stainless steel–filled room in the house, but instead of metal tables, it was stocked with something much worse. Essences. Dozens of them, locked up in narrow plexiglass cages, their faces still and devoid of emotion.

"What the . . ." I wandered through the aisles of caged souls, mouth agape.

Norman Rosenberg, 76, heart attack, unresponsive to #8, 12, 5, Expires: 10.23 read the chart on one.

Juanita Jimenez, 84, pneumonia, success on #4, unresponsive to #7, Expires: 11.16 read another.

"What is all this?" I tapped gently on the glass containing an essence called Martha Walker, but got no response.

"A nightmare?" Conner offered.

I walked back around to where he stood glued to the wall by the door.

"Hey, are you okay?"

"Great," Conner said tightly.

Another contraction grabbed me from within. I collapsed against the wall and moaned.

"Holy shit, Grim, are *you* okay? What happened? Did they shoot you?"

"Contraction," I said through gritted teeth.

"Like, baby contractions?"

I nodded.

"Fuck. Grim. What do I do?"

"Nothing," I said, as the pain slowly began to ease. "This baby is not coming now."

"Like, I don't think you get a choice."

"This baby cannot come now." I was pleading by this point. "This baby can. Not. Come."

I slunk to the floor. Conner sat down beside me. "You really don't want this kid, huh?"

I lolled my head over to face him. "What?"

"The baby. You always talk like you don't want it."

I ran a hand over my stomach. "Of course I want it, Conner. I'm just . . ."

"Just what?"

I bit my bottom lip as the tears rolled in. "Terrified."

"What? Of a baby? You know they're really fucking tiny, right?"

I coughed a laugh through my tears.

"Yes, Conner, I'm familiar with the concept of babies. It's not the baby I'm scared of."

"Then what is it?"

"It's me." I sniffed, snot rattling. "I'm terrified I can't do this. That I'm not going to be any good at it. That I'm not going to be the mom this baby deserves. I've never really done anything well in my life; not school, not marriage, not even work, really, if your case is anything to go by. I'm afraid I'm going to let this baby down."

"Oh," said Conner, "is that all this is?"

"Is that what you always say when someone bares their deepest secret to you?"

"Sorry, it's just that, like . . . Grim, you've been more of a mother to me these past few weeks than my own ever was. Like, holy shit, you care about me. A ton. Enough to risk your job for me, and give up your home, and put your life in danger. I mean, you fucking throttled the bitch who killed me. You played a video game for me, Grim. Kathy." He smiled. "I know you're going to be an amazing mom because you've already been one."

I choked out a tearful, "Really?"

"Yeah. Really."

I reached for Conner's hand. He reached his to meet mine and for a moment I swore I could feel it. I looked up at him, my sobs easing, just as the barn door burst open.

44

Gemma and Dr. Russi were first through the door, Jesse and the armed guard close behind. I jumped at the sight of them, trying hard to scramble to my feet but failing as another contraction took hold of me. I sank back to the cold ground, an agonized wail escaping me.

"What the hell's wrong with her?" Jesse asked from above me.

"She's in labor, dumbfuck," Conner spat back.

Oh no. He was still there, still beside me. He should be running. I tried to say as much, but the words wouldn't come through the pain.

"Labor?" Jesse repeated.

"I can't shoot a woman in labor," the guard said.

"You didn't have a problem shooting at a pregnant woman," Gemma shot back.

"I just thought she was fat," said the guard.

"Enough." I was drenched in sweat as I finally managed to drag myself to my feet, placing my body between Conner and the group at the door. Panting, I looked at Gemma. Properly looked at her. It was like looking at a stranger. All that bright exuberance was gone. She looked as cold and sterile as the walls around us. "Why are you doing this?"

Gemma met my eye, and for a fleeting second I watched some warmth return, but in a blink it was wiped away again. Her lips quivered, pulling up to a smile before falling and then pulling up again. "Because it's important," she said matter-of-factly. "Because it has to be done. Right, doctor?"

"Young Miss Burke has some very different ideas of how to do things," Dr. Russi said. "I assure you I played no part in that boy's death."

I swallowed a lump of rage. "Then why the hell is he dead?"

"It's unfortunate," said Gemma. "Truly. But he saw too much."

"Too much of what?" I demanded. "What is this place?"

"My dear, this is Core Labs," said Dr. Russi. "The home of New Biology."

I clenched my jaw, saying nothing. This was the very subject for which he had been shunned from the scientific community, but it meant nothing to me. The doctor continued.

"We have spent thousands of years studying the human body to learn how it works and how to keep it working, and we've come a very long way. But there are limitations to studying the body alone. It is also necessary to study the soul. Our core. What makes us . . . us. Imagine a world where we could live on after we've outgrown our shells. Where we can remain, not as trapped spirits, but as autonomous energy without the burden of flesh."

"You know, Kathy, we spend every day with cores, souls, essences, whatever you want to call them," said Gemma, her voice softening again. "But we know so little about them. About what's within us. But it doesn't have to stay that way."

"So you . . ." I couldn't process any of this. "You steal souls? And experiment on them like lab rats?"

"It's not that simple."

"Oh, I think it is," I said. "This is your stock, is it?" I waved my arm at the encased essences behind me. "And what happens when you're done with them? You couldn't take them to processing, could you? That would be too conspicuous. Which means they never move on, unless . . . Do you use Jesse's position at S.C.Y.T.H.E. to get around that? Have him fill out some paperwork so the case numbers and dates aren't questioned?"

Gemma shook her head, but Jesse looked away. There may have been a flicker of shame in his eyes, but I couldn't be sure.

"So, what *do* you do with these souls once they're no longer of use to you, doctor?"

"I'm afraid they must be destroyed," said Dr. Russi.

"But it's all for the greater good," Gemma added quickly. "Casualties of progress, Kathy. I thought you'd get that. When I found out it was you on case 507032, I thought, 'thank god, someone who will understand, or at least be smart enough to leave well enough alone.' But then you started snooping around. That was a mistake I truly wish you hadn't made, because it complicated things. I like you, Kathy. You're fun, in a spinster-aunt kind of way. I've liked being your friend. And hey, that doesn't have to end. It's up to you, really. Just step away from the boy and we can talk this out."

"You know I'm not going to do that," I said.

Gemma sighed. "Yeah, I guess I didn't really think you would." She turned to the guard and yanked the rifle from his hands. "You know, it's funny," she said, aiming the gun at me. "All my life I've been pretty enough that no one thought I was all that smart. Insulting, yes, but it comes with perks. If I didn't look like I do, I doubt Jesse would have gone along with any of this, would you, babe?" She looked over her shoulder. "Or that I could have enticed Dr. Russi out of scientific exile to finish the work I knew he was meant to do. But in the end, no matter how many blinded idiots fall in line to help me, I seem to end up doing everything myself. I didn't want it to come to this, I swear I didn't. I didn't want to hurt the boy. But needs must, and I truly believe this is a need. Science should never be halted due to a bit of squeamishness. For centuries, that squeamishness kept cadavers from being studied. Just think of all the people who suffered for it. And now souls, like the boy's, and these in here, and my poor dad, they're relegated either to an afterlife trapped on earth or in some other place we know nothing about. Well, I'm here to see that it doesn't always have to be that way. I'm here to make sure an afterlife is still a life. And I'm sorry, Kathy, truly, but I can't let you stand in the way of that."

By now I was staring down the rifle's barrel, knees weak, heart throbbing. I turned away; turned over my shoulder, but when I glanced behind me, Conner wasn't there. Thank god. If I had to die, at least I would die knowing he'd gotten away. I held my breath and faced forward again just as the shot rang out.

45

fell to the floor, gasping, as the pain took hold of me. But this was pain I knew now. Not the pain of a bullet, but labor pain. Above me I could hear grunting and shoes squeaking on the linoleum floor. I glanced up. Gemma was tangled in a web of grasping arms, her stolen rifle at the center of a deadly tug-of-war. The details of the scuffle were blurred by the pain of the contraction, but as the pain eased, I realized it was Jesse on the other end of the struggle. Gemma sank her teeth into Jesse's arm and the two flung apart, the gun flying out of both their grasps and sliding across the room.

"You monstrous bitch," Jesse shouted, pressing a hand over the bite on his arm. "You told me no one else would get hurt. You promised. I trusted you. I loved you."

I crawled on hands and knees towards the gun, but Gemma was already on it. I kicked her hard in the stomach from my place on the ground, sending her doubling over with a gasp. She still held the gun. Forcing myself upright, I leapt at her, knocking her down easily before she had the chance to aim the rifle. We tussled for a moment, limbs flailing, before Gemma did something far worse than shooting me. She aimed a kick at my stomach. At my baby. I could see her foot flying towards me before I felt it. For a moment it was as though time slowed; stopped.

Then time seemed to realize what it had done and sped up to make amends for its lethargy. Just before the kick made impact, I rolled onto my side. Gemma's foot connected with my lower back. The pain was sharp, but nothing compared to a contraction. Behind Gemma's figure I spied a pair of jeaned legs. I followed them up as Gemma struggled to regain balance. Conner. He was back. And he was smiling.

My mind was racing. Conner was there. He shouldn't be there. And where was the gun?

I flopped myself onto my bum, half prepared for another assault from Gemma, but not remotely prepared for what I saw instead. Simon was there, in the doorway. And beside him, Stu.

Even stranger, men and women dressed head to toe in black poured into the barn and proceeded to haul Jesse, Dr. Russi, and the guard out of the building. Gemma had tucked herself away behind one of the immobilized essences, just out of sight. I rose, dazed, unable to make sense of anything I was seeing. I was walking blearily towards my husband and, for some reason, my boss, when a clicking sound echoed in my ear.

I turned around. Gemma had the rifle again. And it was pointed at me. Her eyes were aflame, nostrils flared. She looked feral.

"You ruined everything," she barely whispered. And then she pulled the trigger.

46

When I opened my eyes again, I was still there. Still alive. Still in one piece. But it wasn't Gemma in front of me anymore. It was Conner. Well, Conner's back, anyway. He stood directly in front of me, all gangly limbs and unwashed clothes. A bullet hovered in his newly transparent midsection, suspended in the final glimmer of energy from his soul, before falling to the floor with a metallic clatter.

The black-clothed people returned, summoned by the gunshot. I was barely conscious of them taking Gemma away. Of Gemma shrieking, "You see? You see why we have to study them? There's so much we don't understand." Of Simon wrapping his arms around me as we both slid to the floor. All I could focus on was Conner. And how he was fading.

"We need to get him to processing," I said as I returned to myself. I was too weak from shock to stand.

"I'll handle that," said Stu from the doorway. I'd forgotten he was there. It made too little sense to stick in my brain.

"Stu—Mr. Calhoun."

"Valence. I'm glad you're all right."

"What . . ."

"I've been looking into the Gemma situation for a while now. It was you who brought it to my attention, though I couldn't disclose as much for your own protection. I'd hoped you'd be safe if you heeded my warnings, and then again once 507032 was off your hands and you weren't at the office, but clearly I was mistaken."

"And those people in black . . . ?"

"S.C.Y.T.H.E. operates outside the realm of societal authority, so we have some of our own. You're lucky your husband called the office when he did or we might not have made it in time."

I nodded, making a mental IOU to Simon for my eternal gratitude. "I'm taking Conner to processing," I said, trying once again to stand and deciding nothing needed to make sense right now. "You take care of these trapped souls."

"Valence, stop," Stu said, looking over the state of me.

"I'm taking Conner," I said again.

Stu sucked in a breath and gave a tight nod. "I expect a call first thing tomorrow morning."

I tried to say something in the affirmative but couldn't. Another contraction. Shit.

"Kath!" Simon grabbed my hand, brows furrowed in concern.

"Just a contraction," I said as I tried to breathe.

"You're . . ."

I nodded. "Conner," I called behind me, where Conner stood mesmerized at the body-less hands that had stopped a bullet. The flesh of his wrists was losing opacity. "Let's go. Now."

47

Simon pulled the car up to Core Labs, the house now teeming with black-clad personnel, and Conner and I jumped inside. The GPS gave us an ETA of thirty minutes. Neither Conner nor I could wait much longer.

"Conner, I need you to hang in for me, okay?" I shouted to the back seat through another contraction.

"Doing my best, Grim," said Conner. "Keep your legs crossed."

We sailed down the rural highway that had taken us to Core Labs and burst into town, careening through deserted streets as late night turned into early morning. Finally, we pulled into the processing warehouse parking lot. I turned around to see the back seat headrest through half of Conner's face.

"Out," I shouted before the car had fully stopped moving.

We all piled out and ran through the industrial double doors at the front of the warehouse, stopping sharp in front of the man behind the desk.

"We need to get this soul to processing," I panted.

"File number?" said the man.

"507032."

The man's dark fingers danced across the keyboard. "We don't have that case on tonight's schedule."

"Fuck your schedule," I said. "Look at him."

The man glanced up from the computer screen and lowered his wire-rimmed glasses to look at Conner.

"That's a shame, but we—"

"Please," Simon piped up from beside me, catching me off guard. "You need to help this boy."

"It really isn't protocol—"

"Look, my wife is very much in labor right now and she isn't leaving here until Conner is processed, so either take him to processing or get ready to see a baby born on your desk."

The man looked me up and down and grimaced. "I suppose we can make exceptions for emergency situations. Let me get the processor on duty." He rose from the desk and walked through an employees-only door. As soon as he was gone, I turned and planted a kiss on Simon's lips.

"Thank you," I said. "And I am, you know. Your wife."

The man behind the desk returned a moment later with a young woman wearing cargo pants and a baseball cap.

"This is Meg," the man said. "She'll take the soul from here."

I turned back to Conner. As much as I'd known what bringing him here meant, I hadn't prepared—wasn't ready—to say goodbye.

"Just . . . just one sec," I said to Meg before turning back to look Conner in the eye. "You okay?"

He nodded, but his sparkling eyes belied the same heaviness I felt.

"Conner." Where to begin? "Thank you."

"What? I should be thanking you, I—"

"No, no, just listen. Before I met you, I thought my life was what it would always be. I settled. I never took risks because I was afraid I'd make a mess of things. But . . . but you changed all that. You changed me. You made me see that I can do more, can be more than I ever gave myself credit for. You've been the best kid anyone could ask for. Don't tell this baby that. I've . . . I feel so lucky to have known you. And I love you, Conner. I always will."

"Okay, I've really gotta take him now," said Meg, "or else we're gonna lose him."

I nodded, wiping away tears.

"Just, uh . . ." Conner paused as he reached the door. "Look, all my life, all I wanted was someone to care about me. I never thought I'd get that, and then I died, and I was sure of it. But you gave me that, Grim. And you and Simon and Jo made this weird sort of family for me. I never thought I'd know what it was like to have one. A real one. But now I do, and it's like . . . I dunno, it's like I feel complete somehow. And I'm not scared now. Of this. Whatever this is. This next thing. And I . . . I love you too, okay?"

I smiled as the tears poured down my cheeks. Meg opened the employees-only door, and in a blink, Conner was gone.

48

The contractions were coming on more frequently now. I barely had a few minutes between them as Simon rushed us to the nearest hospital, but my mind wasn't on the pain. It was on Conner, and on what he had said. There was something in his words that poked at me, but I couldn't untangle it while my insides were being ripped apart.

"Breathe, sweetie. Deep breaths," Simon coached as he ran over the curb at the emergency room entrance and left the car parked across the sidewalk. He raced to my side and helped me out of the car and in through the hospital's automatic doors.

"Baby," he shouted at the first person in scrubs he spotted. "She's having a baby. Right now."

Moments later, a sea of scrubs surrounded me, whisking me off to a crisp white room and stuffing my thick calves into stirrups. If I never saw another sterile room filled with stainless steel again it would be too soon. The contractions were constant now, everything below my belly button in raging agony. I barely paid attention to the doctor introducing herself to me from between my legs. All I felt was pain. And Simon's hand, holding tight to mine. And Simon's fingers, pushing back my sweaty hair. And Simon's eyes, never leaving me.

I heard the word "push" from somewhere above me, but my body was already giving me the same order. I grunted a push, and then another, exhaustion hitting me like a cartoon anvil.

"One more," said a voice.

I had already been shot at tonight; wasn't that enough? I relented and gave one last push as the pain and the pressure that had taken over my lower half eased.

A high-pitched cry filled the room, booming and beautiful. I closed my eyes and let it fill my every pore.

"Would dad like to cut the cord?" the same voice asked. A quick snip echoed in my ears. I tried to see over my stomach, but the doctor had whisked my baby off to the side. When she returned a moment later, she held a small, squishy thing.

"Would you like to hold your baby, Mrs. Valence?"

I nodded dumbly as the doctor placed the baby, my baby, on my chest.

"Congratulations, you have a son."

I looked down at my little boy, the newest little human in the world, a new soul. He looked back up at me and my breath caught in my throat. My son's dark eyes were sparkling with life; so vibrant, so familiar, looking up at me now with the same warm intensity they'd held from beneath the frame of a gray hood. I felt a tear roll down my cheek as I held my child closer.

"I promise you'll always know you're loved," I whispered against my baby's soft head. Simon climbed into bed next to us and ran a finger down our baby's tiny cheek.

"We made that," he said.

"Not a bad collaboration," I said.

"How about another?"

I looked at him with daggers in my eyes. My vagina was still broken, for god's sake.

"No, no," Simon added quickly. "A different kind of collaboration. I was thinking maybe a wedding?"

I lay back against Simon's arm. "Can you have a wedding if you're already married?"

"A vow renewal, then? Or . . . I just, I'd like to be a family again. We don't need to be fancy about it."

I looked at him, Simon, short, round, bald, and perfect. Just like our baby. "Yeah, I'd like that. But not the wedding part. I'm not wearing Spanx if I don't have to." I ran a hand over his cheek. "Thank you for loving all of me."

49

There was no need for me to call Stu the next day. He showed up at my hospital room at promptly nine a.m. wearing a pale pink Oxford shirt and an unreadable look. I glanced down at the exposed boob my son was nursing on and considered covering it before deciding I didn't care. Stu wasn't looking at me anyway. He was slowly pacing the small space around my bed, hands clasped behind his back.

"Congratulations," he said, tipping his head towards the baby on my chest.

"Thanks," I said. We slipped back into silence. "His name's Owen," I said after a beat, trying to fill the air with something other than awkwardness. "Owen Conner Valence. Simon wanted 'Elmer' after his great-uncle, but I told him he can use that when he squeezes a human being out of his body." I caressed Owen's tiny cheek. Finally, I bit the bullet. "So am I fired?"

This stopped Stu's pacing. He looked at me for a moment before easing himself into the chair beside my bed. He scratched his temple. His bicep gave an uncomfortable bounce, as if it would rather be in any other arm right now. I braced.

"No," Stu said at last. "You're certainly not fired. In fact, I've come to apologize." He cleared his throat. "I didn't have enough faith in you on this case. But the way you looked after that boy's essence, it impressed not only me but the higher-ups as well. You've proved to be . . . rather remarkable, Valence."

I blinked. That was not an adjective I had ever heard in conjunction with my name before. Stu continued. "There's an opening for manager of the Murder department, as I'm sure you know. What with Jesse gone. I've been asked to see if you'll take it."

"Me?" I could feel my heart tick faster under Owen's small body.

"Yes, you."

I took a deep breath. "No," I said.

"No?"

"Not unless some serious changes are made," I clarified.

"Changes?"

I nodded. "I've been thinking. In a way, Gemma was right."

Stu opened his mouth but I hurried on. "No, let me finish. She's right that we don't know enough about essences. We work with them every day, and yet they're still a mystery to us in so many ways."

Stu stroked his chin. "I hate to admit it, but Core Labs had made some impressive headway on that front. Between some sort of chemical substance to keep souls forgetful and complacent, and those glasses for laypeople to see and hear essences without S.C.Y.T.H.E. clearance, they certainly knew what they were doing."

"But I'm not talking about any of that," I said. "I don't want to keep essences complacent. They're scared for a reason. I've never taken one to processing who wasn't nervous about it. Until

Conner. And he told me exactly why he wasn't scared to move on, I was just too busy laboring to put it together. What if forty-five days isn't some arbitrary grace period? What if it's there so they can finish up whatever unfinished business they had in life? So they can go on to the next stage with a clean slate?"

Stu sat back in his chair, sucking on his teeth, considering. "What you're suggesting would change the entire business model of S.C.Y.T.H.E., you realize."

"Maybe it needs changing," I said.

"How long are you staying home with—?" He gestured again towards my baby with his chin.

"Six months, maybe a year," I said. I would be around to watch Owen grow for as long as I could.

"That should give us enough time to put some new systems in place. If the higher-ups agree."

Stu studied me. I studied him right back. That bicep held no more fear for me. Not much did anymore. Stu rose to his feet.

"Rest up, Valence. Kathy. I'll see you in a year."

I bent my face to Owen's and breathed him in. Stu had a year before I sprang the idea of working from home on him. That should be enough time to get his biceps back into check. I'd be ready.

Moments after Stu left, Simon returned with a white paper bag, our breakfasts steaming inside.

"Was that . . ." He jabbed a thumb over his shoulder at the door.

"Yup," I said.

"He has so many muscles," said Simon. "I always forget how many muscles he has. I didn't even know the body had that many."

"Yup," I said again.

Simon shrugged and climbed onto the bed beside me. "Breakfast sandwich or a blueberry muffin? Or both? You made a human, you deserve both."

"I love you," I said, snatching the bag from his hand and curling into him. And I did love him, and Owen, and our little family, and my little life. For the first time ever, I truly loved it all. With my entire soul.

ACKNOWLEDGMENTS

Wow, hi! You're here reading the acknowledgments. That's so cool of you! Thanks for sticking around for what is essentially an Oscar speech with no music to play me off. I'll try (and probably fail) to keep it snappy all the same. First and foremost, thank *you*! Yes, you, the person who is currently reading the acknowledgments of this book. Because that probably means you read the actual book too, and getting to share this little word baby of mine has been my dream since I was seven. You just made seven-year-old me incredibly happy. She also says thanks. Thanks also to my family, who supported me and my overactive imagination. I wouldn't have kept at it without you. To my dream team, agent Melissa and manager Tara. To my incredible editor, Tracy, and everyone at Berkley/Penguin Random House who transformed this from a story into a real-life book. To the P Girls and J Boys for being my chosen family. To Carly and everyone who read this story before it probably should have been read by human eyes. And to anyone I'm foolishly forgetting, because there have been so many important people along the way, please write your name here and know that I love you.

Maxie Dara is from a tiny, Hallmark movie–style town in Ontario, Canada, where she works as a writer and actress, because rejection-heavy careers are her passion. She is also a two-time award-winning playwright. Maxie knew she wanted to be a writer at the age of seven, when she first fell in love with the written word. She also wanted to be a mermaid but has mostly focused on the writing side of things.